MARS ENIGMA

By Ken Warner

Contents

MARS ENIGMA

Prologue

Before the Malor Invasion

Bomani rolled onto his back and heaved a sigh.

"Mm, you give me good lovin'" said the woman lying next to him in the bed.

Although this was their second night together, he couldn't recall her name. She was young and gorgeous, and that was all that mattered. He grabbed his joint from the nightstand and took a long drag.

"Share?" the woman asked. He handed it to her.

The newscaster on the television was rambling on about some breaking news story.

The woman reached over him to put the joint down and then plunged her tongue into his mouth.

"You think you can go again, *old man*?"

"Sure, just give me a few minutes," he said with a grin.

"Aw, but I'm ready now," she replied, kissing him once more.

To be young again, he thought. His libido was always strongest when he mixed marijuana and alcohol like this, but he still needed a *little* time to recharge.

"Okay, you let me know when you're ready," she said, flopping onto her back. "I guess if I were 40,000 years old, I'd need a few minutes, too." She poked him in the ribs.

"What, you still don't believe me?"

"Baby, you make me climax like that again, and I'll believe anything you tell me," she said with a grin. "Atlantis, aliens, the whole shebang."

That was another effect of mixing his poisons: he became loose-lipped. He'd spent millennia hiding his true identity. But for the last few decades, since moving to Bermuda, he'd started telling people his story—women, mostly, whenever he indulged too much. There was something about life on this island that put him at ease.

Nobody ever believed him, anyway. It never ceased to amaze him how readily these humans could deny anything that contradicted their preconceptions, no matter how strong the evidence.

"Oh, my God," the girl said, suddenly sitting up and staring at the television.

Bomani sat up to see what was going on. There was an image of an object moving past Mars—an enormous spaceship.

"Shit," he said, getting out of bed. He threw on his pants and a T-shirt.

"Where the hell are you going?" the girl demanded.

"I need a drink," he said, walking out of the bedroom.

Bomani trotted down the steps to the first floor and out the rear patio doors. He'd owned this beachfront home for nearly twenty years now; it was one of the finest in the area.

It took only a few minutes to walk up the beach to the waterfront bar. There were tables on the patio overlooking the ocean, but he headed inside. He sat at the bar and ordered a rum.

They had the same newscast on the television behind the counter. Bomani had been waiting for this moment since the 1940s when the flying saucer crashed in New Mexico. He knew for sure his people had nothing to do with that craft. And there had been many other sightings since then.

He'd dreaded this day. It seemed likely that the vessels that had visited so far would be scout ships. Long had he suspected that it was only a matter of time before an invasion would begin.

Since the moment the Miami power station had sent up that signal, he'd practically been holding his breath. Whoever had been sending the scout ships would be attracted to that transmission like a moth to light. And he'd wasted no time preparing for their arrival.

The bartender served him his drink. Bomani downed it in one.

"Another."

The bartender filled his glass.

"It's time to get the power station ready," said the man at the end of the bar; Bomani hadn't even noticed him sitting there. He was wearing a black suit and tie—and sunglasses. Why those were necessary in the middle of the night, inside a bar, Bomani had no idea.

"Excuse me?" he said. "How would you know about that?"

"We know quite a bit about you, Mr. Bomani," the man said, getting to his feet and sitting down again right next to him.

"Yeah? How's that?"

"Our people have been keeping an eye on you for some time, now. We know you're not from Earth and that you were one of the inhabitants of Atlantis tens of thousands of years ago. Although we only found out about the power stations fairly recently."

The Miami power station had been all over the news, so that wasn't exactly a secret anymore. But Bomani had no idea how he could know about the Bermuda one.

"I trust, should the opportunity arise, you will use the station's weapon systems to help eliminate this threat?" the man asked.

"Of course," said Bomani. "I've already activated the station."

"Excellent," the man replied. "You've done very well for yourself here, we've noticed."

"Yeah, sure; business is good," said Bomani, uncomfortable with the sudden turn the conversation had taken.

"It would be a shame if the authorities were to learn about the nature of your, ah, business," the man said with a smirk.

"I don't know what you're talking about," said Bomani, his pulse rising.

"Let's be frank, Mr. Bomani. We both know that you are the primary importer and distributor of cocaine, heroin, and other illicit substances on this island. Now, I am willing to keep this information to myself—for a price."

"You're trying to blackmail me, now?" Bomani demanded. "I'm not giving you a dime—you can't prove a thing."

"Oh, the price will not be monetary in nature," the man said with a grin. "We may require your services in the coming days. All we ask for is your cooperation in exchange for our silence. And as for proof, you are quite mistaken. We have your bank records, Mr. Bomani. As well as recordings of your phone conversations with your supplier in Puerto Rico. I believe he would be quite disappointed with you if he were to be implicated, as well."

"Oh, come on," said Bomani, his heart racing now. "How could you possibly have recordings like that—I don't even know the guy's name!"

"We do."

Bomani took a deep breath.

"Look, man—I don't want any trouble. What... what do you need me to do?"

"That remains to be seen. It may be nothing; we'll let you know."

"Alright, fine—whatever. But you need to keep my shit quiet!"

"Very good," the man said with a grin, getting to his feet. "I'll be in touch again very soon."

Bomani downed his drink.

"Who exactly are you, anyway?" he asked, turning to face the man—but he was gone. "What the hell?"

He looked all around the bar and ran out the door to check outside, but the man in black had disappeared.

Bomani went back inside and ordered another drink.

Chapter One: Space

After the Invasion

Malia Kwan sat next to her brother, Jaden, staring out the window of the Othali warship. Only minutes had passed since their departure from Earth. Malia felt like this was a dream, and any minute now, she'd wake up, and it would be time for school. It was difficult to process everything that had happened and all the things they'd learned in a matter of only days.

The Malor had arrived and destroyed Miami and Washington, D.C. Malia and her brother had found out that they were created from genetic samples left in a secret chamber inside the Great Pyramid more than 10,000 years ago—by their mother, who, they had discovered, was not from Earth. She had come with a group of colonists tens of thousands of years ago from a planet called Othal—which had since been annihilated by the Malor. In the end, with Jaden and Malia's help, this very warship had managed to destroy the Malor. And now it carried the only survivors from Othal to a new planet capable of sustaining life.

Their mother, Melissa Kwan, and Nadia, one of the Othali, came to find them a few minutes later, snapping Malia out of her reverie.

"Let's go, you two," said Melissa. "Nadia's going to show us to our new quarters."

Malia and Jaden got up and followed them out of the conference room. Nadia led them through the ship to the area that housed the crew quarters.

"They didn't design this vessel with families in mind," Nadia told them. "It was supposed to be used for short-term combat missions defending Othal, not an extended interstellar journey. But we were able to assign you adjoining rooms."

They arrived at their new quarters, and Nadia opened one of the doors for them. Malia followed Jaden and Melissa inside. It was a single room with an attached bathroom. There were a couple of chairs, a small table, a desk, and a bunk bed against the far wall.

"That leads to the second room," Nadia said, pointing to a door inside the room.

"Dibs," said Jaden, moving into the adjoining area. "You two can room together."

"You get your own room?" asked Malia. "How is that fair?"

"A young man needs his privacy," Melissa told her.

"I can see about adding a third room if you want," Nadia suggested.

"Yeah—" said Malia.

"That won't be necessary," Melissa replied, cutting her off. "This will do very nicely."

Malia let out a long sigh. Rooming with her mother would not have been her first choice.

"Hey, where's Carl?" asked Jaden.

"He's got a room across the hall," Nadia told him. "Melissa, if you'd like, I can show you to the medical bay?"

"Mom, what's wrong?" asked Malia. "Are you sick?"

"No, no," she replied. "I'm going to go back to work! Nadia was telling me they don't have a doctor on board, so I volunteered."

"I hope that doesn't mean me and Malia have to go back to school," Jaden said from the next room with a groan.

"There's no school on the ship," Nadia told him. "You two are the only minors on board, so we haven't needed for one..."

"No other kids?" asked Malia. She felt like she should have realized this before but simply hadn't thought about it.

"Don't worry, we'll be making arrangements for the two of you to continue your education," Melissa said.

Jaden groaned again.

Nadia showed them to the medical bay next, where they found a man on duty.

"Melissa, this is Ensign Fareed," said Nadia. "He was a field medic back on Othal, and until now has been a one-man show."

"It's an honor to meet you," he said, shaking Melissa's hand.

"These are my children, Jaden and Malia," she told him.

"It's nice to meet you," said Malia.

"Hey," added Jaden.

Fareed showed them around. Beyond the reception area, there were four exam rooms and a small office.

"As with everything on board, the designers planned for this to be a short-term facility," he told them. "Nobody ever imagined this would have to serve as a full medical bay. But we've made do."

"It's very impressive how you've all been able to adapt," said Melissa.

"Well, it'll be a relief to have a real doctor on board," Fareed replied. "My training was limited—I don't have a medical degree or anything."

"Fareed has done an admirable job taking care of us," said Nadia, patting him on the shoulder.

"I'm officially starting tomorrow," Melissa said to Fareed. "But I thought I could stop by this afternoon, and maybe you can get me up to speed with operations here? I've never worked on a military vessel before!"

"Sounds good," Fareed replied with a smile.

Nadia showed them to the mess hall next.

"We get our meal schedules on our duty roster," she told them. "But as you three are civilians, you can come down to eat any time you'd like."

"Terrific," said Melissa. "You know, it just occurred to me, the only clothes we own are the ones we're wearing..."

"Ah," said Nadia. "We can take care of that. Come with me."

She led them to the ship's store.

"My shift is coming up in a few minutes, so I need to get going," she said. "Will you be okay if I leave you here?"

"Yes, I think we can manage," said Melissa. "Thank you for everything!"

The crewman minding the store helped them pick out new

wardrobes. There wasn't much of a selection, and the colors were drab, but Malia knew fashion wouldn't be much of a priority on a military vessel. She was just glad she wouldn't have to wear the same outfit for the rest of the journey.

Once they had their clothes, they made their way back to their quarters. Jaden started climbing up to the top bunk.

"Hey, get down—that's my bed!" said Malia.

"Fine," he said, crashing on the bottom bunk instead. Malia busied herself putting everything away in the closets and drawers.

"How are you two feeling about all of this?" Melissa asked them, sitting in one of the chairs.

"Which part?" asked Malia, taking the seat across from her.

"I don't know," she said. "Any of it."

"I'm not gonna lie," Jaden replied from the bed. "This whole thing is weird. Like, it's gonna take a long time to get used to it. Finding out we're half-*alien*, and now living on a *spaceship* for who knows how long... I don't know."

"We'll be fine, Mom," Malia told her. "He's right; it *is* weird. But we're together, and we're safe, so..." She shrugged.

In truth, Malia felt deeply apprehensive but didn't want her mom to worry. She'd left her friends behind, for one thing, and would never be able to speak to them again. All the milestones she'd looked forward to for years—getting her driver's license, going to prom, enrolling in college—none of it would ever happen now. But she'd already resigned herself to accepting this new reality; she had no choice.

"I'll be okay with most of it," said Jaden. "But I miss Dad."

Malia teared up instantly at his words.

"Yeah, me, too," she agreed. "We'll get used to everything else. But that's the toughest part."

"I know," Melissa told them. "I wish he could be here with us."

"Why aren't there any other kids here?" asked Jaden.

"Well, supplies are limited on a ship like this," said Melissa. "Having children in these circumstances would strain their resources. Don't worry; I'm sure once we arrive at the new world, people will start having babies again."

"What were your other kids like?" asked Malia. "Back in ancient Egypt?"

Melissa sighed, thought for a moment, and then smiled.

"Rashida was playful," she said, "and inquisitive. She was always smiling or laughing. You could call her a 'free spirit.' She was very outgoing and wanted to talk to everyone she met."

"What about the boy?" asked Malia.

"Nour was shy. He was more of an introvert. Highly intelligent—he was very curious about the world around him."

"Hmm," said Malia.

"What?" asked Melissa.

"Well, it's funny that this time, the *girl* is the smart one," she said, staring pointedly at Jaden.

"Shut up, Malia," he said. "They had powers like us? Like telekinesis and telepathy?"

"Yes," Melissa confirmed. "They were telepathic only with each other and the Othali. And they both had telekinesis."

"Did they have any other powers?" asked Jaden.

"They did," she said, taking a deep breath. "Rashida and Nour were both able to heal themselves. Faster than normal, that is—much faster."

"From injuries, you mean?" asked Malia.

"Wait, you mean like if one of them broke an arm, they could fix it just by thinking about it?" Jaden asked before Melissa could answer.

"Yes, they could repair injuries consciously," said Melissa. "Or illnesses—I don't fully understand how, but they were able to will their immune system to eliminate contagions."

"But they couldn't stop the rapid aging?" Malia asked.

"No. They did try, but their ability to self-heal did not include genetic manipulation."

"Do you think *we* have healing powers, too?" asked Malia.

"Most likely," said Melissa. "You have the same extra chromosomes that they did."

"Wait a minute," said Jaden. "When they caught us at Area 51 and did those experiments on us, they didn't test us for healing powers."

"No, and you can thank your father for that," said Melissa. "He had the foresight not to include that ability in the official documentation for his research."

"Why?" asked Jaden.

"He knew that once the two of you grew into your powers, there would be a testing phase to evaluate your abilities," said Melissa.

"And evaluating your telepathic and telekinetic skills is one thing, but ethically, to *cause you injury*—well, that's wrong. And it would be the only way to test the self-healing."

"So, Dad didn't tell anyone about that because he was afraid someone would try to hurt us to see if we could do it?" asked Malia.

"Yes, exactly."

"But Brian told us that Dad trusted the government and never thought they'd kidnap us the way they did," said Jaden.

"That's true, but the government still provided the funding for his research," she explained. "He worried that even with him in control, they might try to force him into experimenting with your self-healing abilities. To play it safe, he chose to withhold that particular information from the official record."

"That worked out for the best," Malia said earnestly.

"Yeah," Jaden agreed. "Who knows what kind of sick shit that Babcock guy would have tried with us if he knew about that!"

"Other than the self-healing, did they have any other powers that we don't?" asked Malia.

"No, that was it," said Melissa. "But remember, they only lived for ten years, and the powers they had didn't manifest until after they turned eight. Had they lived longer, it's possible other abilities would have emerged—there's no way to know."

"So, Malia and me might be able to do other stuff we don't know about yet?" asked Jaden.

"Quite possibly," Melissa said with a smile. "But listen, I have a meeting with Commander Anhur, so I need to get going. Promise me you two will stay out of trouble?"

"That's tough," Jaden said with a grimace, "I can't make any guarantees."

"I'll make sure he behaves," Malia told her, glaring at Jaden.

"Hey, she wasn't only talking about *me*!" said Jaden.

Melissa shook her head, saying, "Heaven help me," as she left, closing the door behind her.

"That's pretty cool," said Jaden. "Self-healing. I hope we do develop other powers eventually."

"Like what?" asked Malia.

"I don't know, use your imagination! I mean, think of all the things people can do in the movies, like Star Wars and X-men—maybe we can manipulate people's minds, like the Jedi! Or control metal, like Magneto! Or even *fly* like Superman!"

Malia rolled her eyes.

"We can already fly like Superman, dummy," she said.

"What? No, we can't."

"Yes, we *can*! Don't you remember after we rescued Mom, and I dove into the water so I could see the shuttle and move it to safety?"

"Yeah..."

"The waves kept washing over me, and you were no help, so I ended up using my telekinesis to fly back up to the shuttle. Remember?"

"Oh, damn—that's right! I gotta try that!"

"But anyway, none of that other stuff is real," she said. "It's all fiction."

"Come on, seriously," he said. "You think it's crazy, but look at what we can do already! Anything is possible."

"I guess," she replied. "But we don't exactly have an owner's manual for ourselves. We'll have to keep trying things and see what happens."

"Well, I don't know about you, but I'm starving," said Jaden. "Let's go check out that cafeteria and see what they have to eat!"

They left their quarters, but it became apparent that Jaden had no idea where he was going.

"You got us lost," Malia complained.

"No, I didn't," he said, looking up and down the corridor. "Okay, maybe I did..."

"Follow me," she said. "I'm pretty sure it's this way."

Within minutes they arrived at the mess hall. Someone was working at the buffet, and there was food, but nobody else was here.

Malia followed Jaden across the room, and they each grabbed a plate.

"Uh... I don't know what any of this is," said Jaden, scanning the trays. "This one looks like scrambled eggs... sort of..."

"Well, we'd better get used to it, whatever it is," said Malia, filling her plate. "It's either this or starve to death."

They sat down to eat. Malia tried each item on her plate. She couldn't identify any of it, but most of it tasted pretty good.

"This one reminds me of barbeque chicken," she said to Jaden.

He was staring at his food with a sad expression on his face, not touching any of it.

"Oh, get over yourself," she said. "Just eat."

By the time Malia finished, Jaden had eaten only half of his food and didn't seem interested in the rest.

They went to drop off their plates, and Malia noticed Jaden grabbing a clean knife and sliding it into his pocket.

"What are you doing?" she demanded.

Jaden shushed her.

They went back to their quarters. Jaden pulled the knife out of his pocket and sat down.

"Time to practice a little self-healing," he said with a grin.

"You've got to be kidding me!"

"What? How else are we supposed to learn how to do this?"

"This is dumb—you're gonna cut yourself just to see if you can heal it? What if you can't—you'll bleed all over the place!"

"One way to find out," he said.

Jaden grabbed the blade of the knife, closing it in his fist. With his other hand, he pulled it out with a wince. When he opened his hand, Malia could see that he'd sliced it open.

"Okay, genius," she said. "Let's see you heal it."

He stared at his hand, brow furrowed, but nothing happened. Blood began dripping onto the floor.

"Uh-oh," he said, looking worried now.

"You're an idiot," she chided him. "Go wash that, and I'll see if I can find you a bandage—and you'd better clean up the blood on the floor!"

Malia left their quarters and made her way down to the sickbay. She found Fareed and asked him for a bandage.

"Everything alright?" he asked, handing it to her.

"Yeah, my brother cut himself... by accident. But, uh, could I get a few more of these, just in case?"

Malia returned to their quarters and gave Jaden one of the bandages.

"Where's the knife?" she asked.

Jaden handed it to her.

"What, are you gonna try it now?" he asked.

Malia didn't reply. She washed the knife in the bathroom sink and then sat down and stared at it. This still didn't seem like a smart idea, but healing wounds and injuries could be extremely useful.

Malia brought the blade against the side of her index finger and sliced. The cut began bleeding immediately. She focused, imagining coagulant streaming to the wound. At first, nothing happened. She wiped the blood away with a bandage and then concentrated again. This time, the cut closed itself, and the bleeding stopped. She could see the surface of her skin knitting itself back together over the wound.

"Why is it you're always the one who gets this stuff first?" Jaden demanded. "This was *my* idea!"

"Girls mature faster," she told him with a fake smile. "You should know that by now."

"Yeah, whatever," he said. "Tell me how you did it!"

"Simple. I imagined the coagulant moving through my bloodstream to the injury."

"What the hell is coagulant?"

Malia sighed.

"It's the protein that causes clotting. It thickens the blood so that the bleeding stops."

"How do you always know stuff like this?"

"Maybe because I pay attention in school? You should try it sometime; then you'd know stuff, too."

Jaden shook his head.

"Maybe I would if we had school anymore. But which damn class taught us about *coagulant*? I don't remember anything like that."

"Health class, dummy," she said.

"Oh. Well, I *did* pay attention in that class..."

Malia giggled.

"Yeah, but only to the section on sex ed."

She went to the bathroom and washed her hands. Returning to her seat, she watched for a few more minutes as Jaden focused on his hand, trying to heal the wound. The bleeding seemed to stop after a few minutes, but not any faster than usual.

"Hey, the bleeding stopped," said Jaden. "I think I got it!"

"You're such a moron," she muttered. But before Jaden could respond, the ship began shaking, like an airplane moving through turbulence.

"What the hell is that?" said Jaden, looking scared.

The shaking stopped, but a siren sounded, and a red light above the door began flashing.

"I don't like this," said Malia, getting to her feet. "Something's wrong."

She moved out to the corridor. Jaden followed, hastily putting the bandage on his hand.

Carl emerged from the doorway across the hall.

"What just happened?" he asked. "Everything started shaking, and then this siren went off!"

"No idea," said Malia. "Let's go to the bridge and find out!"

"Great!" Carl replied. "And... which way is that?"

"Follow me!" said Malia, striding off, Jaden and Carl close behind.

Chapter Two: Breakdown

Malia walked onto the bridge and stopped in her tracks. Jaden bumped into her, almost knocking her down.

"Watch it!" she scolded him.

The entire bridge crew seemed agitated, everyone rushing around doing something—Malia had no idea what. Melissa was standing off to one side; it looked like she was trying to stay out of the way.

"Will someone shut off that damn noise!" Anhur yelled over the commotion.

A moment later, the siren stopped blaring.

Melissa joined Malia, Jaden, and Carl.

"Mom, what's going on?" Malia asked.

"I'm not sure," said Melissa.

"Lieutenant, status report," said the commander.

"No change," said the lieutenant. "We are no longer accelerating, but the main engines still show fifty percent thrust."

"That's impossible," said Anhur. "Increase engines to seventy percent."

"Yes, sir."

"Why is that impossible?" Jaden whispered to nobody in particular.

"If their engines are generating thrust, then we should be accelerating," said Carl.

"So we've stopped moving?" asked Jaden.

"No," said Malia. "Acceleration is the rate of change in velocity. It's like driving down the highway in a car—if you floor it, your speed keeps increasing. But if you ease up on the gas, then your speed levels off."

"No, if you do that, then the car slows down," said Jaden.

"Yes, because of the force of friction between the tires and the pavement," said Carl. "But space is a vacuum, and so there is no friction. Without engines, we'd keep going at the same velocity forever—well, unless we ran into something, of course!"

"So, basically, they're giving it gas, but we're not speeding up anymore?" asked Jaden.

"Right, exactly," said Malia.

Nadia joined them on the bridge, and Bomani showed up a moment later.

"Still no acceleration," the lieutenant reported.

"Increase to ninety percent," said the commander.

"Yes, sir," said the lieutenant. "Ninety percent."

"Sir, I just came from the engine room," said Bomani, "and they said main engines are completely offline."

"Gauges show ninety percent thrust," said the lieutenant.

"Your gauges are wrong," said Anhur. He tapped a button on his console. "Engineering, report."

"We have a problem down here," a voice said from the console.

"Main engines have gone into safe mode. We can't get them back online until we figure out what caused the fault."

"Understood," said the commander. "Keep me updated, please."

"Yes, sir."

"Lieutenant," said Anhur, "reboot control systems."

"Yes, sir."

"I thought you were a geneticist," Carl said to Bomani. "What brought you down to the engine room?"

"Well, when we journeyed here from Othal, there wasn't much need for a geneticist," he replied. "My skills didn't come into play until we reached Earth. So, during the voyage, I learned systems engineering to keep myself useful. But my knowledge is severely out of date, so I figured I'd brush up now that we're going off-planet for a while."

"Control systems are back online," said the lieutenant. "And now I'm showing engines offline, locked into a maintenance cycle."

"Very well," said Anhur.

"Bridge, this is engineering," said a voice over the intercom.

"This is Anhur; go ahead."

"Sir, we believe the engines must have taken some damage during our engagement with the Malor. We can't nail it down, but it seems like there are at least three different issues at play here. And a sensor is down, as well—maybe more than one, making diagnostics difficult at this time."

"How long to repair?" asked Anhur.

"Sir, we don't even know what we're dealing with yet. We may be looking at a complete teardown."

"Keep me apprised."

"Commander, with engines offline, navigation is going to be severely limited," said the lieutenant. "We're coming up on Mars, and without engines..."

"Understood," said Anhur. "Calculate a trajectory to place us in a stable orbit."

"Yes, sir."

"We're going to Mars?" Jaden asked quietly. "What for?"

"Well, the plan was to use the planet's gravitational well to boost our acceleration," said Nadia.

"Huh?"

"Have you ever tried holding a tennis ball on the top of a basketball and then dropping them?" asked Carl.

"Sure," Jaden replied with a chuckle. "When they bounce, the tennis ball shoots off like a bullet."

"Yes, and that's essentially how a gravitational slingshot works," said Carl. "It's a little more complex, but the idea is the same. They can use the gravitational well to siphon off a tiny amount of momentum from the planet and add it to the spacecraft, giving it a great boost in velocity."

"Oh... yeah..."

"But without engines, we can't do that," Malia observed. "So, what now?"

"We'll need to move into orbit around the planet," said Nadia. "That'll give us time to repair the engines. But that's going to be easier said than done..."

"I'd imagine so," said Carl. "We must be moving much too fast for that by now."

"Wait, what?" asked Jaden.

"The velocity we'd want for interstellar travel is vastly greater than that of an orbiting body," said Nadia. "We're moving well beyond the planet's escape velocity. If something in orbit of Mars were to accelerate to our current speed, it would shoot off into space."

"So we need to slow down somehow?" asked Malia.

"Yes, precisely," said Nadia. "And I'm not sure how we're going to pull that off without engines..."

"Not only that," added Carl, "but our orbital insertion angle will have to be *just right*. Too steep, and we crash into the planet. Too shallow, and we zoom off into space!"

"This doesn't sound very encouraging," said Malia.

"Sir, I've calculated our trajectory," the lieutenant reported. "This is going to be tricky. We can use maneuvering thrusters to slow down a bit, but it won't be enough. We'll need to dip into the atmosphere to achieve orbital velocity."

"Proceed," said Anhur.

"Hold on, what?" asked Jaden. "What does he mean by *dip into the atmosphere*?"

"Friction," said Malia. "There isn't any in space, and that's why we'd keep going at the same speed forever. But if we drop into Mars' atmosphere, there will be a *lot* of friction with the air, and that will slow us down."

"Air has friction?" asked Jaden. "How? Air is like... nothing."

"Sure, when you're walking around, you'd never feel it because you're not moving very fast," said Malia. "But don't you remember when we moved down to Earth in the shuttle? We were engulfed in fire because there's so much friction from the atmosphere."

"Oh..."

"That's correct," said Nadia. "It's dangerous, but it's the only way we can bleed off enough speed. As Carl pointed out, we have to get the angle exactly right to enter orbit."

"Course laid in, sir," said the lieutenant.

"On screen," said Anhur.

The viewscreen came up, and Malia could see empty space on one side, with a point of light in the center, and a graphic on the other side showing their course.

"Magnify the planet," said Anhur.

"Yes, sir," said the lieutenant.

The point of light grew until Malia could see that it was Mars. On the other side of the display, she could see their ship growing ever closer to the planet.

As the minutes went by, the bridge grew quiet. Malia could feel the tension in the air as the crew kept their eyes on the display.

"Entering the atmosphere now," the lieutenant reported.

Malia could see an orange glow around the edges of the viewscreen. It expanded until flames engulfed the entire display. The ship began to shake.

"Steady at the helm," said Anhur.

"Yes, sir."

The shaking grew more violent, and the flames on the display intensified. Malia felt herself quivering with fear. She grabbed her mother in a hug, and Melissa held her tight.

"Commander, our velocity has decreased too much," said the lieutenant. "Our altitude is dropping."

"Fire all thrusters," said Anhur. "Get us higher!"

"Yes, sir!"

Malia felt terrified. She squeezed her mother tighter and kept her eyes glued to the display. Slowly, the shaking diminished, and the flames on the viewscreen dissipated. Malia could see the red planet below them.

"Commander, we've entered Mars orbit," said the lieutenant.

The bridge crew cheered and clapped. Malia let go of her mom and breathed a heavy sigh of relief.

"What happened back there, Lieutenant?" asked Anhur.

"I'm sorry, sir," he said. "I neglected to add the mass of the additional passengers we picked up on Earth."

"Maybe you need to go back to school with Jaden and Malia," said Nadia, earning a chuckle from some of the bridge crew.

"Engineering," said the commander into his console, "we've entered orbit. Proceed with your repairs."

"Yes, sir," came the voice over the intercom.

"Commander, I'm getting some unusual readings from the planet," said the lieutenant.

"What have you got?"

"There are surface structures... they don't appear to be naturally occurring."

"On screen."

Malia saw the display change, now showing the surface of Mars. She could make out a human-looking face and a five-sided pyramid.

"What the hell?" said Nadia. "I thought this planet was lifeless!"

"So did I," Melissa agreed.

"I'll be damned," said Carl, staring at the screen.

"What is it?" asked Nadia.

"Back in the 1970s, the United States sent the Viking probes to Mars," he explained. "The first one sent back images that showed what appeared to be a humanoid face and a pyramid nearby. NASA told us it was merely a trick of the lighting and that there were only naturally occurring rock formations there.

"And, in fact, later missions sent by both NASA and the European Space Agency seemed to confirm this. The cameras on the Viking probes were very low resolution. But the imagery from the later probes showed the region in much greater detail, and it no longer looked like there were any artificial structures."

"Those don't look natural to me," said Malia, staring at the screen in awe. The face looked like it had eroded over time, but the eyes, nose, and mouth were very clear. And the pyramid, while also eroded, appeared to be symmetrical.

"I agree!" said Carl. "They must have doctored those later images! It was a government cover-up—I should have known!"

"You mean you never saw anything like this at Dreamland?" asked Malia.

"No, we weren't involved with any of the planetary missions. That must have been a different department. I never guessed that the newer Mars images were fakes!"

"You're slipping," said Jaden. "The government's *always* trying to cover up stuff about aliens!"

"I know!" said Carl. "And your uncle was always telling me I was paranoid! Here's more proof I was right!"

"Sir, I'm detecting a vast underground structure beneath those formations," said the lieutenant.

"Explain," said Anhur.

"I can't, sir. Sensors can penetrate only about a hundred meters below the surface. But it appears whatever's down there goes much deeper."

"And I'm guessing it's not naturally occurring?" said Anhur.

"I don't think so, sir."

"Any life signs?" the commander asked.

"No, sir. Based on the surface erosion and the chemical makeup of the atmosphere, I'd estimate those structures are... several hundred thousand years old, at least—possibly much older."

"Commander, we should go down to the surface to investigate," said Nadia.

"I don't think so," said Anhur. "If there was life down there at one time, it's long gone. There's nothing for us to see here."

"Sir, I respectfully disagree," said Nadia. Malia thought she could detect a note of frustration in her voice. "There must have been a highly advanced civilization here at one time to build such an underground structure. We've never encountered a star system where more than one planet has developed advanced intelligent life. This is a unique opportunity."

"Very well," said Anhur. "Assemble a team."

"You're going down there?" asked Jaden. "Can we come?"

"Yeah," said Malia. "I want to go, too!"

"As do I!" added Carl.

"Mom, can we go?" asked Malia.

"It's alright with me..."

"Commander, permission to take *two* shuttles down to the surface?" said Nadia with a grin.

"Granted," said Anhur. "Lieutenant, be aware, without engines, we won't be able to rescue you should anything go wrong. And while we're on the far side of the planet, we'll be out of communication range. You'll be on your own, so I would *prefer* that you take two shuttles."

"Understood, sir," she said. "Alright, let's meet in the shuttle bay in one hour," she added to Jaden, Malia, and Carl. "We'll have to get you suited up before we leave."

"Hey, mind if I join you, too?" said Bomani. "I've always wanted to see some other planets in this system."

"Sure," said Nadia. "We could use a bioscientist on this mission.

"We'll probably be gone for several hours," she added to the group, "so I'm going to head down to the mess hall for some food before we go. Anyone care to join me?"

"Hell, yes," said Jaden, rubbing his stomach.

"We ate already!" Malia reminded him.

"Yeah, so? I'm hungry again."

Malia and Jaden joined their mother and Carl and followed Nadia down to the mess hall. Unlike earlier, the area was crowded now. Nadia led them to a table in the far corner where a man was just sitting down to eat.

"Everyone, this is my husband, Awan," Nadia told them. She introduced each of them.

"It's nice to meet you all finally," he said. "Nadia's always talking about you guys!"

The rest of them went to the buffet to grab some food, then came back and sat down at the table. Malia wasn't hungry yet, so she grabbed only something that resembled an apple.

"So, what is all of this stuff?" asked Jaden, who had loaded his plate again.

"Every item you've got there is a synthesized compound of proteins, carbohydrates, and fats," Awan told him, "formulated to provide the nutrition your body needs. We've got algae growth chambers on board that provide the basic building blocks."

"Yuck," said Jaden.

"The food is identical to dishes we used to eat back on Othal," Nadia said.

"It is *not* identical," Awan retorted. "It's a rough approximation and mostly tastes awful."

"I thought it tasted pretty good when we were here earlier," said Malia.

"*Real* Othali food is better," said Bomani, as everyone started eating. "But I'll take it—tastes like home cooking after so many eons of Earth food!"

"Yeah, I could see that," said Awan.

"So, Bomani," said Melissa. "You said you were living in Bermuda this whole time? Ever since the war?"

"Almost," he confirmed. "I spent a couple of years trying to find you. But I settled down in Bermuda after the Roswell crash in 1947 to be near the power station in case of an attack."

"It's a good thing you did!" said Carl.

"You *expected* an attack?" Malia asked.

"That ship that crashed in New Mexico, as well as many others that came later, seemed like they were probably scout ships," said Bomani. "I always had a feeling that whoever sent them would come calling eventually."

"You didn't get to travel in that whole time?" asked Melissa.

"Oh, I did a fair bit of traveling over the years," he said. "Got to see most of the U.S., Europe, parts of Asia. I went on a safari in Africa once—that was fun. Oh, and I did make it to Australia once, too."

"Sounds like you traveled quite a lot," said Carl. "More than I have, certainly. But you always came back to Bermuda because of the power station?"

"In part," he said. "But to be perfectly honest, I liked it there. It was peaceful. Laidback. That's one thing I came to dislike about humanity after so much time—the conflict. The wars. The fighting. On every level—superpowers building up their nuclear arsenals, neighbors having petty arguments, and strife at every stage in between. It's enough to make you crazy, you know? But Bermuda's different. It's live and let live there—very refreshing."

"That's very true," said Melissa. "Humans are so combative!"

"Do you mean to tell me Othal didn't have wars?" asked Carl.

"We did," said Nadia. "Long ago. We weren't so different from you. But that was way before my time."

"Our people learned to set aside their parochial concerns for the greater good," Bomani agreed. "But I know our history. Sure, we had our share of conflict before the planet united. But things never got so bad on Othal as they have on Earth. Between weapons of mass destruction, climate change, and general hunger and poverty, humanity seems determined to destroy itself."

"Did your planet ever have climate issues?" asked Malia.

"No, we managed to avoid that," said Melissa. "We only ever used renewable energy sources, like wind, solar, and hydropower. Personal transportation was electric from the beginning."

"Believe it or not, nearly forty percent of cars on Earth were electric at the turn of the twentieth century," said Carl. "Petroleum won out in the end, of course, but it didn't start that way!"

"But Othal probably didn't have dinosaurs, right?" asked Malia. "So they *couldn't* have developed fossil fuels."

"That's a myth," said Carl. "Petroleum does *not* come from dinosaurs! It's made from plankton, algae, and bacteria and largely formed millions of years *before* the dinosaurs. And I'm guessing Othal probably did have plankton and bacteria, or something quite similar, anyway."

"We did," Nadia confirmed. "And we very well could have used petroleum the way Earth did—it just happened not to go that way."

"That's not true," said Bomani. "It was a choice. Our people *did* consider using petroleum, but our scientists realized the damage it would do to the environment. They decided to use other alternatives."

"So, what—humans are all bad people?" asked Jaden.

"I wouldn't go that far," said Bomani. "But as a species, they do make some *awful* decisions!"

Once they'd finished eating, Nadia said, "Alright, those of us who are going to the surface had better get moving."

"Be careful, you two," Melissa said, giving Jaden and Malia each a hug. "And behave—I want a good report when you get back!"

"Don't worry," Bomani told her. "I'll keep an eye on them."

Chapter Three: The Face

Nadia led them down to the shuttle bay. There was a large chamber on one side that housed equipment and spacesuits.

"Alright, we'll need to get you all fitted," said Nadia.

"Fitted for what?" asked Jaden.

"Spacesuits!" Nadia replied.

"Why do we need spacesuits?" he asked.

Malia rolled her eyes and let out a long sigh.

"Because the Martian atmosphere is mostly carbon dioxide, so we can't breathe down there," she told him. "Not to mention that it's so cold, we'd die in seconds without a suit."

"And don't forget the radiation!" said Carl. "Mars' atmosphere is much thinner than Earth's, and the magnetic field is minimal—and that's what protects us from all that radiation back home."

"What radiation?" asked Jaden.

"From the sun," Malia told him with another sigh. "We *definitely* need to get you back to school!"

"Shut up, Malia," he said, glaring at her.

Nadia led them into the equipment room. An enclosure at the far end housed the spacesuits. She handed smaller ones to Jaden and

Malia, grabbed medium-sized ones for herself and Bomani, and gave Carl a large.

"One piece," Carl observed, examining the suit. "This is very thin and light—reminds me more of a wetsuit than those bulky outfits our astronauts wear. Feels kind of like rubber, too."

"Yes, it's meant to be form-fitting," Nadia told him. "There are only three sizes—the suit will expand or contract as necessary within a certain range. It retains heat and deflects radiation. The seams will form an airtight seal, and oxygen is stored within the material itself."

"Fascinating," said Carl. "How long does the oxygen supply last?"

"Well, that depends," said Nadia. "In open space, it would give you about sixteen hours of breathable air. But it can last longer in a planetary atmosphere. Mars doesn't have enough oxygen for normal respiration, but there is *some* oxygen down there. The suit will use that to constantly replenish itself. On Mars, that should buy you an extra four hours or so."

"Incredible!" said Carl.

"You still remember how to put one of these on?" Nadia asked Bomani.

"Sure do," he said.

"Great, why don't you give Jaden and Carl a hand, and I'll help Malia," she suggested.

Jaden and Carl followed Bomani into the men's changing area; Malia went with Nadia to the women's room.

"Okay, so... how does this work?" Malia asked.

"You'll have to remove your clothing," Nadia told her.

"Underwear, too?"

"Everything."

Nadia removed her clothes and put on the spacesuit. She pulled on the bottom section like a pair of pants and then the top and the attached helmet. Malia copied her the best she could. The suit felt loose at first, but she felt the entire thing contract as she pulled the helmet over her head.

"Now, I'll need you to seal me in," Nadia said, turning her back to Malia.

"Uh... how do I do that?"

Malia could see that Nadia's suit had contracted, too, but there was an opening that ran up the middle of her back.

"Pull the flap from the left side across to the right, then run your finger from the base of my spine up to my neck," Nadia told her.

"Okay..."

Malia pulled the flap across Nadia's back and pressed it to her right side. It clung to the material there in a way that reminded Malia of staticky clothes. She touched her finger against the base of Nadia's spine and dragged it up to her neck.

"Perfect," said Nadia. "Now you have to seal the back of the helmet the same way."

Malia found a flap hanging down from the back of her helmet. She pressed it against Nadia's shoulders and then ran her finger across it from left to right.

"That's it," said Nadia, turning to face her. "Turn around, and I'll do yours."

Malia felt Nadia run her finger up her spine and then across her shoulders. Malia felt her ears pop as the suit formed a seal.

"There," said Nadia, as Malia turned to face her. "How's that feel?"

"Good. It's skin-tight!"

"You can change the temperature here," said Nadia, showing her buttons on her right forearm. "It'll maintain oxygen levels on its own. The visor on the helmet will automatically adjust to lighting conditions, but you can adjust the brightness with these two buttons. The suit has built-in voice communication that will allow you to talk to anyone else in the party. You can adjust the volume here."

"What about these last three buttons?" asked Malia.

"Oh, I almost forgot," said Nadia. "The visor serves as a display. These two buttons allow you to zoom in and out—but if you've zoomed in on something, don't forget to zoom out before you start walking around again. It can become quite disorienting if you forget to do that! And that last button turns on the heads up display."

Malia tapped the last button. Suddenly she could see an array of symbols around the edges of her field of view.

"I can't read any of this," she said.

"Yes, it's in Othali," Nadia told her. "We'll have to adjust a few suits at some point to show the data in your native language."

"What does it say?"

"It provides ambient conditions—temperature, light, and radiation levels, that sort of thing. And if you use the zoom function, it will provide you with the distance to whatever object you're looking at."

Malia tapped the button to zoom in and suddenly found she

was looking at a closeup of Nadia's face. The visor had overlaid a measurement grid on her field of view, and the symbols around the edge had changed.

"Wow," said Malia, zooming back out again. "This is neat. But what happens if I accidentally hit my arm against something?"

"The buttons will only respond to your touch," Nadia told her, "so you don't have to worry about that."

They went back out to the equipment room and joined the others, then Nadia led them into the shuttle bay. There was another crew waiting for them there. Malia recognized their pilot, Madu, from her last shuttle mission

"Everyone ready?" Nadia asked. The others nodded. "Let's go!"

Jaden and Malia boarded one shuttle with Nadia, Bomani, and Carl, while the other crew climbed into a second shuttle. Bomani sat up front in the cockpit with Nadia. Malia took a seat in the rear along with Jaden and Carl.

"You remember how to fly one of these?" Nadia asked Bomani.

"Pretty sure I do," he said. "Doesn't look like *too much* has changed since my day."

"Then, she's all yours," said Nadia. "Take us out!"

"Oh, man," he replied, taking the controls. "I hope I don't screw this up!"

"Don't worry, I'll take over if you do," Nadia told him.

The shuttles left their berths and headed out of the bay. Malia could see Mars growing larger in the window as they descended toward the surface.

"I've got a question," she said to Carl. "Back on the ship, you said that you suspected that Othal had plankton and bacteria like Earth. Why would that be?"

"A question for the ages," he replied with a chuckle. "Well, it starts with the laws of physics. Take gravity, for example. We would expect gravity to work the same way everywhere. And so far, our measurements of the observable universe would confirm this to be true."

"So would ours," Nadia added from the cockpit.

"Centuries ago, people believed that the Earth was the center of the universe," Carl continued, "and that the Sun and all the planets revolved around us. But in time, of course, we figured out that the Sun is actually in the center of our solar system and that the Earth—along with all the other planets, revolve around the Sun.

"In other words, we discovered that we were not as special as we thought we were. But then, we discovered that other stars—possibly *most* other stars have planets, too. And with recent events, we have finally confirmed that life—and intelligent life has come to exist in at least two other places."

"Making Earth even less special," said Malia.

"Precisely," said Carl. "Even before the arrival of the Malor, many scientists had begun to postulate that life—simple life, at least, if not advanced, intelligent life—may well be as common as planets."

"How can that be?" asked Jaden.

"Well, take chemistry. We know that most of the elements are created inside of stars. Many of the heavier elements are formed in neutron star collisions, and others by supernova explosions. But once the elements were created, chemical interactions between them began happening all on their own. Hydrogen and oxygen combined to make water—and not only on Earth. We've detected water ice on comets and water molecules in interstellar clouds. It's a chemical process that will happen wherever suitable conditions exist.

"And what is life, but a collection of ever more complex chemical reactions? What if the interactions that ultimately produce DNA and simple single-cell organisms are just as universal as those that create water—again, given the right conditions?"

"Then life would probably exist wherever there are planets," said Malia.

"Precisely!" said Carl.

"Our scientists came to the same conclusion," said Nadia. "We have direct experience with four solar systems that developed technologically advanced life—this one, Othal, the Malor homeworld, and the planet we found that the Malor had destroyed. Add to that the planet we're traveling to now, and that makes five separate star systems where we've confirmed the presence of life. We believe simple life has probably evolved in *most* star systems where planets have formed, as a natural result of complex but common chemical processes."

"And so you would expect to find organisms like bacteria and plankton in those places," said Malia.

"But only on planets with conditions similar to Earth," Carl pointed out. "Othal has even more water than our planet, and so I figured they'd have that same sort of basic life—to provide a long answer to your simple but profound question!

"But I'm extremely curious to see what we're about to find on Mars. Conditions here have been dry and arid for at least two billion years."

"So, we're probably not going to find any plankton?" asked Malia with a grin.

"Ah, no," said Carl. "I suspect not."

"Our scientists have long suspected that it should be possible for technologically intelligent life to develop on more than one planet in the same system," said Nadia. "But we've never found evidence to support the idea—until now. So, I'm interested to see what we're going to find here as well."

As they moved into the atmosphere, flames engulfed the exterior of the shuttle. Once they cleared, Malia noticed that it was dark outside.

"It's nighttime now?" asked Jaden.

"Well, it is here," Nadia confirmed. "But our warship has moved on and is still over an area with daylight."

She turned on spotlights on the shuttle's underside, and Malia could see the landscape flying by beneath them. It looked like the entire planet was one big desert. A few minutes later, she could feel them slowing down.

"We're here," Nadia announced.

"I'll be damned," said Carl, gazing out the window.

The shuttle had come to rest hovering directly in front of the five-sided pyramid they'd seen from space.

"That thing is *huge*!" said Jaden.

"That looks way bigger than the Giza pyramid," Carl observed.

"Yes, it's roughly twice as high," Nadia confirmed.

The pyramid was the same reddish color as the rest of the landscape. It looked like it had eroded significantly—the edges of each side were rounded, but unevenly so, and the flat surfaces had crumbled in places. It almost looked like the entire structure was being reclaimed by the surrounding desert.

Malia looked past the pyramid and could see the face in the distance, protruding from the Martian surface. It looked larger than the pyramid. In the space between the pyramid and the face were a handful of much smaller structures.

"What are those other formations?" she asked. "I don't remember seeing those from space."

"I'm not sure," said Nadia. "They're rectangular cuboids—I don't think they're naturally occurring, either."

"They look like regular buildings," said Jaden.

"Take us in closer to the face," Nadia said to Bomani.

The shuttle moved across the area. Bomani took them up and over the structure so that they were looking down on it.

"Wow," said Malia.

"This is *crazy*," said Jaden.

Up close, Malia could see the same erosion on the surface of the face that she'd noted on the pyramid. Areas that looked like they were probably smooth at one time had become rough and pockmarked as if the face had a bad case of acne.

The shuttle moved down by the left side of the structure, where the ear would be, but there was no ear. From there, they headed down around the chin and up the right side.

"That's good," said Nadia. "Set us down here."

"I'll give it a shot," Bomani replied, "but be ready with those controls. Landing was always the hardest part!"

"You'll be fine; just take it slow."

Bomani ended up having no trouble setting them down on the surface. Malia saw the second shuttle land nearby.

"This is it," said Nadia. "Check each other's suits and make sure the seams are sealed. There's very little oxygen out there, and the surface temperature is only about 190 Kelvin."

"What the hell is Kelvin?" asked Jaden.

"Universal temperature scale," said Carl. "Zero Kelvin would be what they call 'absolute zero'—a temperature so cold that atoms would stop moving."

"Okay, so what does 190 Kelvin translate to in normal terms?" asked Jaden.

"It's about a hundred degrees below zero," Carl replied.

"Maybe I'll stay in the shuttle," Jaden said.

"Don't be silly," said Nadia. "Your suit will keep you warm."

Once everyone confirmed their suits were airtight, Nadia opened the hatch and led the way outside. Malia stepped off the shuttle and gazed around in wonder. The floodlights from the shuttles illuminated the area, and it looked like a desert as far as she could see.

"Okay, now *this* is crazy," said Jaden. "We're the first Earthlings to visit Mars, right?"

"Yes, Jaden," Malia replied.

"This is a dream come true," said Carl. "But I never thought it would happen."

"I feel light," said Malia. "Like my feet are hardly touching the ground.'

"The gravity on this planet is only a little more than a third of what we're used to back on Earth," Carl told her.

"Watch this," said Jaden, before leaping straight into the air. He rose just over Malia's head before returning to the ground.

"Whoa," said Malia. "Do that again!"

He jumped, and this time Malia reached out with her mind and lifted him higher.

"Hey! Cut it out!" Malia laughed at him. "Come on, now—I'm not kidding! Put me down!"

"You sound scared," she chided, holding him about twenty feet in the air.

"This isn't funny! I might float off into space!"

"Oh, there's too much gravity for that," said Carl.

Malia finally relented and set him down on the ground. But then she ran toward him and jumped right over his head. Not to be outdone, Jaden launched himself into the air and flew right over her.

"I'm Superman!" he yelled.

"Alright, you two," Nadia said with a grin. "That's enough of that."

They met up with the crew from the other shuttle. Nadia held a device in one hand that resembled an iPhone. She pointed it at the face and gazed at the display.

"This is astonishing," she said. "We weren't able to calculate the age of this structure too accurately from orbit. But according to my readings, the face is somewhere between seventy-five and one hundred *million* years old!"

"Which would mean someone built this when the dinosaurs still roamed the Earth," noted Carl.

"There's a massive structure beneath the face," Nadia told them, gazing at the display on her device. "It's at least a hundred meters deep. And it extends laterally far beyond the face."

"It would seem this is only the tip of the proverbial iceberg," Carl observed.

"Let's get closer," Nadia suggested. She led the group right up to the structure. Up close, it looked like nothing more than a giant stone wall.

Malia reached out to it with one hand but stopped before making contact.

"Is it okay to touch it?" she asked.

"I think so," said Nadia. "Why?"

"Well, I remember the last time one of us touched something built by aliens..."

"Yeah, the power station," said Jaden. "Doing that brought the Malor here."

"I'm not detecting any circuitry or anything," said Nadia. "It's just stone."

Malia touched it, only with her fingertip at first, pulling it away immediately as if she'd been shocked.

"What happened?" asked Jaden.

"Nothing," said Malia, feeling embarrassed. "I'm just nervous."

"Give me a break," said Jaden, placing his palm against it. Nothing happened. "See? Just stone."

Malia touched it again, rubbing her hand along the surface.

"Just stone," she repeated.

"Let's take a walk around the perimeter and see what there is to see," Nadia suggested.

She led the way around the structure. The surface remained mostly smooth as they walked, but it became rougher in some places, and big chunks were missing in others. The terrain around the face was primarily flat, but they encountered small peaks and valleys in some places where they had to climb a bit. Slowly, their path curved to the left as they reached the forehead area of the structure.

Nadia stopped when they reached the crown of the head.

"What is that?" she asked, pointing to the base of the formation.

Malia could see something protruding from the stone. It looked metallic.

Nadia squatted down and began sweeping sand and dust away from the object. As she worked, it became ever more apparent that some sort of structure was attached to the rock.

"That's as far as I can go by hand," Nadia reported, straightening up. "We'll need tools to go any deeper."

Two of the crew members from the other shuttle ran back to get the necessary equipment. Meanwhile, Nadia and Bomani cleared the sand away farther to each side of the hole she'd dug. Within a few minutes, it became apparent that the metallic object was circular.

The crew members returned, each carrying a crate. They set them down on the ground and opened their lids.

"We should start with shovels," said Nadia. "It appears to be compacted sand below the area we dug out. Let's see how much we can clear away."

Several of the Othali began digging. Malia watched their progress with the others. More and more of the metallic object became visible as they worked. But eventually, they reached harder stone, and the shovels became useless.

Nadia removed a device from one of the crates.

"That looks like a ray gun," said Carl.

Nadia chuckled.

"It's a laser," she said as she tapped the display on its top surface. "I'm programming it to emit a frequency that will vaporize the rock but not affect the metal."

"Well, that's useful!" Carl replied.

Nadia programmed a second device and handed it to Bomani.

"Everyone stand back," she advised the group.

Malia moved away with the others. Once they were clear, Nadia and Bomani went to work with the lasers. They started up close to the face, slowly backing up as they cleared a broader and deeper area. This process sent a cloud of smoke and dust into the air, making it impossible for Malia to see what they were uncovering.

Once they'd finished, Nadia and the crewman rejoined the rest of the group. Slowly the dust cloud dissipated, revealing the area of the face they'd exposed with the lasers.

"Extraordinary," said Carl.

A giant archway was embedded in the crown of the face's head, with a solid metal door in the middle.

Chapter Four: The Hatch

"Looks like we've found the entrance to... whatever is in there," Nadia observed.

She held up her device for a moment.

"I'm detecting circuitry in the walls around the aperture," she told them, "but no current."

"You're not detecting any kind of signal?" asked Bomani. "No carrier wave?"

"No, nothing," said Nadia. "I've tried emitting signals on various wavelengths, too, thinking perhaps we could trigger a response. But I'm not getting anything."

"This is a motorized electric door?" asked Carl.

"It would seem so," she said. "Hang on; I'm going to try inducing an electric current."

She tapped on her display for a moment. Suddenly, Malia heard a grinding sound coming from the hatch, but nothing else happened.

"Well, that didn't work," Jaden observed.

"Thank you, Captain Obvious," Malia muttered.

"I'm not too surprised," said Nadia. "After millions of years, I wouldn't expect this to work anymore, but it was worth a shot."

"We could try prying it open," Madu suggested.

"Let's do it," Nadia agreed.

Madu and two of the other crew people grabbed crowbars from one of the crates and tried to open the hatch. This didn't work, either. Next, they used the lasers to try cutting a hole through the metal but had no better luck with this.

"I can't identify this alloy," Nadia said, tapping the display on her device. "Without that, it'll be impossible to find the right frequency for the lasers."

"I can try running a more extensive analysis on the metal," Bomani suggested. "If we can identify it, then we should be able to tune the lasers to cut through it."

"Great idea," said Nadia. "While you're doing that, I'm going to take a walk. Anyone care to join me?"

"Oh, hell yes," Jaden replied.

Malia, Carl, and Jaden went with Nadia. They walked back to the shuttles and then to the smaller structures they'd seen earlier.

They were rectangular, roughly twice as tall as Malia. There were no openings or markings on their sides, and they appeared to be made of stone.

"What do you make of these?" asked Carl.

"I'm not sure," said Nadia, holding her device toward one of them. "I'm detecting circuitry and heavy wiring inside. I'd guess these must be power junctions of some kind."

Jaden ran toward one and leaped into the air. Malia could tell he'd used his telekinesis to make it up to the top of the structure. She shot into the air and landed next to him.

"Anything interesting up there?" Nadia asked.

"No, it's stone, just like the walls," Malia replied.

She and Jaden jumped back down to the ground, and they proceeded to the pyramid. The structure seemed even larger from the ground than it had from the shuttle.

"There are open cavities inside of this," Nadia told them, scanning the structure with her device. "Lots of technology inside there, but none of it active."

"It's astounding that all of this is here, but we never found it from Earth," said Malia.

"Well, we *did* see it from Viking," said Carl. "But then the government covered it up and doctored the images from the more recent orbiters."

"Sure, but why didn't they ever explore this area with the landers?" she asked.

"I'd imagine whoever released the fake images made sure the space agencies didn't target this area with the surface probes," said Carl.

"But, why?" asked Malia. "Even if they kept it a secret, wouldn't they have wanted to explore this area up close, after those first images?"

"Your guess is as good as mine," said Carl.

"Is it possible that they *did* send a lander here but kept the mission a secret?" asked Malia.

"I suppose anything is possible," said Carl. "But I'd tend to doubt it. Sending a probe to another planet requires an enormous investment of money and human resources. It took thousands of people back on Earth to bring each lander mission to fruition and thousands more to operate it over the course of its lifetime. Doctoring some photos and classifying the real ones is one thing, but I doubt it would be possible to keep such a massive undertaking a secret.

"Hmm," Malia replied.

"I wonder why the folks who built all of this decided to construct a humanoid face," said Carl. "That would make it seem like they *wanted* to pique our curiosity—or someone's at any rate—human beings didn't yet exist when they built it."

"It does almost seem like they intended it to announce their presence here, doesn't it?" said Nadia.

"Indeed," Carl agreed. "Any intelligent species seeing that face from space would surely want to come and investigate, one would think. Ironic that humanity never did."

"But if humans didn't exist when they built it, how could they make it look like a *human* face?" asked Jaden.

"Strictly speaking, they didn't," said Carl. "I would call it *humanoid*, not human. After millions of years of erosion, most of the details have worn away. Its basic shape is similar to a human face, so our brains fill in the details to match our expectations. Were those details still present, it may not look remotely human. But this would seem to suggest that whatever technologically advanced life developed here did resemble humans at least in the broad strokes."

They walked around the perimeter of the pyramid. The terrain here was somewhat less level than that around the face, so they had to climb or jump in some places. But they made it around the entire structure without finding any openings or surface features.

"There's an enormous canyon about a hundred meters over that way," Nadia told them, pointing off in the distance. "Care to have a look?"

"Yeah, I'm game," said Malia.

Nadia led the way. Most of the land between the pyramid and the canyon was a flat plain, and the going was relatively easy. As they drew closer, Malia could see that the canyon formed a horseshoe shape, and they were approaching from one end of the horseshoe.

"Wow," said Jaden. "I've never seen anything like this."

"This must be bigger than the Grand Canyon back home," Carl observed.

"It's twice as deep," Nadia confirmed. "And it's roughly twice as far across. But it's only about half the length."

"Fascinating," said Carl. "The reduced gravity of this planet allows taller mountains and deeper valleys to form here. Earth's greater mass tends to keep things more homogenous, relatively speaking."

As Malia gazed across the canyon, she spotted a darker area halfway down the face of the far side.

"What is that," she asked, pointing to the area.

"What?" asked Jaden. "Where?"

"Hang on," said Malia, tapping the button to zoom in with her visor. It looked like there were long, flat openings in the rock face. "They look like caves, maybe."

"I see it," said Nadia. "Almost reminds me of docking ports for spacecraft."

"I'm sorry, how are you two able to see that far?" asked Carl.

"Yeah, what the hell?" Jaden demanded. "I can't see shit!"

"Didn't Bomani show you two how to use the controls on your suit?" asked Malia.

"What controls?" asked Jaden.

Nadia took a minute to show them how to use the buttons.

"Whoa," said Jaden once he'd zoomed in on the openings.

"I'd agree," Carl added. "Those do look like aircraft hangars."

Nadia scanned the area with her device.

"They may well be," she said. "Those openings connect to a vast network of tunnels and cavities inside the bedrock in that area."

"Does that connect to the structure beneath the face?" asked Carl.

"It may," said Nadia. "I'm not able to penetrate far enough into the rock to tell." She continued to look out across the canyon for a moment longer, then added, "Why don't we head back and see how they're making out with the hatch?"

They followed Nadia back to the pyramid, and then to the face, and around to the hatch at the top of its head. Madu and Bomani were standing there with the rest of the crew, staring at the hatch. There were tools scattered about on the ground and black marks on the door, but not much else had changed.

"No luck?" asked Nadia.

"Well, we were finally able to identify the alloy they used for the door," Madu told her. "So, we were able to tune the lasers to the proper frequency. But the handheld units aren't powerful enough to cut through it. We just gave up a few minutes ago. I think we should try the shuttle's lasers, but wanted to run it by you first."

"I agree," she said. "I don't see how else we're getting through this. Let's give it a try."

Madu ran off to fetch one of the shuttles.

"Everyone should stand back for this," Nadia said to the others. "And once the shuttle gets here, you'll want to dim your visors. The laser will be emitting much more power than the handheld units, and it could blind you if you look directly at it."

Malia moved away with everyone else. Moments later, the shuttle moved into view. Madu had it hovering a few feet from the ground, its floodlights illuminating the hatch. Malia dimmed her visor.

"Go ahead, Madu," said Nadia.

He opened fire. There was a humming sound as the laser beam hit the hatch. Madu moved the beam slowly, and it seemed to be working. Malia could see the glowing line he was tracing along the outline of the door.

Once he'd finished, he backed the shuttle away from the face and set it down, and rejoined the group.

"I think that did it," said Nadia. "Let's see if we can knock it in."

She approached the hatch with Madu. The two of them pushed the door, and it fell inside the structure.

The others joined them. Nadia shone a light through the doorway.

"This looks like an airlock," said Carl.

Malia had to agree. There was a chamber inside, more or less circular, and roughly twenty feet across. The walls were white and metallic-looking. There was a small window on the far side.

"Everyone, wait here," said Nadia, before going inside with Madu.

Malia watched as they moved across the chamber. Nadia peered through the window, shining her light into the area beyond. The two of them spent a few minutes examining the area around the window before returning to the others.

"It does seem to be an airlock," Nadia told them. "And possibly an elevator as well. There's a hollow shaft below the chamber—I couldn't tell how deep it goes. We found another door on the opposite side, and there's a large open area beyond that. But the door is sealed shut."

"Can we get through it with the shuttle's laser again?" asked Bomani.

"Yes, I think so," said Nadia. "Let's all get out of the way, and we'll give it a shot."

Everyone else moved away while Madu boarded the shuttle. He lifted off and hovered up close to the opening. Moments later, he fired the laser into the chamber. After a few minutes, he cut the laser and landed the shuttle again. Smoke poured out of the aperture in the side of the face.

"Alright, let's move inside," Nadia said once the smoke had cleared.

Nadia and Madu led the way. Malia followed close behind with Jaden, and the rest of the crew came behind them.

The inner doorway had fallen on its own. They climbed through the opening, and Malia found herself in a much larger, oval-shaped chamber. There was a long counter at the far end and windows along part of the far wall.

Malia went straight to the windows, but it was dark, and she could see nothing beyond them. Nadia joined her and shone her light through the window. Malia gasped. The chamber overlooked a vast chasm. Nadia's light did not penetrate the darkness far enough to see the bottom.

Looking across the chasm, Malia could see that structures covered the walls. It looked like a massive underground city.

"Incredible," said Carl. "This place could be as big as Manhattan, but all underground."

"Bigger, possibly," Nadia replied. "It's several kilometers across. We still can't tell how deep it goes, but it's at least a few kilometers."

"Well, this certainly explains a lot," said Carl. "This planet has been a barren desert world for *billions* of years. But seeing this, I wonder if most, or perhaps all advanced life here evolved to live underground. We've known for a long time that Mars does have water—mostly locked in the polar ice caps, but surface conditions are not exactly hospitable to life."

"The airlock seems to be the only way to access the lower areas from here," Madu reported. "I don't see any other openings."

"We can't go that way," said Nadia. "I wasn't able to power the control system. But even if we could get the chamber to move somehow, I wouldn't trust it. Given the age of this structure, there's a good chance we'd end up plummeting to our deaths."

"We could probably blow out these windows," said Madu. "But then we'd be forced to rappel down into the chasm."

"No, thank you," said Nadia. "We found docking bays in a cliff face nearby. Let's take the shuttles in there and see if there's another way inside."

Everyone moved out of the chamber and boarded the shuttles. Once they were airborne, Nadia pointed out the canyon to Bomani.

"Ah, yeah, I see it."

They flew over the plain and descended into the canyon. Once they'd reached the other side, Bomani flew them inside the docking bay. The shuttle's floodlights illuminated the area. Malia spotted at least two dozen saucer-shaped craft sitting at the far end of this area.

"Those resemble the Malor scout ships," said Carl, "only sleeker."

Bomani set the shuttle down, and they disembarked. The other shuttle landed nearby.

Nadia and Madu led the way, and the rest of the group followed them across the docking bay. A thick layer of red dust covered everything, including the spacecraft. Sand drifts had piled up against the walls of the area. Beyond the saucers, they found several large bay doors.

"This is our way in," said Madu, "but I don't know how we're going to get these doors open. I'm pretty sure we'll need to cut through them with the shuttle's lasers again, but these saucers are in the way. I don't know how we'd get the shuttle close enough."

"Let's see if we can access the power system first," Nadia replied, "or perhaps pry one of these open."

Madu went back to the shuttles to retrieve the crowbars. Nadia pulled out her scanner and tried to find a way to provide power to the control units. Madu returned, and he and another crew member tried to pry one of the bay doors open.

"These circuits are beyond dead," Nadia said after several minutes. "I can't get a signal or induce any current."

"Not too surprising after millions of years," said Carl.

"The doors won't budge," Madu told them. "And these doors are thicker than the ones for the airlock, so there's no way the hand lasers will have any effect."

Nadia looked around the hangar.

"Let's have a look around and see if there are any other openings that *wouldn't* require us to move these saucers," she said.

They spread out to search the hangar, but the bay doors were the only openings they could find.

"Well, this is it, then," said Nadia, as they regrouped by the bay doors. "What will it take to move these saucers out of the way?"

Madu scanned the saucers for a minute.

"We should be able to do it with tow cables," he said.

"Let's make it happen," said Nadia. "I think we should only have to move a few of them, right?"

"That should do it," Madu agreed. "We only need enough room to have a clear shot with the shuttle's lasers."

Madu moved his shuttle into position to move the first saucer.

Two of the crew members got to work attaching the tow cable to the spacecraft's landing gear. Once everything was ready, they secured the line to the shuttle. Everyone cleared the area, and Madu moved the shuttle forward. A groaning sound came from the saucer as it started to move. But moments later, the landing gear broke off, and the saucer crashed to the hangar floor.

"So much for that idea," said Carl.

Madu joined them again.

"Now what?" asked Nadia.

"Well, I don't see anywhere else we can attach the cable," he said. "But even if we could, we may run into the same problem again. These spacecraft are so ancient; who knows how much corrosion there is. The whole thing could come apart. I think our best option is to use the shuttle like a plow and just push the saucers out of the way."

"I agree," said Nadia. "I'll assist with the second shuttle."

Nadia started by the left end of the bay door. She brought the front of the shuttle into contact with one of the saucers and slowly applied thrust. The saucer began to move, its landing gear making a screeching sound against the hangar floor. Moments later, part of the landing gear collapsed, but Nadia kept pushing it forward.

When the saucer she was pushing made contact with the next one, she increased the shuttle's thrust. Both saucers began to buckle, but they both moved. When they hit the third saucer, she had to boost the thrust again. But within minutes, she'd created a large space in front of the left end of the bay door. Madu had done the same on the right side.

Next, they cleared away the saucers from the middle area. Sure enough, each lost pieces as they worked. But they'd opened up a large enough space to take the shuttles in closer.

Nadia turned her shuttle toward the bay door. She fired the laser.

"Madu, I don't have enough power," Malia could hear her say in her headset. "We're going to need both shuttles."

Madu moved his shuttle next to hers and fired his laser. Slowly, they cut out a large oval in the metal. But when they finished, the section in the middle didn't move. Nadia moved her shuttle forward and used it to knock the door down. Malia could feel a rush of air blowing out of the opening. Nadia and Madu moved the shuttles out of the way and set them down.

"Alright," said Nadia once they'd rejoined the rest of the group. "Let's go inside."

Chapter Five: The City

Once again, Nadia and Madu led the way, shining their lights ahead of them. Malia crossed the threshold and found that they had entered a cavernous area. Most of the walls were rock, except for the one abutting the hangar, which was metal. There were many more saucers here and heavy equipment that looked like it was probably used for digging.

On the far side, there was what looked like an enormous vault. There were giant bay doors on the front that had been left open.

"What is that?" asked Carl, indicating the vault.

"Good question," said Nadia. "Let's get a closer look."

She scanned it as they approached.

"The walls are several feet thick," she told them. "It's made from some sort of lead alloy."

They peered inside, but it was empty.

"What do you think they used this for?" asked Malia.

"I'm not sure," said Nadia. "It's big enough that they could have fit at least a few of these saucers inside. The wall thickness would suggest they wanted to protect whatever was inside from impact, and the lead alloy would have shielded the contents from any kind of radiation."

"Fascinating," said Carl.

"There's a tunnel over there," said Nadia, pointing across the expanse, "that appears to lead to the main part of the complex."

They followed her across the area. Minutes later, they arrived at the tunnel entry; Nadia led them inside. Several smaller tunnels and corridors led away from the central shaft, but they stayed the course. It turned several sharp corners but continued to lead in the same general direction.

"I'm detecting an enormous cavity up ahead," Nadia told them after several minutes. "It's several kilometers wide and at least as deep."

"Is it the same one we encountered earlier, inside that airlock?" asked Carl.

"No, it can't be," she replied. "That's back in the other direction."

They emerged from the tunnel and arrived at a terrace that extended for at least a hundred meters in either direction. Malia and Jaden followed Nadia to the far edge. Malia was thankful that there was a thick stone railing here—the terrace overlooked a chasm. Nadia's light could not reach the bottom.

Malia looked up and saw that the cavity extended far above them as well. Nadia's light reached the top—there appeared to be a roof of solid stone over the entire area.

Looking around the area, Malia could see numerous other terraces overlooking the cavity from all sides. The area's shape reminded her of an amoeba.

The rest of the group joined them by the railing.

"Let's look around and see what we can find," Nadia said to them. "I'd like to find some sort of computer interface so we can retrieve some information about the beings who lived here and what happened to them. It would also be useful to find a power source or controls to turn on some of the systems. I don't know how much we'll be able to find on this level, so it would also be helpful to locate a way to get to the lower levels."

"Any kind of elevator we find will be unsafe," Madu added. "So, we're probably looking for... well, stairs."

"And let's do this in pairs," Nadia concluded. "Just to play it safe. You two are with me," she added to Jaden and Malia.

Nadia led them away from the edge, and they moved to the far end of the terrace. There, they found an opening leading to a set of chambers. They had windows looking out over the chasm.

"This looks like it could have been a dwelling," Nadia suggested.

"You mean this was someone's house?" asked Jaden.

"There's no way to know for sure," she replied, "but that would be my guess."

A panel on one wall looked like it could have been a computer terminal of some kind. Nadia scanned it but was unable to activate it or provide power to the unit.

They moved back out to the terrace. A little farther along the wall, they found a tunnel, smaller than the one from the hangar, that led off behind the chambers they'd explored. Malia and Jaden followed Nadia into the tunnel.

There were numerous sets of chambers beyond the first one.

Nadia found power lines and consoles that appeared to be computer terminals in each but could not activate any of them. They were not able to find anything that would provide access to other levels.

"Let's head back to the terrace," Nadia said finally. "I don't think we're going to find much more down here."

They returned to the promenade area, where they met Madu and another crew member.

"We found what appears to be an elevator shaft," Madu told them, "but no sign of a carriage. We didn't see any stairways."

"Neither did we," said Nadia. "There are consoles all over the place that would appear to be access points to a computer system, but they're all dead."

The rest of the teams returned over the next few minutes. Nobody had found any kind of power source or any viable access to other levels.

"Could we get one of the shuttles in here?" asked Bomani. "We could use that to get down to the lower levels."

"There's plenty of room to maneuver inside the chasm here," said Madu. "But we'd never get it through that tunnel. It's too long to fit around some of those corners."

Malia went to the edge of the concourse and gazed down over the railing. There were smaller terraces directly below—many of them, going down as far as she could see.

"Jaden and I could get us down there," she suggested to the others.

"Using your telekinesis, you mean?" asked Nadia. She peered over the edge. "That might work..."

"It'll work," said Jaden. "Let me show you—I'll drop down to that next level and then come back up again."

"Your mother would kill us if anything happens to you," said Nadia.

"You have nothing to worry about," he insisted. "This'll be *easy.* Look, Malia can bring me back up if something happens."

Nadia considered it for a moment longer and then said, "Alright, let's see what you've got."

Jaden vaulted over the railing and dropped down to the terrace below. A moment later, he took himself back up to the main concourse.

"See? Easy."

Nadia took a deep breath.

"Move me down there," Madu suggested. "Malia, *please* be ready in case he can't get me back up!"

"I'm on it," she said.

Jaden focused for a moment, then reached out with his mind, raised Madu into the air, over the railing, and down to the terrace.

"Alright, I'm convinced," he said. "Now, bring me back."

Jaden brought him back up.

"This is the only way," Madu said to Nadia.

"I agree," she said. "I want to minimize the risk, though. Bomani and I will go down with the twins. The rest of you stay here—Madu, why don't you get the shuttles ready for a quick departure, just in case something goes sideways."

"Any chance you could take Madu with you and let me stay up

here?" said Bomani, backing away from the edge. "I'm, uh... well, a little afraid of heights..."

"Seriously?" asked Malia. "You didn't seem nervous on the shuttle."

"Sure, because there's no risk of *falling*!" he said. "Dropping into a bottomless chasm is an entirely different matter!"

"Very well," Nadia said with a chuckle. "You can get the shuttles ready. Madu and I will go into the abyss."

Malia and Nadia went to the railing and looked down.

"Do you think you could move both of us at the same time?" Nadia asked.

"Yeah, definitely."

"How far down do you think you could go in one shot?"

"As far as you want," said Malia. "If we get tired, we'll let you know, and we could take a break on one of the terraces. But we probably won't need it. Going up is harder."

"Very well," said Nadia. "I'm going to keep an eye on the temperature on the way down. This area is up to 300 Kelvin, and it's likely to get much hotter down there."

"What is that in Fahrenheit?" asked Malia.

"About eighty degrees," said Carl.

"Wait, what?" said Jaden. "It was a hundred *below zero* outside—how can it be that warm in here?"

"This pit here goes very deep into the planet's crust," said Carl. "It may be hundreds of degrees at the bottom, depending on how far down this goes. And heat rises, so this chasm has likely provided heat for the entire city the whole time it's been here. If anything, they would have needed a cooling system!"

"I don't get it," said Jaden. "Why would it be so hot down there?"

"Like most rocky planets, Mars has a molten core," Carl told him, "in large part because the weight of the entire planet pushes down on the center, creating tremendous pressure. That heat radiates up into the mantle and then into the crust."

"So, you're saying the center of the planet is lava?" Jaden asked.

"Much hotter than the volcanic lava you're probably imagining," said Carl, "but yes. That's the idea. Liquid iron, primarily."

"How much heat can our suits handle?" asked Malia.

"The suits are rated to 600 Kelvin," said Nadia.

"That's a little over 600 Fahrenheit," Carl added. "The two scales line up with each other at about 575 degrees."

"I'll keep an eye on it," said Nadia. "Malia and Jaden, be ready to stop our descent if it gets too hot." They both nodded. "Let's do it. Everyone ready?"

"As ready as I'll ever be," said Madu, gazing over the edge.

"You're not having second thoughts, are you?" Nadia chided.

"Who, me? Nah, not at all..."

Malia focused, then lifted herself and Nadia up and over the railing and down into the chasm. Jaden followed close behind with Madu. Nadia pointed her light below them.

They descended dozens of levels at a walking pace. Still, there was no sight of the bottom.

From this vantage point, Malia noticed tracks running up and down the walls. Were they on the ground, she would have described them as sidewalks. She had no idea what purpose they might have served.

"Would you two feel safe going a little faster?" asked Nadia.

"Hell, yeah," said Jaden; he and Madu fell away from them like a couple of stones. Malia could hear Madu's scream receding into the depths, and she had to laugh. She let herself and Nadia drop, too.

"Whoa!" Nadia yelled. "This doesn't feel too safe—how quickly can you slow us down?"

Malia stopped their motion and held them steady ten feet out from the nearest terrace.

"Alright, good enough," Nadia said with a nervous chuckle. "Go ahead."

Malia let them drop again; Nadia screamed.

Terraces went streaking by for several minutes. Malia guessed that they must have dropped hundreds of levels; still, they kept going.

"The temperature's rising," Nadia said, "but we're still well within the suits' limit."

Looking down, Malia could see Madu's light—it was only a pinprick; they were far ahead now. A few minutes later, the walls changed—the terraces were much larger down here.

"We're getting close to the bottom now," said Nadia, tapping at the display on her scanner. "Maybe we should slow down?"

"You got it," Malia replied and decreased their speed.

Minutes later, they reached the bottom. They joined Jaden and Madu, who were nearby, looking around.

"We're roughly thirty kilometers below the surface," Nadia told them. "It's about 400 Kelvin down here—that's roughly 260 degrees in your Fahrenheit scale."

"Good thing for these suits!" said Malia.

Nadia scanned the rest of the area.

"We've reached the very bottom. I don't see anything but solid rock below us. There's a chamber at the far end of this cavern that houses what appears to be the computer core. Let's go see what we can find."

They followed her across the space. The floor was solid stone; there was some debris strewn about here and there, but the area was mostly clear.

It took them a half hour to reach their destination. The chamber was built into the rock wall, and the openings had no doors. Nadia led the way inside. The chamber's vaulted ceiling was several levels above them. There was a massive tower in the center.

"That's the core, I think," said Nadia.

They proceeded around the tower to the far side of the chamber. There, they found several consoles on the wall that looked like terminals.

"Madu, why don't you see if you can get one of these to activate. I'm going to try to find the power generator."

"Yes, ma'am," he said.

Malia and Jaden followed Nadia back out into the cavern. She scanned the area for a minute, finally saying, "This way."

She led them into a wide tunnel; it took several minutes to get there. It didn't go very far before they found themselves inside of another open chamber. In the center, there was a structure that reminded Malia of a giant electrical transformer. It filled the majority of the area and had numerous cylindrical coils protruding along its top.

"I think this is it," said Nadia examining her scanner. "There are conduits underneath this thing that tunnel even deeper into the ground. My guess is that this structure converts geothermal energy into electrical power, but it's dormant now. Let's see if we can find a way to activate it."

They walked around the perimeter of the structure. There were consoles embedded in the walls at regular intervals but nothing that functioned. Finally, they found a giant lever protruding from the stone wall at the far and of the chamber, pointing down toward the floor.

"I think we found the main power switch," said Nadia. "Let's turn it on."

"Do we think this is a good idea?" asked Malia. "This thing has been shut off for millions of years, right? Could it overload or something if we turn it on after all this time?"

"Maybe," said Nadia with a shrug. "But if it does, we can turn it off again."

Malia still thought this might prove dangerous, but Nadia didn't seem too concerned.

"I hope you're right," she said.

Nadia tried to flip the lever up, but it wouldn't budge.

"Give me a hand, you two," she said.

The three of them together still couldn't move the lever.

"Let us try it using telekinesis," suggested Malia.

"Great idea," said Nadia.

"You ready?" Malia asked Jaden.

"Let's do it."

Malia reached out with her mind and could feel Jaden doing the same. Together they willed the lever to move. It let out a metallic screeching noise and began to shift. Slowly, they managed to get it to the upright position.

"Nice work," Nadia told them, turning to scan the generator. It started making a deep humming noise, but Malia couldn't sense anything else different. "It's working," Nadia told them. "It's generating power, and the output is climbing. Let's go see how Madu's doing!"

They hurried back to the computer core.

"Hey!" Madu said when they arrived. "Did you do something? Because this thing was completely dead no matter what I tried—until a few minutes ago. Then it came to life all on its own—and it certainly wasn't from anything I did."

"We turned on the main power, I think," said Nadia.

"You did?" asked Madu. "That seems a little risky, no? I mean, given its age?"

"We'll turn it off again if anything goes wrong," said Nadia. "And besides, it's purely geothermal. It's not nuclear, so there's no chance of a meltdown or anything like that. Have you been able to access the system since it came online?"

"You'd better believe I have," he replied. "The wall consoles still won't activate, but take a look at this," he added, showing them his scanner.

They gathered around Madu, and he turned the device around to show them the display. Malia watched as a video started on the screen. It was a person—or a being of some kind, who did look humanoid, but also lizard-like. The face did have roughly the same shape as the one on the planet's surface, but the skin was scaled, and the pupils were slits. The being seemed to be speaking into the camera, but she couldn't hear what he was saying.

"There's no sound," Malia observed.

"Yeah, the computer system is a mess," Madu replied. "After so much time, there's extreme degradation to the storage media. I was only able to retrieve some small fragments of data. Most of it wasn't identifiable, but then I found this!"

"Advanced humanoid," said Nadia. "Great work, Madu. Let's see what else we can find!"

The two of them spent the next several minutes scanning the computer core.

"Take a look at this," said Nadia. They gathered around her, and she showed them her display.

"It looks like a map," said Jaden.

"Yes, this appears to show the entire complex," Nadia agreed. "Three different chasms. This one is underneath the face on the surface. Here is where we are now, and there's a third in between the two."

"It looks like they built them around the edges of the canyon," said Malia.

"It does," Madu agreed.

Malia could see the hangars in the cliff face, the power generator, and the computer core represented in the diagram.

"What do you think this is?" she asked, pointing to a square area below their current location.

"I have no idea," said Nadia. "Other than the geothermal conduits for the power generator, it looks like it's the only thing that goes any deeper than this level. Let's see if we can find it."

Madu stayed behind to keep working on the computer core. Malia and Jaden went with Nadia. Using her scanner, they made their way across the cavern until they found what resembled a manhole cover near the middle.

"There's a shaft underneath this," said Nadia. "Looks like it goes about fifty meters into the bedrock."

"What's at the bottom?" asked Malia.

"I'm not sure," she said. "This leads to the area we saw on the map, but something's blocking the scanner. And there are no handles to open this."

"I'll do it," said Malia. She focused on the cover, lifting it out of the shaft with her mind. It was a solid metal cylinder, roughly two feet deep. She set it down on the ground.

They gathered around the shaft and peered down into the darkness.

"No stairs or ladders anywhere in this place," Nadia observed. "Makes one wonder how they got around."

"Are we going down there?" Malia asked apprehensively.

"I'm not detecting anything dangerous," said Nadia, using her scanner. "I'll take a look—if one of you can lower me down there?"

"Sure," Malia replied. "Are you ready?"

Nadia nodded. Malia moved her into the shaft, lowering her slowly. Nadia's light gave her a view of the interior, but she couldn't see past her.

"There's a cavity down here," she said over their headsets once she'd reached the bottom. "Roughly six feet high. I'm pretty sure I'm standing on the top of the chamber we saw on the map. The walls are some sort of lead alloy, just like that vault in the hangar bay—the scanner can't penetrate it. There's an opening into the chamber, but there's another metal cover, and I can't get it open."

"We'll be right down!" said Jaden.

Malia watched him lower himself into the shaft, but she was hesitant to follow. She wasn't ordinarily claustrophobic, but the idea of going so deep into this narrow opening was making her extremely uncomfortable.

Jaden noticed the look on her face.

"What's wrong?" he asked.

"I don't like this," she told him. "What if we get trapped down there?"

"You worry too much," he said, disappearing into the shaft.

Malia took a few moments to work up her courage and then followed him down.

Chapter Six: The Vault

Malia lowered herself down the shaft; she felt her heart racing. She was afraid of being trapped in such a small space and scared of what might be lurking beneath them. Although she tried telling herself these fears were irrational, she couldn't help it.

She pressed the button on her forearm to lower the suit's interior temperature. Despite its being climate controlled, she felt hot.

Minutes went by, and finally, she reached the bottom. She'd emerged into what looked like no more than a small cave carved out of the bedrock. The cave floor was different from the walls—it was flat and smooth and appeared to be metallic. Jaden and Nadia were standing over what resembled another manhole cover. Its diameter was larger than the one at the top.

"I still can't get any readings in there," Nadia told them. "Can you two open this?"

"Are we sure this is a good idea?" asked Malia. "We have no idea what might be inside—what if they were keeping something dangerous in there?"

"Well, I guess that's possible," said Nadia. "But this seems like a vault—I think there was something in here they were trying to protect."

"Let's just open the cover," said Jaden. "You'll be able to use your scanner then, right? And we put the cover back if there's anything bad inside."

"Yes, I should be able to get some sort of reading through the opening," Nadia confirmed.

"Alright," Malia said with a sigh.

Malia and Jaden focused on the cover. Slowly, they lifted it out of the opening. It was quite a bit longer than the first one and barely fit inside the cave. They moved it aside and let it topple over. The three of them squatted down around the opening.

Nadia shone her light down into the space below. The chamber's ceiling was so thick that they could see only a small circle of the floor.

"I'm not detecting anything dangerous," Nadia told them.

"So, are we going down there?" Malia asked, both knowing and dreading the answer.

"Of course, we are," said Jaden. "We came this far, might as well!"

"I'll go first again," said Nadia.

Malia lowered her to the floor. Jaden followed, and then Malia. Nadia swept her light slowly around the chamber; it was roughly a square, perhaps fifty feet to a side. Cylindrical structures lined most of the walls, each approximately eight feet high.

"Oh, my God!" Malia yelled with a little scream.

Lying in the middle of the floor were a dozen skeletons.

"Whoa," said Jaden, moving toward them.

Nadia went with him, tapping away on her scanner's display. Malia followed reluctantly.

"How long have these been here?" Jaden asked.

"It's difficult to say precisely," said Nadia. "But it appears these beings died only about eighty years ago."

"*What*?" asked Malia. "How can that be? Everything else we've found has been dormant for tens of millions of years. These bones should have turned to dust long before now!"

Nadia walked around the chamber, scanning the cylinders along the walls.

"Most of these are empty," she said, moving up close to one of them. "But many are still occupied."

"Occupied?" said Malia. "By what exactly?"

"Come have a look."

Malia and Jaden joined her. Looking through the cylinder's glass cover, Malia could see a figure inside, humanoid in shape, with the same scaled skin as the being they'd seen on the video.

"Is he... alive?" asked Jaden.

"No, he's been dead an extremely long time—at least a million years. But this chamber has kept him perfectly preserved."

"How is that possible?" asked Malia. "There was no power here—he should have disintegrated into dust by now."

"This unit is active; power conduits come up to it through the floor," said Nadia. "I would guess that there's a separate, independent power generator for this chamber that's been operational this entire time."

"Is this some sort of cryogenic cell?" asked Malia.

"Yes, that's precisely what I think," Nadia confirmed.

"What does that mean?" asked Jaden.

"It's a kind of suspended animation," Malia told him. "They've experimented with this on Earth. If someone's got an incurable illness, they can put them into a kind of deep hibernation. They're still alive, but their bodies are frozen. The idea is that maybe in the future they'll find a cure, and then they bring the person back to life and make them better."

"But this one is dead?" he asked.

"Yes," Nadia confirmed.

They circled the perimeter of the chamber. There were forty-five cylinders in total. Twenty-one contained dead bodies; the rest were empty.

"Twelve skeletons on the floor, and twenty-one dead ones inside the cylinders... what happened to the last twelve?" asked Malia.

"That's an excellent question," said Nadia. "They must have left."

"Where did they go?" asked Malia.

"I don't have an answer," Nadia said with a shrug.

"And why did they put them into a cryogenic sleep in the first place?" asked Jaden.

"Another great question," said Nadia.

"Let me get this straight," said Malia. "Millions of years ago, forty-five people went into cryogenic sleep in this chamber. Over time, twenty-one of them died. But eighty years ago, the remaining twenty-four woke up? And half of them died here, while the other half went... somewhere else?"

"So it would seem," said Nadia.

"Man, it's too bad we're not going back to Earth," said Jaden.

"Why do you say that?" asked Nadia.

"Because this would be the discovery of the millennium!" he said. "We'd be winning Nobel prizes for this!"

"How could they have kept them alive for *millions* of years?" asked Malia. "That seems like it should be impossible."

"I agree," said Nadia. "And it would appear that only about a quarter of them survived that long. They do seem to have gone to great lengths to maximize their chances, though. They gave this chamber an independent power supply, so even though they cut the main power in the rest of the complex, that didn't affect this area. And although the scanner can't penetrate the floor, I have a suspicion that every one of those cylinders has its own separate power source."

"So, even if one cylinder loses power, the rest are fine," said Malia.

"Yes, exactly. And each cell has six redundant control consoles—again so that if one failed, others could take over. They also enclosed this chamber in six-foot-thick walls, constructed of some sort of lead alloy, that would shield it very effectively against any kind of radiation. That's why the scanner won't work. And they buried this place more than thirty kilometers underground, which would be more than sufficient to protect it from even a large asteroid strike."

They had one more look around the chamber, but there was nothing else to see. A few minutes later, they made their way to the top and then back up to the larger chasm, replacing the covers in both shafts as they went.

Meeting up with Madu, they told him what they'd found.

"That's incredible!" he said when they'd finished. "I wonder what happened to the survivors?"

"Me, too! Have you found anything else in the computers?" asked Nadia.

"No, sadly not," he replied. "Little fragments of data, a few more images of the inhabitants, but that's about it. The decay in the storage media is too severe, and the circuitry itself is barely functional. It's almost miraculous that the little I have found survived as long as it did."

"Nothing that might give some insight into what happened to their civilization?" asked Nadia.

"Not even close," said Madu. "There's not enough information for our translation algorithms to decipher their language—and even if there were, there's nothing here to translate. You'd get random scraps of sentences, at most."

"What a shame," said Nadia. "An entire civilization has been lost, without so much as a record of their demise. Well, I think we're done down here. Let's head back up to the hangar level."

At that moment, a siren sounded out in the chasm, echoing off the stone walls.

"What the hell is that?" asked Madu.

Nadia took out her scanner and moved out into the central chasm, staring at its display.

"Uh-oh," she said, running off toward the power generator.

"What's going on?" Madu yelled after her as he, Jaden, and Malia followed her.

They caught up to her in the power chamber.

"Oh, damn," she said, staring at the display on her scanner.

"Are you going to tell us what's happening, or just keep us in suspense?" asked Madu.

"It would appear the geothermal conduits we found earlier tap into an area of molten rock," she explained. "And the baffles that control the flow down there have failed."

"We need to shut down the generator!" said Madu.

The four of them dashed around the chamber to the main power switch. Nadia and Madu tried to turn it off, but the lever wouldn't budge.

"Jaden, Malia!" Nadia yelled.

Malia nodded to her brother. They reached out with their minds and pushed the lever down.

Nadia took a look at her scanner again.

"We're in trouble," she said. "Cutting power didn't make any difference. There's molten rock flowing up the conduits! Let's go!"

They ran across the room. As they crossed the threshold, Malia turned in time to see lava oozing out from under the generator.

"Quick, get us out of here!" Nadia said to Malia and Jaden.

Malia reached out to her with her mind and launched Nadia and herself up to a terrace a dozen levels above the rock floor. Jaden followed close behind with Madu.

Looking down, they could see the cavern floor filling with magma.

"Bomani, we've got a situation down here," Nadia said. "Are the shuttles ready to go?"

"They are," he said over their headsets.

"Good—get everyone boarded and be ready for an immediate departure when we get there!"

"Yes, ma'am!"

"Wait," said Jaden. "We're like thirty kilometers underground. Is there any danger of the lava getting that high?"

"There's no way to know," said Nadia. "We don't know how much there is, and we don't know how much pressure it's under. On top of which, we have no way of knowing what effect the molten rock will have on the city's superstructure—the entire thing could collapse! Let's not take the risk!"

Malia peered over the edge again and saw that in only a few moments, the magma had risen nearly to their level.

"She's right," she said. "Let's get out of here!"

Malia grabbed Nadia with her mind and began their ascent. She lifted them through the chasm as fast as she could, but working against gravity meant it was slower going than the way down had been.

Malia needed to rest after a few minutes, so she set them down on a nearby terrace. Jaden and Madu landed right next to them. Moments later, Malia noticed a deep rumbling noise.

"What's that sound?" she asked.

Nadia scanned the chasm below them.

"The foundation is melting, and the entire city is starting to sink," she said. "The ambient temperature here is roughly 550 Kelvin."

"Didn't you say our suits can only handle 600 Kelvin?" Malia asked.

"We need to move," Nadia said with a nod.

They resumed their ascent. Malia and Jaden need to rest every few minutes. Malia felt exhausted now, and it was sweltering—she could tell her suit was reaching its limit.

She was about to launch again from one of the terraces when Jaden put his hand on her shoulder. Turning to face him, she realized he looked terrified.

"I can't go any farther," he told her. "I'm spent, Malia—my telekinesis..."

Malia looked up; she could see the large concourse where they'd started, maybe twenty levels higher.

"We're almost there," she said to her brother. "Just a little farther!"

"No, you're not getting it," he said. "I literally *can't*!"

"Crap!" she said. "Okay, wait here—I can't move more than one of you at a time. Let me get Nadia to the top, and I'll come back for you."

Malia reached out to Nadia with her mind and powered up to the main concourse. When they landed, she dropped to her knees; she felt weak.

"Malia, I'm sorry, honey, but you've got to hurry," said Nadia.

She looked around and realized that the entire concourse was listing toward the chasm.

"Oh, no!"

Malia got to her feet, took a deep breath, and jumped over the edge. She waited till she was close to Jaden's level before using her power to slow down and land on the terrace.

"Madu, you're next," she said.

"Not a chance—get your brother out of here first!"

Malia nodded. She reached out mentally to her brother and slowly raised them both into the air. It was a struggle; she was so tired that she could only move them at a snail's pace.

"Jaden, you've got to help," she said. "I can't do it!"

She could feel him adding his power to hers. He didn't have much left, either, but they moved more quickly. Finally, they reached the concourse, and both fell flat on their backs.

Malia felt exhausted. She didn't know if she had the energy to stand, much less make another trip down to rescue Madu.

"Malia, we can't go back down," Jaden told her. "We'll never make it back up again."

"If you work together, can you bring Madu up from here?" Nadia asked.

"We have to try," said Malia, struggling to get to her feet.

The concourse was tilted perilously into the chasm now. She worried that it might soon become too steep to climb.

"Let's go into that dwelling we found earlier," she suggested. "Even if we can get Madu up here, we'll be stuck on this terrace!"

"Yeah, good thinking," Nadia agreed, gazing around the area.

They made their way up to the hangar level and had to resort to crawling on all-fours to avoid slipping down the slope. There was a breach in the floor where the terrace was breaking away from the rest of the level. They made it over that and then hurried into the chambers at the far end. Looking down from the small terrace in that area, they could see Madu.

"Ready?" Malia asked her brother.

Jaden nodded.

"Madu, they're bringing you up from here," said Nadia.

"Understood," he replied on their headsets. "Not to rush you, but it's mighty hot down here."

Though it had slowed down, Malia could see that the magma had risen nearly to his level. Together with Jaden, she reached out, and they started lifting Madu out of the pit. Malia felt so drained; it took every ounce of her concentration to keep Madu moving toward them.

Suddenly, there was a crashing sound—the main concourse had given way and was falling into the chasm.

"Jaden!" Malia screamed.

He'd seen it, too—they moved Madu out of the way in the nick of time as the stone terrace hurtled past him.

"I've got nothing left!" said Jaden.

"Don't let go!" Malia yelled back. "We've almost got him!"

Seconds later, they got Madu onto their terrace, and the three of them collapsed on the floor.

"I hate to be the bearer of bad news," Nadia told them, "but the heat in here is now beyond tolerance. We've got to move!"

Nadia helped Malia get to her feet, and Malia slung one arm over Nadia's shoulders. Together, they hobbled out of the chamber and into the tunnel leading to the hangar. Madu followed close behind, helping Jaden.

They stopped to rest halfway down the tunnel. Nadia checked her scanner.

"I think we're out of immediate danger," she told them. "The molten rock has stopped rising a few levels below us."

"That was too close for comfort," said Madu.

"Agreed," Nadia replied. "Let's get moving again—we have no way of knowing how stable this area might be."

They pressed ahead and made it back to the docking port. Bomani had moved the shuttles to the outer hangar, out near the canyon.

Madu boarded his shuttle, while Jaden and Malia followed Nadia to theirs. Carl was waiting for them inside. Nadia climbed into the cockpit, and Jaden and Malia took their seats in the main cabin. Carl closed the hatch behind them.

"What the hell happened down there?" Bomani asked.

"Get us out of here," Nadia replied. "I'll fill you in on the way up to the ship."

But at that moment, there was an explosion somewhere outside in the hangar bay. Looking out the window, Malia could see that the second shuttle had gone up in flames.

"Oh, my God!" she screamed.

Nadia jumped out of her seat, popped the hatch, and rushed out of the shuttle. Jaden and Malia made to follow, but Nadia said, "No—you two stay here!" Carl went with Nadia.

Malia tried to get a better view of what was going on, but suddenly, the hatch closed, and their shuttle lifted off, hovering ten feet off the ground. She turned to see Bomani at the controls.

"What the hell are you doing?" Jaden demanded. "Where are we going?"

The shuttle turned to face Nadia and Carl. Malia could see Nadia waving her arms at them.

"Bomani, what are you doing?!" Nadia shouted in their headsets.

"I'm sorry, Nadia," Bomani replied and fired the shuttle's lasers. The beam hit Nadia in the chest; she fell to the ground and didn't move.

The shuttle flew out of the hangar and rose into the Martian sky.

Chapter Seven: Loss

Carl dropped to his knees by Nadia's side, gently shaking her shoulder.

"Nadia! Can you hear me?"

There was no response to stimuli; he couldn't feel her pulse through their spacesuits.

Carl regained his feet and stared up into the sky, tracking the shuttle's progress.

"Bomani! What did you do?"

There was no reply.

"Come back! You can't leave me down here!"

Still, no one answered.

"Malia, Jaden—can you hear me?"

Only silence met his pleas as he watched the shuttle climb ever higher.

Suddenly, there was an explosion. As the fireball cleared, there was only a clear sky beyond. The shuttle was gone.

"NO!"

Carl fell to his knees and wept. How could things have gone so wrong? Of the two shuttle crews that had landed on the Martian surface, Carl was the only survivor. His initial assumption had been that the first shuttle was an accident. But after seeing Bomani shoot Nadia, he now believed he'd probably sabotaged that craft.

But what about *his* shuttle? What could have happened up there?

Carl moved toward the burning shuttle wreckage, but there was nothing he could do. The explosion had destroyed it.

"Hello, Othali warship, this is Carl—can anyone hear me up there? Hello?"

There was no answer. Carl guessed they must have been on the other side of the planet. He returned to Nadia's side, but there was no change in her condition.

Taking a seat next to her, he stared into the sky and waited. Minutes went by, but he had no way of tracking the time.

Finally, he heard a female voice in his headset.

"Landing crew, come in."

"Hello! Yes—this is Carl, from Earth. There's been a disaster down here! Both shuttles have exploded—Nadia and I are the only ones left, and she's been injured. I'm afraid she might be dead!"

"Hold on, please."

"Okay, I'll hold, but this is terrible! Can you folks send someone down here?"

There was silence for a moment.

"Carl, this is Commander Anhur. Can you tell me what happened down there?"

"Yes—we were leaving, and the other shuttle exploded! Everyone on that ship is dead. And then, Bomani took off in the other shuttle—he took the twins, and he fired on Nadia! I think she might be dead, but I can't tell for sure. But then, Bomani's shuttle exploded in midair!"

Carl heard the commander sigh.

"I'm alone down here, Commander. I don't know what to do..."

"Hang tight, Carl. We're sending a shuttle down to you now."

"Thank you!"

He sat by Nadia's side while he waited. It might have been twenty or thirty minutes later when he saw an Othali shuttle move into view. It landed in the hangar bay. The hatch opened, and three people disembarked.

Two of them examined the charred remains of Madu's shuttle, while the third approached Carl and Nadia.

"Hello, Carl," he said, dropping to his knees next to Nadia. "I'm Ensign Fareed—I'm the field medic."

"Nice to meet you."

"I understand Nadia took a laser blast at point-blank range?" he asked as he scanned her body.

"Yes, that's correct—from the other shuttle's laser. Is she alive?"

"She is, but only barely," Fareed told him. "We need to get her up to the medical bay immediately."

He joined his companions, and then they came back and moved Nadia into the back of the shuttle. Carl climbed in with her and Fareed. The other two sat in the cockpit. They closed the hatch, and the shuttle lifted off.

Minutes later, they left the Martian atmosphere, and Carl could see the warship up ahead of them. They docked in the shuttle bay.

Three Othali were waiting for them there. Two of them moved Nadia from the shuttle to a gurney and wheeled her out of the shuttle bay. The third greeted Carl.

"I'm Lieutenant Bukhari," she said. "Commander Anhur wants to see you right away—if you can take a moment to change out of your spacesuit, I'll escort you up to the bridge."

"Yes, of course," said Carl.

He went to the equipment room and changed back into his regular clothes. Bukhari escorted him up to the conference room behind the main bridge. Commander Anhur was sitting at the head of the table, the pilot from the rescue mission in the adjacent seat. Lieutenant Bukhari sat across from the pilot, and Carl took the seat next to her.

"You've met Ensign Shurani?" the commander asked.

"Not by name, but yes," said Carl.

Shurani nodded to him.

"Carl, I'd like you to take us through everything that happened on the mission, from the moment you left this warship," said Commander Anhur.

Carl recounted the entire experience.

"You don't know what sort of emergency they encountered underground?" the commander asked when he'd finished.

"Nadia never had the chance to tell us," he said. "As I said, we did feel a minor earthquake—or Mars quake, I guess, shortly before she told us to prepare the shuttles. But I don't know if that was related to whatever happened down there."

"Did Bomani do or say anything during the mission to make you suspicious before commandeering the shuttle and gunning down Nadia?" asked Anhur.

"No, nothing," said Carl. "The only thing I can't understand is why I couldn't communicate with the twins after he lifted off."

"Chances are he'd cut off communications by then," said Shurani.

"And you didn't encounter any life forms during the mission?" asked Anhur.

"None whatsoever. That underground city must have been constructed by technologically intelligent life, but there was no evidence that any life still exists down there."

"Let's see what you recovered from the flight recorder," Anhur said to Shurani.

The ensign tapped on the console in front of him, and then a holographic video appeared above the table. The images were only two-dimensional; they were rotating, so Carl could see the footage clearly only when it turned to face him. It showed a humanoid figure with scaly skin.

"I'm sorry, what is this?" Carl asked.

"We recovered it from the onboard flight recorder on Madu's shuttle," the commander told him.

"It survived the explosion?" Carl asked.

"Every Othali spacecraft possesses a recording device in a protected area that's designed to withstand a disaster," Bukhari told him.

"Ah, yes—we would call that a black box back home," said Carl.

"This footage came from Madu's scanner," said Shurani. "It would have been uploaded automatically when he boarded the shuttle."

"You didn't see this while you were down there?" Anhur asked.

"Certainly not," said Carl. "They kept trying to power up the systems, but they're millions of years old. Nothing worked."

"They must have activated a power source on the lower levels," Bukhari suggested.

"There's very little data from Madu's scanner," said Shurani. "Most of it is only fragments and doesn't yield anything meaningful. I would guess that they probably did manage to activate a computer terminal somehow, but the data had degraded after so much time."

"Well, this would seem to confirm advanced technological beings did inhabit this planet in the ancient past," said Carl. "Were you able to recover Nadia's scanner?"

"It wasn't on her, and we didn't see it while we were down there," Shurani replied. "We believe it's most likely on Bomani's shuttle."

At that moment, Melissa Kwan entered the conference room and sat down next to Carl. He squeezed her hand; she acknowledged him with a smile, and he could see tears in her eyes.

"How's Lieutenant Bashandi?" asked Anhur.

"She's sustained massive damage to every organ system," said Melissa. "I've had to put her into a medically induced coma. She may yet recover, but it's going to take time. It's a wonder she survived the initial laser blast."

"Very well; keep me posted on her progress," said Anhur.

"Commander, do we know what caused the shuttles to explode?" Melissa asked.

Anhur nodded to Bukhari.

"Nothing conclusive," he said. "The flight recorder from Madu's shuttle only shows a sudden, massive overload in main engines an instant before the explosion."

"Any idea what caused the overload?" asked Anhur.

"No," Bukhari replied. "All systems were normal until then."

"Could it have been sabotage?" asked Melissa.

Shurani let out a long sigh.

"There's no evidence of that on the flight recorder. But our shuttles had perfect safety records before today. There hasn't been a malfunction like this in a century, at least. To have two of them destroyed within minutes of each other..." He shrugged. "The evidence is purely circumstantial, but I don't see what else could have caused this *but* sabotage."

"Why take out his own spacecraft?" asked Anhur.

"Commander, I don't think he did," said Melissa. "We don't have any evidence that shuttle was destroyed."

"We'll go back for a more thorough investigation, of course," said Anhur, "but we do have an eyewitness."

"Yes, one who is completely unfamiliar with our technology—no offense, Carl," she said, patting his arm.

"None taken," he said.

"He saw an explosion, and then he *couldn't* see the shuttle anymore," said Melissa. "That's hardly conclusive. Bomani made sure to take out Nadia but keep Carl conscious. I think he *wanted* a witness, but only one he could fool. If Nadia had been able to see what happened and report back, she probably would have seen through whatever ruse he employed to make it appear that the shuttle exploded."

"She has a point," said Shurani. "Bomani could have detonated a torpedo and then raised the shields."

"That would have made them invisible," said Bukhari. "Nadia could have used her scanner to detect the ship's exhaust or its wake turbulence. But, of course, Carl doesn't know how to use the scanners."

Anhur considered everything for a moment.

"Ensign, I want you to go back down there," he said finally. "Take Carl with you. Have him show you precisely where they went inside that complex. And run a complete scan of the area around the hangar bay. See what you can find."

"Commander, I'd like to go with them," said Melissa. "If my kids are down there, they may be able to reach out to me telepathically."

Carl knew they'd be able to contact any of the Othali that way if they were still alive but didn't say anything. He understood Melissa's need to go down there herself.

Anhur nodded.

"Take two soldiers as well. If Bomani is down there somewhere, we need to consider him armed and dangerous."

Everyone got up and left the conference room. Carl and Melissa went back down to the shuttle bay with Ensign Shurani, where they met two soldiers. Everyone suited up and boarded a shuttle; Carl sat up front with the ensign.

"It's been a while since I've worn one of these," said Melissa.

"They're amazing!" said Carl. "Our astronauts back home would be jealous!"

The shuttle left the docking port and made its way down to the planet's surface. As they approached the underground complex, Shurani brought them to rest across the canyon from the hangar bays.

"Carl, can you tell me exactly which way Bomani's shuttle went?" he asked.

"Well, sure," said Carl. "I was down there in the docking port, and he moved straight across the canyon here, on a steep upward trajectory."

Shurani flew them slowly around the area and then out across the plain beyond the pyramid and the face.

"I'm detecting trace alloys on the ground that must have come from Bomani's shuttle," Shurani told the others. "But there's no debris field, which is what I'd expect to find if the ship itself had exploded. The material on the ground doesn't have nearly enough mass to account for an entire shuttle. But the alloys I found would also be consistent with a torpedo detonation."

"Then, the shuttle is still intact somewhere," said Melissa.

"That's likely the case. But I couldn't find any evidence to indicate where it might have gone."

"No trace of exhaust in the atmosphere?" asked Carl.

"Too much time has passed," said Shurani. "The exhaust has become diluted in the atmosphere. But the warship is monitoring from orbit for any new signs of exhaust or wake turbulence. If he flies again, they might find him."

"If they happen to be on the same side of the planet when he does," Carl pointed out.

Melissa closed her eyes. Carl figured she was probably trying to communicate with the twins. But she looked at him a moment later and shook her head.

"We'll find them," Carl assured her.

Shurani headed back toward the hangar bay. But as they moved across the canyon, he said, "Hold on—what is that?"

"What is what?" Carl asked.

"I'm detecting something on the canyon floor… it looks like one of our scanners. I'm going to take us down."

"Nadia must have dropped it when she was hit," said Carl. "We were pretty close to the edge—it must have fallen."

They descended into the canyon. The floor was too rocky and uneven to touch down, so Shurani hovered a few feet above the ground. One of the soldiers popped the hatch and jumped out. She retrieved the scanner and climbed back aboard. Shurani took them up to the docking port and landed inside.

"Let's see what we've got here," he said, trying to activate the scanner. "Hmm… The fall must have damaged it. We can retrieve its data back on the warship."

They disembarked from the shuttle. Carl let them through the bay doors into the inner docking port. He pointed out the vault they'd found in the back of this area.

"There's a tunnel here on the far end that leads into the complex," he said, leading the way.

Shurani grabbed him by the arm.

"One of the soldiers will take the lead," he said. "Just in case."

"Right, of course," said Carl.

The soldier moved ahead, and Carl pointed out the tunnel entrance to her. They walked across the hangar and entered the tunnel.

"Temperature's rising fast in here," said Shurani. "We're within tolerance, though."

They moved through the tunnel toward the main concourse Carl had visited earlier. When they arrived, Shurani cautioned the others to stay inside the tunnel while he advanced with one of the soldiers. They returned a few minutes later.

"This is incredible," he said. "It looks like an underground city."

"Yes," Carl agreed. "That's what we thought, too."

"Whatever happened in there released magma from somewhere deeper inside the planet," he told the others. "It's risen to fill most of the chasm in there. The air temperature here is very close to our suits' limit, so we should move back to the hangar."

"That entire space is filled with magma?" said Carl. "Something catastrophic must have happened!"

"Let's get back to the ship," Shurani replied. "Hopefully, we can retrieve the data from Nadia's scanner and get some answers."

They returned to the warship. Once they'd changed out of their spacesuits, Shurani, Carl, and Melissa regrouped with Commander Anhur and Lieutenant Bukhari. Shurani told them everything they'd found.

"Well done," said Anhur. "Let's see what's on the scanner."

"Yes, sir," said Shurani. He placed it on the table and tapped on his console.

A holographic image appeared over the table; like last time, it was two-dimensional.

"This appears to be a map of the complex," Shurani told them. "Three separate chasms, each several kilometers across, and a little over thirty kilometers deep."

"Astonishing," said Bukhari. "That's quite the feat of engineering. This image came from the Martian computers?"

"That's correct," said Shurani.

He tapped on his console again. A new image formed above the table, this one three-dimensional.

"Nadia took these images inside a vault that was buried beneath the chasm," Shurani told them.

"What are those cylinders along those walls?" asked Carl.

"You're not going to believe this," said Shurani.

The image changed, now showing a being inside one of the cylinders.

"Oh, my God," said Carl. "It's a Martian—he looks like the one in the video from Madu's scanner."

"Are those cryogenic capsules?" asked Melissa.

"That's what they would appear to be," said Shurani. "And take a look at this."

A new image formed, showing twelve skeletons on the floor of the vault.

"The bones are still intact," Melissa said. "They cannot have died very long ago."

"Nadia's data indicates that they passed away roughly eighty years ago," Shurani confirmed. "There were forty-five capsules down there. Twelve of their occupants dead on the floor, twenty-one dead inside their cryogenic chambers—who appear to have died millions of years ago—and twelve who are missing."

"Missing?" asked Anhur. "Where did they go?"

"There's no way to know," said Shurani. "The saucers they left behind are derelict. But there was a vault inside the docking bay where they might have stored a few of them. It might have preserved them from decay—they could have used those."

"So we have twelve missing Martians who left this planet eighty years ago," said Anhur, "and a renegade Othali who has absconded with two of our people."

"We don't know that the Martians left Mars," said Bukhari. "There could be another complex somewhere on the planet; if so, they might have gone there."

"Commander, Jaden and Malia must be our priority!" said Melissa. "They're out there somewhere—we have to find them!"

"I agree," said Anhur. "The Martians are an interesting mystery, but they are not our concern."

"Well, who knows," said Carl. "If there *is* another complex somewhere down there, maybe that's where Bomani took the twins. We don't know if he left the planet or not, either."

"I think he took them back to Earth," said Melissa.

"That would seem likely," said Bukhari. "I don't see anywhere else in this star system he could have gone, and the shuttle doesn't have the range to go any farther."

"There are a couple of moons orbiting the two gas giants that could harbor life," said Shurani. "If the Martians settled there, and Bomani was in league with them somehow, he could have taken the children there. But I agree that Earth does seem like his most likely destination."

"Well, engineering tells me they're going to have to do a complete teardown and rebuild of our main engines," said Anhur. "That's going to take a few weeks at least. So, in the meantime, we're not going anywhere. We can search the planet from orbit and send down teams in shuttlecraft if we find anything interesting."

"And if we *don't* find anything here, on Mars?" asked Melissa. "Then what?"

"Then we make that decision when the time comes," said Anhur.

"Commander, with all due respect, that's not good enough," Melissa told him. "I need a commitment from you that we will find Jaden and Malia before we leave this solar system."

Anhur stared at her for a moment. The other two officers had averted their eyes; Carl suspected they had never heard anyone speak to the commander with that tone before.

"Very well," Anhur said finally. "I will agree to that. They're Othali; we won't leave until we find them."

"Thank you," Melissa replied, with a long sigh of relief.

Chapter Eight: Betrayal

Malia stared out the window at Nadia's body lying on the hangar bay floor. Their shuttle left the docking port and rose into the Martian sky.

"You killed her!" Jaden screamed.

Bomani flew out of his seat, slammed into the cockpit roof face first, and stayed there as if physically attached. His nose began bleeding.

"Jaden, no!" said Malia, realizing her brother had attacked him with his telekinesis.

"Think it through," Bomani said. "I'm the only one who knows how to fly this thing. If you don't return me to the controls, we're all going to die in here."

"*Mom! Mom, can you hear me,*" Jaden called out telepathically.

"The warship will see us," Malia said. "They'll rescue us."

"Oh, no, they won't," Bomani replied. "I calculated their orbit while you were underground. They're on the other side of the planet right now with no way to see us or contact us."

"*She won't be able to hear us from here,*" Malia told Jaden telepathically.

"Why not? Nadia heard you from lightyears away before they got to Earth!"

"Only because of Earth's magnetic field—it boosted my abilities. You heard Carl—Mars has a weak magnetic field. There's nothing here to provide that boost!"

"So, you want me to let him go?" Jaden demanded.

"I don't see what choice we have. He's right—we have no idea how to control the shuttle."

"Fine," Jaden said out loud.

Bomani fell to the floor. He got to his feet, removed the helmet of his spacesuit, and wiped the blood from his nose.

"That's better," he said, returning to his seat. "Now, you two might want to hold on back there. It's going to get a little bumpy."

"Why?" asked Malia. "What's happening?"

Bomani didn't answer. Moments later, there was an explosion outside the shuttle. The shockwave rocked the spacecraft back and forth. Malia looked out the window to see a giant fireball between them and the ground.

"What the hell was that?" Jaden demanded.

"I dropped a couple of torpedoes and detonated them at the minimum safe distance," Bomani told them. "And made us invisible at the same moment."

"For what purpose?" Malia asked.

"Because now, when the warship comes to rescue your buddy Carl, he'll report that our shuttle exploded in flight. There won't be any reason for them to come looking for us if they believe we died here."

"Wait, what?" said Jaden. "Why would Carl tell them that?"

"From the ground, he would have seen the shuttle disappear in a fiery explosion," Malia replied. "What would you think if you saw that?"

"Oh... damn."

Looking out the window, Malia watched as they left the Martian atmosphere and entered orbit around the planet. She took several deep breaths to stave off the sense of panic that was threatening to overwhelm her.

"*Mom! Can you hear me*?" Malia cried out telepathically. "*Commander Anhur, are you there*?"

There was no answer.

Malia focused, trying to reach out with her mind and return the shuttle to the ground. But she couldn't do it—she'd never been able to move a vessel from the inside of it. In theory, she felt sure it *should* be possible. But she had some sort of mental block with this.

"*Jaden—try to use your telekinesis to move the shuttle back to the ground*!" she called out in her mind.

"*Okay,*" he replied. He focused intently, but nothing happened. Then he closed his eyes, and Malia knew he was trying again.

"*Damn—I can't do it*!"

"Where are you taking us?" Malia asked Bomani.

"Well, for now, we'll be doing a couple of orbits to build up our velocity," he replied. "And then, we'll be using that to slingshot us back to Earth."

"Why?" said Jaden.

"Let's just say I know someone who requires your services."

"Who?" asked Malia. "What are you up to?"

Bomani ignored her. Malia watched out the window as they circled Mars, and the landscape far below went from daylight to darkness and back again.

Finally, she felt them accelerating and knew they were leaving orbit. Over time, Mars receded in the window.

"*Jaden, can you hear me*?" she asked telepathically.

"*Of course, I can.*"

"*Listen to me. The moment we land on Earth, we have to strike. We can't touch him now because we don't know how to fly this thing. But once we're on the ground, we need to get away from Bomani before he has a chance to deliver us to... whomever.*"

"*Yeah, I agree,*" he replied.

"*Okay, good. So, the instant we touch down, we act. We need him incapacitated so he can't just come after us.*"

"*I can handle that.*"

"*And then we run. We'll have to use our powers to get as far away from this shuttle as we can, as quickly as we can.*"

"*I got it.*"

"Bomani," said Malia out loud, "why are you doing this? You were our mom's only companion for what, thousands of years? How can you betray her like this?"

Malia had touched a nerve.

"Betray *her*?" he said, turning to face them. "Are you kidding me? She left *me* for dead in a Nazi concentration camp! She fled and didn't bother coming back to rescue me!"

"Mom thought you were dead, man," said Jaden. "I mean, it was the *Nazis*! Why would anyone go back to rescue someone they thought was dead? That would be suicide!"

"She didn't know for certain that I was dead—she should have checked up on me! I would have done it for her," Bomani insisted. "We spent *centuries* together on this god-forsaken planet. I never thought she'd abandon me like that."

"Are you taking us to Babcock?" asked Malia.

"That tool? No, it's not him. He represents everything I've come to despise about humanity."

"What is that supposed to mean?" asked Jaden. "What's wrong with humanity?"

Bomani shook his head.

"It's like I said earlier, back on the warship," he said. "The human species has a death wish. I've witnessed civilizations rise and fall for eons, and that entire time, it always comes back to the same thing. Those in power do everything they can to *keep* that power, and to seek more, all the while keeping the rest of humanity down. Over and over again, they make war and decimate entire populations: Rome, Genghis Khan, Hitler, the United States—"

"You cannot possibly include the U.S. in that group," said Malia.

"Oh, no? Have you studied history, Malia Kwan? Tell me the only power in the history of Earth that's used *nuclear weapons* against an enemy?"

Malia glared at him but didn't know what to say to that.

"*Who*?" Jaden asked her telepathically.

"*The U.S., dummy,*" she said. "*We dropped two atom bombs on Japan at the end of World War II—when a lot of historians say they were ready to surrender anyway.*"

"Despite that, the U.S. has done a lot of good in the world," Malia said out loud.

"After what Babcock's CIA did to the two of you, how can that be your conclusion?" Bomani demanded. "That organization has trained death squads that suppress dissent against U.S.-backed dictatorships in Latin America. They supported the Taliban's rise to power in Afghanistan. They've tortured prisoners in their supposed 'war on terror.'

"And that's just the CIA. What about the 'war on drugs'? After enslaving African Americans for centuries, they came up with that one as an answer to the civil rights movement—ultimately imprisoning countless thousands of Black people for minor drug offenses. Why do you think they have a 'war on drugs' but no war on poverty? They'll do anything to keep the Black man down!

"And all the while, they keep providing tax cuts to the ultra-wealthy, driving income inequality to levels unprecedented in the country's history. On top of that, they continue distributing subsidies to the mega-rich oil companies, who do nothing but destroy the already-fragile climate. And you know who that affects the most? You guessed it, the most impoverished people around the world.

"The U.S. does not deserve your loyalty. It's an evil empire and only the latest in a long string of evil empires that have plagued your planet."

"Then who is it you're taking us to, if not Babcock?"

Bomani chuckled.

"You sure are persistent, little lady. Alright, I'll tell you. In the midst of the chaos with the Malor, this man paid me a visit down in Bermuda. I don't know how he knew about me, but frankly, I don't care."

"He knew you're an alien?" Malia asked.

"Sure did. Knew my age and that I lived in Atlantis. And he was aware of the power stations—and the two of you."

"What?" said Jaden. "Some random guy knew about Malia and me? How?"

"No idea. But he asked me to fire up the power station and be ready to join the fight. Woulda done that anyway once I saw those Malor bastards destroy Miami. But then, after they wiped out D.C., he contacted me again. Told me there were a couple of kids mixed up in this whole thing—Earth kids, who had telekinesis due to some top-secret government project. Said he needed to acquire them and believed I might find myself in a position to help him out.

"Now, I've got no idea how he could've known any of that, so don't ask. But I knew it had to be the two of you."

"How could you?" Malia asked. "You hadn't met us yet."

"I spent thousands of years with your mom, waiting for humankind to develop the technology to bring her kids to life—kids who would have telekinesis. *Obviously,* it had to be you. After so much time, she'd finally found a way. And somehow, you'd gotten involved in the Malor mess.

"And then, sure enough, you and your mom showed up to rescue me from that sub. And you were going with the Othali, so I knew that was my chance. If I wanted to get my hands on you, I had to go along."

"Wait a minute," said Jaden. "You said you were glad to be with your own people again! And you hate Earth—I thought you *wanted* to go to the new planet with the Othali?"

"Little man, who ever said I hate Earth? Bermuda is a paradise—why would I ever want to leave? To spend the next hundred years cramped up in that tin can, traveling to a place with no rum, no weed, and no women? You misunderstand—it's the *people* of Earth I hate, particularly the powerful ones. And this man I met belongs to an organization that is plotting to bring about a new order—overthrow the dictators and emperors and finally bring peace to the planet. And he needs the two of you to do it!

"Now, I don't know if he can do what he says. But, the truth is, I don't have any choice but to cooperate. And so, here we are!"

"What are you talking about—why don't you have a choice?" Malia demanded.

"Because he *blackmailed* me, okay? I'm going to spend a lot of time in jail if I don't do what he wants—and quite possibly end up dead. But if I cooperate, they'll let me be. And if his group can do what he says—overthrow the existing hierarchy and save the climate to boot, well, then that's just icing on the cake."

"So, you only joined the Othali to give yourself a chance to take us back to Earth?" said Jaden.

"And if you'd stayed on Earth, I would have, too. But nothing's ever easy, is it?"

"But, wait—what would you have done if the warship's engines hadn't broken down?" asked Malia. "We would have left the solar system if that hadn't happened, and then there wouldn't have been any way to get us back to Earth."

"I thought you were the smart one?" Bomani chided. "The engines didn't break down on their own!"

"*You* caused the failure?" she said.

"I'm afraid I might have overdone it, though," he replied. "I'm not sure if they'll ever get them running again. But, that's life, eh?"

"And then you made sure to go down to the surface with us," said Jaden.

"You sabotaged the other shuttle while we were underground, didn't you?" asked Malia.

"Now, you're catching on," Bomani said before turning back to the controls.

"You're a bastard," she said.

"That may be, my darling, but I'd rather be a live bastard than a dead hero."

They rode in silence for a long time. Malia was lost in thought, thinking through all the events that had led them to this situation. She felt highly anxious but didn't see what more they could do until they landed on Earth. Though she tried several more times to reach out to their mother telepathically, she had no more luck than earlier.

"Mom thinks we're dead," she said to Jaden in her mind. *"And we have no way to tell her the truth."*

"I know. I feel bad—she must be heartbroken."

Hours passed. Malia finally spotted Earth up ahead of them; it was coming up fast.

"Brace yourselves back there," Bomani said once they arrived. "We'll be using the atmosphere to slow down, so it's gonna be a little choppy."

Minutes went by, the planet growing larger in front of them. Finally, Malia saw flames erupt around the edges of the windows. Before long, fire engulfed their entire view. The shuttle shook violently for a few minutes. But then, they rose above the atmosphere again, and she could see the Moon in the distance.

"Are we in orbit?" Malia asked.

"Indeed, we are," Bomani replied. "We'll be completing one orbit, then making our way down to the landing site."

The planet went by beneath them, land and ocean, day and night. Malia couldn't tell where they were. But after a while, they began their descent into the atmosphere. Fire engulfed the shuttle again. This time, when the flames cleared, she could see the ocean flying by below them.

Minutes later, they moved over land. They passed above some mountains, and finally, Malia spotted a land formation she recognized in the distance: Baja, California.

She felt the shuttle decelerating.

"Be ready, Jaden. We're landing soon."

"*Yeah, yeah—I know.*"

Malia watched out the window. Their altitude had decreased significantly—she could see a desert landscape all around them and enormous rock formations not too far away. Finally, they came to rest, hovering about a hundred feet above the ground. Slowly, they descended.

"*This is it*!" she told Jaden with her mind.

Suddenly, Bomani jumped to his feet, pointing a handheld laser at them.

"Shuttle's on auto-pilot for the landing," he told them. "Which means, of course, you'll be losing your incentive to cooperate momentarily. So, we'll consider this your new motivation."

Malia glared at him.

"Shit," said Jaden.

The shuttle touched the ground. Malia reached out with her mind and slammed Bomani's hand into the cockpit wall. The laser fired, hitting the rear window. Bomani lost his grip, and it clattered to the floor.

Bomani reached for it, but Malia reached out telekinetically and threw him into the ceiling. Jaden popped the hatch. Malia grabbed the laser, lowered Bomani with her mind, and smashed his head into the control console. He fell to the floor in a heap and didn't move.

"Nice job!" said Jaden. "Now, let's get out of here!"

They jumped out of the shuttle. Desert surrounded them; the terrain was rocky, with large boulders strewn about. Malia could see the enormous rock formations off in the distance.

"Where the hell are we?" asked Jaden, looking around the area.

"Arizona, I think," she said. "Let's go!"

"How the hell do you know that?"

They ran into the desert, Malia leading the way.

But suddenly, laser fire hit a boulder to their left, spraying dust everywhere.

"Stop right there!" a voice called out.

Malia looked back—it was Bomani. He was standing by the shuttle, bleeding from the forehead, pointing one of the other hand lasers at them.

"Get down," she hissed at Jaden, pulling him down behind a boulder.

They dropped behind the rock just as Bomani fired again.

"How the hell do you work this thing?" Malia asked, showing Jaden the laser she'd taken.

"I don't know," he said. "Point it and pull the trigger!"

Malia peered out from behind the boulder and fired at Bomani. Her shot went wide.

"That was terrible! You weren't even close!" Jaden yelled.

"I've never used a gun before!"

"Give up before you get hurt," Bomani yelled. He was getting closer.

"*Forget the laser,*" Jaden said telepathically. "*On the count of three, you take care of his weapon, and I'll do the rest.*" Malia nodded. "*One... two... THREE!*"

They burst out from behind the rock. Malia reached out with her mind and flung the laser from Bomani's hand. His face registered shock for a moment before Jaden used his powers to throw Bomani into the side of the shuttle.

The man bounced off the spacecraft and hit the ground. He scrambled to his feet, but Jaden grabbed him again. Using his telekinesis, he slammed Bomani's head into the side of the shuttle over and over again. His body went limp, and Jaden threw him to the ground like a ragdoll; he didn't move.

Malia crept up close and squatted down to press a finger to the side of his throat; she could feel his pulse. She rocked him back and forth to make sure he was unconscious this time. Bomani didn't move.

"He's alive," she said to Jaden as she straightened up. "But I don't think he's waking up anytime soon. Let's get out of here."

Chapter Nine: Earth

"Hang on," said Jaden. "Where are we going?"

"I don't know, but we have to get far away from this shuttle, right away," Malia replied. "Bomani was taking us to *someone*. Whoever that is could be here any minute!"

"Okay, I get it—but where are we going?"

Malia looked around.

"See that huge rock formation over there?" she said, pointing out across the desert. "The biggest one in the middle of that group?"

"Yeah..."

"That's where we're going—I'll meet you there!"

Malia launched herself into the sky. Using her telekinesis, she guided herself to the top of the mesa. Jaden landed next to her moments later. She looked around again and spotted another massive rock formation in the distance.

"Let's go there," she said, pointing out the location to Jaden. "But let's meet down by the base—people might be able to see us if we're on top."

Malia took to the air again, directing herself to the base of the next mesa.

"Alright, this should be far enough," Jaden said when he joined her. "Now we gotta come up with a plan. Where the hell are we gonna go? What are we gonna do?"

Malia took a deep breath and let out a long sigh.

"I don't know."

"Let's try to talk to mom," Jaden suggested. "We're on Earth now, so the magnetic field should help now, right?"

"It's worth a shot," Malia replied with a shrug.

"*Mom, can you hear me,*" she called out telepathically. "*Jaden and I are back on Earth. We're safe, but we don't know what to do. Can you hear me*?"

She heard no reply.

"I don't know if this is going to work," she said out loud.

"Why not? Nadia was able to hear you before, and they were way out in space—much farther than Mars, right?"

"Yeah, but Nadia said it was only happening when we were in states of heightened stress," Malia pointed out.

"I'm very stressed right now," said Jaden. "Aren't you?"

"I am, but the other thing is that it was kind of random when it happened with Nadia. I mean, I wasn't trying to reach her—I didn't even know she existed. And it was different than how our telepathy normally works—Nadia only saw images of what was happening here. I don't know—it seems like that kind of telepathy isn't something we can control."

"How does that make sense?" Jaden demanded. "We always control our telepathy. Why wouldn't we be able to in this situation?"

"Think about your breathing," said Malia. "You can consciously control it—you can hold your breath or breathe faster if you want. But most of the time, you breathe without even thinking about it."

"Okay..."

"So, maybe our telepathy is like that. When we're near each other, we can consciously use it to communicate with each other. But maybe for it to work somewhere far away, it only happens subconsciously."

"You're saying we can't reach mom this way on purpose?"

"That's what I'm guessing," she said, sitting down on the ground. Jaden sat next to her. "And the other thing is that it was only one-way with Nadia that time. She saw images from my thoughts in her dreams but couldn't communicate with me. They had to use the ship's technology to send that signal that I heard."

"So, we have to hope that Mom will see what's going on here when we're in danger and realize that we're still alive and on Earth," said Jaden.

"Yeah," Malia agreed. "I think that's right. I've never been able to tap into the magnetic field consciously—even for telekinesis. It's happened subconsciously every time."

"Great. So back to my original question—where are we going?"

"We should try to get to Uncle Brian," said Malia. "Or Sydney."

"Can we call them?"

"With what phone?"

"Let's find the nearest town and steal someone's cell phone."

"You remember their phone numbers?"

"No, don't you?"

Malia shook her head.

"Why not? You know everything!"

"I never memorized their numbers! But even if we could call them, I don't think it's a good idea."

"Why not?"

"That's how Babcock tracked us last time, remember? We need to find a way to get to them on our own."

"Okay… so can we take a plane?"

"I don't think so," said Malia. "I think we'd have to be eighteen to fly without an adult. Or at least have an adult buy the plane tickets for us—I don't think minors can do that. And we'd need an ID to fly, which we don't have."

"What other choice do we have?"

"Bus or train," said Malia. "I know a girl at school who bought her own train ticket to California once. She was sixteen, and she told me you had to be at least that old to do it. But I think we could pass for sixteen. And I'm pretty sure you don't need an ID for that."

"Yeah, probably," Jaden agreed. "But we don't have any money to buy tickets, either. We could hitchhike."

"All the way across the country?"

"Why not? I've heard of people doing that."

"That could be dangerous," said Malia. "What if we get picked up by some psycho or rapist or something? I think we should take the train."

"And what do we do about money?"

Malia considered this for a moment.

"We'll have to steal some," she said.

"Whoa! *You're* saying we need to steal? Miss Prim & Proper? I never thought I'd hear you say that!"

"Shut up, Jaden. I don't see any other way. We can lie about our age to get a train ticket, I think, but to get a job, we'd have to fill out paperwork and prove our age. If you know some other way to get the money, I'd love to hear it."

"Alright, let's do it," said Jaden. "But we gotta find the nearest town—there's nobody to steal from out here in the desert!"

"Right. Let's get to the top of this mesa and see if there are any towns nearby."

But as Malia got to her feet, she saw three Malor running toward them; she screamed.

"What's wrong?" Jaden demanded.

Malia pointed to the aliens.

"Where did they come from?" he said. "I thought we destroyed them?!"

There was a metallic crackling sound, and suddenly something hit the rock face right next to them, spraying debris everywhere.

"Let's go!" said Malia, launching herself into the air. But at that moment, something hit her in the leg. It burned, and she lost her concentration; she fell to the ground.

Jaden had jumped right after her; looking up, she could see him ascending toward the top of the mesa. Malia heard the metallic crackling sound again. Something hit Jaden, and he plummeted toward the ground—without slowing his fall.

Malia reached out with her mind and set him gently on the ground next to her. He was unconscious.

The three Malor arrived; they were pointing some sort of device that she guessed to be their weapons. She reached out with her mind, grabbed them out of their hands, and threw them as far as she could into the desert. The Malor backpedaled, but four more showed up to join them, all brandishing weapons.

Two of the Malor lunged in to grab her. Malia repelled them telekinetically, but three more charged her. She knocked them back but then noticed a whole group of Malor running toward them; this was becoming overwhelming.

Malia turned to run, but two of the Malor grabbed her. Using her mind, she threw them back, then launched herself into the air. She landed fifty feet away and took cover behind a boulder. Peering back the way she'd come, she saw several Malor charging in her direction, all carrying weapons.

"Damn," she whispered.

Reaching out with her mind, Malia tossed their weapons out of their hands. She took to the air and raised herself to the top of the mesa. As she landed, something hit her in the shoulder, and she screamed. She dropped to the ground to assess her wounds.

They'd hit her left calf and her right shoulder; both were bleeding. Malia focused, imagining coagulant rushing to both wounds. In only a few moments, she was able to heal both injuries.

Gazing over the edge of the mesa, she could see roughly twenty Malor moving across the desert. Two in the middle were carrying

Jaden—he was still unconscious. There were two more Malor flanking him who appeared to be looking out for her return.

Malia focused on Jaden and lifted him into the air. The two carrying him plus two more grabbed him and pulled him back down to the ground. Malia started lifting the whole group of them along with her brother, but several more Malor moved in to hold them down.

This was futile. If she managed to bring them all up to her position, then they'd overwhelm her again and capture both of them. Her only choice was to let them take Jaden, track their progress, and then move in to rescue him.

She relinquished her control. The Malor resumed their course, taking Jaden with them. Malia watched for a few minutes as they trekked across the desert. They rounded another mesa, and she lost sight of them.

Malia jumped into the air, landing on a nearby butte. She dropped to her stomach the moment she landed to avoid being seen.

Far below, she spotted their destination: the Malor had set up a camp in the desert. They were constructing a metal building and some sort of tower, and there were three flying saucers nearby.

Malia didn't understand how they could be here. She and Jaden had destroyed their mother ship back in Bermuda. But as she thought about it, she remembered hearing that they had sent scout ships all over the world. This group must have gathered together here to set up a base of operations. They'd been extremely efficient—only a day had passed since the destruction of their mother ship, and the building was already nearing completion.

As she watched, they took Jaden inside the building. Malia knew what she had to do. But rescuing Jaden was going to be tough—they'd be guarding the building entry.

Malia crept across the top of the butte, then dropped to the ground on the opposite side. She hurried around the formation and headed toward the Malor camp.

As she drew closer, she moved around to the rear of the metal building to see if there was any other way inside; she couldn't see one. To be sure, she continued around the far side of the camp, but the entry they'd used with Jaden was the only one she could find.

Most of the Malor she could see were moving about between the building and the flying saucers. She moved back to the opposite side of the building, thinking this would give her the best chance of making it to the entry without being seen.

Malia crept right up to the building and made her way to the front. Peering around the corner, she saw two Malor carrying weapons guarding the entry. Reaching out with her mind, she hurled the two of them into the air, far across the desert.

Malia bolted around the corner and darted inside. This looked like a storage building—she saw equipment and stacks of containers. There were a couple of rooms walled off from the rest of the space. She didn't see Jaden anywhere in the open area and suspected they'd probably moved him into one of the rooms.

But as she moved toward the first room, a dozen armed Malor charged into the building. Malia thought about fighting her way out, but then she'd be back at square one and would just have to find her way back into the building again.

She surrendered, holding her hands above her head.

The Malor surrounded her. One of them grabbed her arms and moved them behind her back, shackling her wrists together. They led her to the room she'd been approaching. As they took her inside, she caught a glimpse of Jaden lying on the floor—he was still unconscious. But a moment later, they tossed her onto the ground and closed the door; darkness engulfed the room.

Malia managed to sit up, her arms bound awkwardly behind her back.

"*Jaden*," she called out telepathically. He didn't answer. "*JADEN*!" It was no use; she couldn't wake him up.

Malia tried to free her arms but couldn't remove them from the shackles. She tried to use her telekinesis, but without being able to see what she was working on, she found this to be impossible. It felt like they weren't standard handcuffs—there was some sort of energy field binding them together. Her fingers tingled when she touched it as if it were some sort of electric current.

"Great," she thought. "Now what?"

Sitting in the darkness, she grew anxious. She'd been so focused on what she was doing until now that she hadn't had time to reflect on her situation or pay attention to her emotions. But now she was scared and didn't know what to do.

Malia tried reaching out to Jaden telepathically every few minutes, but there was no response. She attempted communicating with her mother, too—perhaps now that she was in a heightened state of distress, something would get through. But she had no way to know if that was working.

As time stretched on, she could hear the Malor moving about in the rest of the building. She had no idea what they were doing here, but the ones she'd seen from the outside appeared quite busy.

Malia heard footsteps approaching. Suddenly, the door flew open; three armed Malor were standing beyond it. One of them grabbed her by the arm and led her out of the room.

"Where are you taking me?" she demanded.

The Malor took her to an open area in the rear of the building where several comrades were waiting for them. Floodlights lit the space; coming from the darkness, Malia had to squint to see anything. The Malor formed a circle around her. They all stood there and stared at her.

Malia remembered that they were telepathic and wondered if they were trying to read her mind. She focused on them and said with her mind, "*What do you want with us*?"

They didn't seem to hear her. Instead, she tried listening with her mind, as she did with Jaden when they communicated that way.

Suddenly an image flooded her mind—the Malor mothership in the water off the coast of Bermuda and the tower of flame rising from its center. Malia hadn't thought of this—they had placed this scene in her mind. Next, she saw their camp here in the desert, as if she were looking at it from the air. Although she didn't hear any words, she got the idea that they had nowhere else to go and were trying to rebuild their society here.

Malia was very careful not to project the idea that she and Jaden were responsible for bringing down their mothership. She had no idea if the Malor possessed a concept of revenge but had no desire to find out the hard way.

She remembered seeing the flying saucers outside and had an idea. She focused intently on the Malor and imagined them transporting Jaden and her to the east coast with one of their ships. It didn't seem like she was getting through.

Next, she saw an image of a sprawling complex here—much more extensive than what now existed, and hundreds of Malor moving about. This was what they were doing, she realized.

She tried again to show them an image of them taking her and Jaden to Maryland. But it did not seem the idea was reaching them. It was as if she could see their thoughts, but they couldn't see hers.

Eventually, they took her back to the room. She noted two armed guards standing outside the door. They threw her to the ground and closed the door. Malia tried reaching out to Jaden with her mind again, but it was no use.

Minutes later, the Malor returned. Two of them stayed outside the door, pointing their weapons at her, while two more moved into the room. They picked up Jaden from the floor and removed him from the room. One of the others closed the door again. Malia wondered if they'd try communicating with him, too—did they have a way to wake him up? That could help. If he were conscious when he returned to the room, then they could escape.

A few minutes later, Malia heard Jaden's thoughts.

"*Malia, where are you?*"

He sounded weak, but at least he was awake now.

"*I'm here—I tried to rescue you, but they captured me, too.*"

"*The Malor—they're standing around me in a circle, staring at me. I don't know what they want.*"

"*They're telepathic, too—they're trying to communicate with you. Be careful—make sure you don't give them the idea that we're the ones who took down their ship!*"

"*Okay, I won't.*"

"*But try to show them an image of them taking us to Maryland in one of their saucers!*"

"*What saucers?*"

"*They have three outside this building. Focus, Jaden—this could be our chance. Imagine them flying us to Maryland!*"

"*Alright, I will.*"

Malia started feeling anxious again. But this time, it was different—it was more a nervous hope that maybe Jaden would succeed and the Malor would take them to Sydney. But a few minutes later, the door opened, and they threw Jaden roughly into the room. He fell to the ground next to her.

"Hey, what the hell!" he yelled.

The Malor closed the door, and they were shrouded in darkness once again.

"Are you okay?" Malia asked. "What happened?"

"They kept showing me a picture of an alien city in the desert," he said. "I think that's what they want to build. But then they got frustrated with me and brought me back here."

"Did you show them what I told you?"

"I tried, but I don't think they could see it. It seemed like the telepathy only went one way—them to me."

"Yeah, that's what it felt like to me, too. Well, now that you're awake, let's get out of here!"

"Good idea. Can you get these handcuffs off of me?" he asked.

"I can't see anything—turn around."

"Okay..."

Suddenly, Malia could make out a faint glow in the darkness. Moving closer, she could see Jaden's wrists. The handcuffs did indeed use some sort of energy beam to bind his arms together. There was a metal device between the two beams.

"They're like laser handcuffs," Malia told him.

"Seriously? That's why they feel so strange. I wonder if they have lightsabers, too, like in Star Wars!"

Malia focused on the metal device and imagined it splitting in half. It took all of her concentration, but after a few moments, the object ripped apart. Sparks flew, and then the beams disappeared, and Malia couldn't see anymore.

"Nice!" said Jaden. "Turn your back to me, and I'll do yours."

Malia turned around. Moments later, she felt her bonds disappear.

"Perfect," she said, getting to her feet. "Now we need a plan."

"Simple—get the hell out of this building and fly away!"

"Right, but they're keeping a couple of guards outside our door," Malia told him. "Let's find the door, and the moment we get out of this room, we'll throw the guards out of the way."

"Got it," said Jaden. "And then we need to haul ass out of the building."

"Yes, exactly," Malia agreed. "There's a mesa nearby—once we get outside, I'll meet you up there, and we'll figure out what to do next."

"Great," said Jaden. "Now we just have to find the door..."

This would be easier said than done in total darkness. But Malia held her hands in front of her and moved slowly. Her hands came in contact with the wall. Feeling along its surface, she found the door. There was no handle. She moved her fingers to the edge but couldn't pry it open.

"Jaden—I found the door, but it won't open."

She felt him bump into her a moment later.

"Let's use our powers," he suggested. "Rip the thing open."

"I'll do it," she said. "Get out of the way."

She felt him move to her other side. Malia focused on the door with her mind and ripped it away from the wall.

The guards turned and pointed their weapons at them. Malia tossed them across the building.

"Let's go!"

Malia and Jaden ran to the exit. They met a few more Malor on the way, but Jaden hurled them out of the way. When they reached the opening, they launched into the air.

Chapter Ten: Flight

Malia landed on the top of the nearby mesa. Jaden joined her moments later.

"Let's go to that next one," she said, taking in their surroundings. "We should put more distance between us and that camp."

"Hang on," said Jaden, sitting down on the ground. "I feel kind of weak still. They messed me up with that weapon—I'm groggy."

"Alright, I'll take us both there—can you stand?"

He got to his feet, and Malia raised them both high into the air. She guided them to the next mesa and set them down on the ground.

"Okay, this should be far enough," said Jaden, sitting down again. "I gotta rest before we go any farther."

"Flying like that is harder here than it was on Mars," she replied. "The gravity is so much stronger. I'm feeling a little tired myself."

She sat down next to him.

"Let's figure out our plan," she said.

"We gotta get to Maryland and find Sydney," Jaden said. "She can take us to Brian."

"Yeah, but how do we do that?"

"I was starting to think maybe we could use our powers and fly the whole way there," said Jaden. "But I don't think that'll work."

"Not a chance," Malia agreed. "It takes too much energy—we'd never make it that far. I still think a bus or train is going to be the best way."

"You still okay with stealing some money for the tickets?"

"I don't like it, but it's the only way," she said with a sigh. "We need to go somewhere with a lot of people—we're going to have to find the nearest town somehow. And we have to get access to the internet somehow, too."

"What for?"

"To find the nearest bus or train station. And to find out how much tickets will cost—otherwise, we won't know how much money to steal."

"Good point," said Jaden. "We're gonna need to get some clothes, too—we'd look pretty strange traveling across the country in these!"

"You're right," said Malia. "I'm so used to this spacesuit now that I forgot I was wearing it! We're definitely buying clothes!"

"Hey, do you think we have to worry about those Malor coming after us?"

Malia considered this for a moment.

"I don't think so... they set up their camp way out here in the middle of nowhere. It seems like they don't want to be found. And we didn't see any other humans in there. I think they were just patrolling the area, and we had the misfortune of getting caught."

"Right, but wouldn't they be worried that we'll run and tell someone about them? They might want to capture us again to make sure we can't report them to the army or anything like that."

"Yeah, you might be right; we should get moving as soon as you're feeling up to it."

"I'm good, I think," he said. "We can rest again if I get tired."

"Alright. Now we need to figure out where we're going."

Malia got to her feet and gazed out across the desert, turning slowly. She couldn't see any towns or people in any direction.

"We're way out in the desert. Hang on—I'm going to go higher and see what I can find."

She launched into the air, lifting herself higher and higher. Then she turned herself slowly in a circle, gazing out in every direction. There were a couple of buildings not too far away, but that was it—they seemed isolated. Rising even more, she tried again. This time, she saw what looked like it might be a town. Tapping the button on her arm to zoom in with her visor, she could make out buildings.

"That's it," she said to herself.

There was also a road out to the west that led toward the town. She noted its position relative to the sun, then descended back to the mesa.

"I found a town," she told Jaden. "It's roughly southwest from here, maybe south by southwest."

"How do you know the direction? You have a compass I don't know about?"

"No, dummy. But you can figure it out using the sun."

Jaden thought about this for a moment.

"How?"

"It's morning here, and the sun rises more or less in the southeast this time of year. The town was that way," she said, pointing in the direction she'd seen it. "So I think it's south by southwest."

"If you say so," he said.

"I saw a road not too far from here that goes in that same general direction," she told him.

"Can we use that?" asked Jaden. "Maybe we can catch a ride."

"I think we should stay away from the road," said Malia. "Don't forget, Bomani was taking us to someone—whoever that is might be watching it. But we can use it to navigate if we need to."

"Okay, that makes sense."

"And listen, we need to stay off people's radar as much as possible," she told him. "We can't contact Brian or Sydney—there's a good chance Babcock will be monitoring them after everything that happened. And that means we can't get arrested or anything, either—or show up on the news, or anything like that. If we do the slightest thing to make Babcock realize that we're back, then making it to Sydney's is going to get way harder than it already is."

"I get it," he said. "That guy would do anything to get his hands on us. We'll be careful. Are you ready?" She nodded. "Lead the way!"

Malia shot into the air. She moved in the direction she'd seen the town, keeping them well to the east of the road. After only a few minutes, she found herself growing weary—fighting Earth's gravity to stay airborne was taking a tremendous amount of energy. She picked a spot far from the road and returned to the ground. Jaden landed next to her moments later.

"That's tiring," she said.

"Yeah, it is," he replied, dropping to the dirt and sprawling out on his back. "I need a break."

Malia sat down next to him.

After a few minutes, they took to the air again and continued toward their target. They ended up needing to rest several more times. But when they landed on the outskirts of the town, Malia suggested walking the rest of the way.

"Why walk—we're almost there," said Jaden.

"Yeah, exactly—which means if we keep flying, someone's bound to see us landing. That's going to raise some uncomfortable questions, don't you think?"

"Oh, right. Well, now that you mention it, these suits are gonna raise some questions too."

"Probably, but there's not much we can do about that till we get some money."

"Yeah, you're right. Going naked is the only other way, and we're not doing that!"

"Um, no. But let's take off the helmets, at least."

Malia removed hers, but it was attached at the front. She thought it looked odd hanging there, but at least they'd be able to talk to people this way. Jaden removed his, too, and then they set off.

Malia led the way. They stayed in the desert, keeping the road in sight. She was still worried about Bomani's contact finding them, but at least like this, they had a way to navigate.

A few minutes later, they passed some mobile homes. Malia guided them onto the road.

They walked for a few miles without encountering anyone else on foot. A few cars passed by, but nobody seemed to take any notice of them. Finally, they met an old lady walking her dog.

"Excuse me," said Malia. "Can you tell me if there's a public library nearby?"

The woman took in their appearance but didn't comment on the spacesuits.

"Sure, Kayenta public library is in the center of town," she told them. "It's next to the post office, behind the town hall."

"Great," said Malia. "And... where is the town hall?"

The woman gave her a funny look but said, "This here is Route 163—keep following it, and the town hall will be on your right, a little before you hit 160."

Malia said "Thank you," and then they continued on their way.

"We look weird," said Jaden.

"I know, but at least she didn't ask any questions."

They walked into town. More people were out and about here, and several did give them strange looks, but nobody tried to talk to them.

Once they'd reached the town hall, they moved to the driveway and walked to the rear. They found a couple of metal buildings, but they appeared to belong to the town hall. Beyond those was a mobile home.

"I don't see a library," said Jaden.

"Hang on, there's a sign on the mobile home," Malia replied, moving closer. "This is it—the sign says Kayenta Community Library!"

They found the entrance and walked inside. The woman sitting at the desk across from the entry smiled at them for a moment, then noticed what they were wearing and quickly looked down at her work.

Books lined the walls. There were a couple of small tables in the middle, and one hosted a computer. Malia walked over to that and sat down; Jaden took the seat next to her.

"Perfect," she whispered, moving the mouse around. "It's got internet access."

She looked up the rules for airplane flights first.

"Yep, we'd need IDs to fly."

Next, she looked up train tickets.

"We could travel on our own if we were sixteen," she read from the web page she'd found. "And it doesn't say anything about providing ID."

She found a website for bus tickets next.

"We have to be seventeen to take a bus on our own. And they're much stricter about it—sixteen-year-olds can travel alone, but only if a parent or guardian fills out a special form for them to travel as an unaccompanied minor. And we'd need ID to get on the bus to prove we're seventeen."

"Well, we're more likely to pass for sixteen than we are for seventeen," Jaden whispered. "And we don't have any ID or anyone to sign a form for us."

Malia went back to the train website.

"The closest train stations are in Flagstaff and Winslow." She checked Google Maps. "It would take about two and a half hours to get to Flagstaff... and closer to three hours to Winslow."

"But Winslow looks closer," said Jaden.

"Yeah, but I think we'd have to take backroads the whole way to get there, so it would take longer."

"We could fly..."

"Maybe, but that's a lot farther away than it was coming here," said Malia.

"Oh, then that's not gonna work," said Jaden. "We'd die of exhaustion before we got there."

"I think we should go to Winslow," said Malia. "Flagstaff's a much bigger city. Whoever is looking for us will probably monitor the train and bus stations and are more likely to look for us there. Winslow's a little hole in the wall."

"Alright," Jaden agreed. "How much money are we gonna need?"

Malia checked for train stations near Sydney's house.

"Well, Washington is gone... that would have been our best bet. Now, it looks like we'd have to go to Baltimore. Looks like we'll need close to $400."

"Okay," said Jaden, getting to his feet. "Let's go... uh... raise some funds!"

"That's a nice way to put it," Malia replied with a frown.

They left the library and went back to the road. Malia scanned the area in both directions.

"I think we should go back the way we came," she said. "There was a café and a restaurant that both had outdoor patios. It'll be easier to pull this off there than it would be inside, I think."

"What? How?"

"If we want to do this without getting caught, we should use our powers and pull some wallets out of women's purses. If we take a wallet out of a guy's pants, he's way more likely to notice. And if we go inside wearing these suits, people will be staring at us. It's going to be hard to pull this off without someone realizing what we're doing. We can do it from farther away outside."

"You've put a lot of thought into this," Jaden remarked, nodding appreciatively. "Let's do it."

They reached the café a few minutes later. The patio was in front of the business. Several people were seated at the tables there, and Malia spotted an older woman who had her giant pocketbook sitting on the ground by her feet. They moved up the driveway and stopped just beyond the edge of the building.

Malia peered around the corner. The older woman had left her pocketbook unzipped—sticking out of the top of it was what looked like a wallet. Malia focused and slowly worked the wallet loose. Keeping it near the ground, she brought it over to them; nobody seemed to notice it flying by.

She opened the wallet; the woman had only a twenty and a couple of singles.

"Damn," said Jaden. "I figured she'd be carrying a lot more cash!"

"Me, too," Malia replied. "Let's put this back before she notices it's missing."

Jaden held onto the cash. Malia moved the wallet back into the woman's purse.

They repeated the process twice more and managed to collect

$120. But then the older woman opened her wallet and realized that her money was missing.

"We'd better get going before the other two figure out what happened," said Malia.

They walked around behind the building and moved farther up the street. The restaurant was in a standalone building with outdoor seating on one side. They hid behind some bushes near the back of the patio.

In only a few minutes, they added another $230 to their total. But then one of the women realized her cash was missing. She stood up and yelled, "I've been robbed!"

"We gotta get out of here!" Jaden hissed, looking ready to bolt.

"Yeah, but without anyone seeing us!" Malia replied, grabbing his arm. "This way!"

She led them around the rear of the building. They continued behind the next couple of buildings, then crossed the road.

"Give me the cash," said Malia. Jaden was holding it rolled up in his fist; he handed it to her. She stuffed it down the front of her spacesuit. "Nobody will see it this way."

"Good thinking," said Jaden. "We're still $50 short. And we're gonna want a little extra for clothes and food and stuff," he added, looking up and down the street. "I've got an idea—follow me!"

He led them to a building a little farther down the road.

"Jaden, no!" said Malia. "We can't rob a bank! We'll get caught for sure!"

"Trust me," he said. "This way!"

They walked past the bank and around behind the adjacent building. Jaden took her behind a dumpster. From there, they had a clear view of the bank's drive-through ATM.

"What are you up to?" she asked.

"Hang on," he said with a grin. "You'll see."

There was a minivan at the ATM. Jaden didn't do anything. But a minute later, a convertible Mercedes pulled up behind the minivan.

"Now we're talking," said Jaden.

"I wish you'd tell me what you're planning," said Malia.

"For once in your life, just go with it," he replied.

The man driving the Mercedes put his card into the machine and tapped on the display. A few moments later, he tapped some more and then took his card back. As he reached to grab his cash, it flew out of his hand, as if taken by a strong gust of wind. The money flew all over the place—the man swore loudly and got out of his car. He ran around, trying to grab all the bills. Most of the money gathered in a cloud above the building and moved north—Malia noticed this, but the man did not; he kept chasing down stray bills near the ground.

"Let's go," Jaden said with a chuckle, moving around the dumpster and heading toward the parking lot behind the adjacent building.

Malia followed. Jaden kept the cash cloud in the air as they continued behind the next few buildings. Finally, they ducked down behind some bushes, and he brought the money into his hand. He counted it and handed it to Malia.

"Another $310," he said. "Now we have more than enough. Let's buy some clothes!"

"Yes, agreed. I saw a little secondhand store on the way down here—let's go see what they have."

"Secondhand? No way—there's a strip mall on the corner down there. They must have at least a few good stores."

"It's going to be too expensive," said Malia. "We can get stuff way cheaper at the shop I saw."

"We're gonna look like bums wearing other people's old shit," Jaden complained.

Malia stood firm; Jaden finally relented.

"Not the underwear, though!" he said. "That's gotta be new—I'm not negotiating on this!"

"Ew—used underwear," Malia replied, crinkling her nose. "I don't think so."

They bought new underwear at a store in the strip mall, then walked up to the road to the place Malia had seen. In only a few minutes, they were each able to find jeans, a T-shirt, and sneakers that all looked new. Malia also found a backpack.

"We can use this to carry the spacesuits," she whispered to Jaden. "Who knows—they might still come in useful."

The cashier gave them a strange look but didn't say anything. They paid for everything, used the fitting rooms to change into their new outfits, and then left the store.

"Alright, I'm starving," said Jaden. "We gotta find some food before we do anything else."

"Yeah, I'm pretty hungry, too."

Despite Malia's objections, Jaden insisted on McDonald's. They ordered their food and sat down to eat.

"I was thinking," said Jaden. "How long have we been up, now? I'm getting kind of sleepy."

"I'm not sure," Malia replied. "I think it's been almost a full day. But we can sleep on the train. Let's get out of here."

They threw their trash away and went outside.

"That's it," said Malia, slinging the backpack over her shoulder. "Time to find the train station. Have you ever hitchhiked before?"

"No, have you?" Malia shook her head. "Right, stupid question. Well, how hard can it be?"

"We've got to keep our eyes open—hitchhiking is illegal," she told him. "So, if we see a police car or anything, we have to pretend we're just walking."

"Got it," he said.

They walked south to Route 160 and turned right. Jaden looked back and held out his hand with his thumb sticking up.

"I think this is how you do it," he said.

Malia giggled.

"That's how it works in the movies!"

They walked for about twenty minutes without any luck. Plenty of cars went by, but none stopped. Finally, a red pickup truck pulled over a little ahead of them. Malia and Jaden ran up to meet it.

There was an older man in the driver's seat. He rolled down the passenger-side window.

"Where you kids headed?"

"Winslow?" Malia told him.

"I ain't goin' that way, but I can get y'all as far as Route 41—you'll want to take that to get the rest of the way to Winslow."

"Yeah, that works!" said Malia.

"Get in," the man said.

She opened the door, and the two of them climbed into the cab.

Chapter Eleven: Fight

Malia sat in the middle, Jaden to her right. He closed the door, and the man merged onto the road.

"So, what are you two goin' to Winslow for?" he asked.

"Train station," said Malia.

The man nodded. They rode in silence for several minutes.

"I gotta fill her up," he told them, pulling over at a gas station—one of the last buildings on the outskirts of town. He stopped next to one of the pumps and got out.

"Oh, good—they've got a convenience store," said Jaden. "Give me some of the money—I'm gonna go in and get some food."

"We just ate!"

"Yeah, but it's a long ride to Winslow," he said. "Come on, fork it over!"

Malia handed him a ten. Jaden got out of the truck and ran into the store.

Moments later, the man got back in the truck and started the engine.

"That was fast," Malia commented; she hadn't even seen him pump the gas.

The man put the truck into gear and pulled up to the road.

"Wait—my brother went inside to get some food," Malia said.

"We don't need him," the man said, patting her on the knee. "You and me can have a little fun now."

He turned onto the road and accelerated hard. Malia was scared but felt confident she could handle this.

"What are you doing?!" she said, scooting over to the passenger-side door. "We have to go back for my brother!"

The man only grinned at her.

"Stop the car now!"

"Be patient, little lady," he said. "My place is just a few minutes away."

"*Malia, where the hell did you go*?" Jaden said in her mind.

"*This creep drove off with me*!"

"*What the hell?*"

"If you don't pull over *right now*, I'm calling the police!" she said out loud.

"No, you're not," he said. "You ain't got a cell phone. And besides, the police don't take too kindly to hitchhiking in these parts."

Malia had enough. She grabbed her backpack, opened the door, and launched herself into the air. As she left, she heard the man swearing at her. She set herself down on the shoulder; the truck's tires screeched as the man pulled over. He got out of his vehicle and moved in her direction.

"Get back here, you little bitch," he called out to her.

Malia strode toward him.

"Leave me alone, or you're going to regret it," she said.

"Oh, we'll see about that," he said with a chuckle.

Reaching out with her mind, Malia flung him into the back of his truck. The man slammed into the vehicle and fell to the ground.

"How the hell did you do that?" he said, scrambling to his feet, fear in his eyes now.

"Get back in your truck and go home, or I'll do worse," she said, moving toward him, with the meanest glare she could manage.

"Alright, sweetheart," he said, hurrying to get back in his truck. "No need to get your panties in a bunch!"

"Do *not* call me 'sweetheart,' you pervert."

The man got into the driver's seat, slammed the door shut, and took off down the road.

Malia watched him drive away for a minute, then turned to head back to the gas station.

"*I got rid of him,*" she said telepathically to Jaden.

"*Good—where are you?*"

"*Not too far up the road.*"

"*Stay put—I'll be there in a minute.*"

Moments later, Jaden dropped out of the sky right next to her.

"Jaden! Don't do that in public! What if someone saw you!"

He looked up and down the road.

"Like who? There's nobody nearby. You need to relax!"

She glared at him for a moment longer, then said, "We need to get a ride again."

"Are you alright?" he asked. "Did that asshole hurt you?"

"No," she said with a grin. "I kicked his ass."

"Good, he deserved it!"

"This was exactly the kind of thing I was worried about—hitchhiking really isn't safe! But it feels good knowing we can handle it."

They walked along the road for several minutes. Only a few cars went by, and none of them would stop. But finally, an older woman pulled over. Jaden and Malia got into the backseat of her car.

She was only able to get them as far as Route 41. They got out there, and she kept going west on 160. Malia and Jaden walked along Route 41 for almost a half hour without seeing any cars go by.

"This sucks," said Jaden. "We should fly for a while."

Malia looked up and down the road. There was only desert as far as the eye could see, but random buildings were scattered about.

"I don't think so," she said. "There aren't a lot of people around here, but there are *some*. We can't risk someone seeing us and calling the police!"

"Ugh, fine."

They kept up a brisk pace for another twenty minutes. Malia did want to use their powers to expedite this process. Every time they moved beyond the view of any buildings, she considered trying it, but then invariably, they'd come upon another structure.

Finally, they spotted a car approaching in the distance.

"Alright, here we go," said Jaden. "We gotta get this one to stop—look as sad and pathetic as you can!"

"Let's hope it's not another pervert," Malia replied.

As the vehicle drew closer, they could see it was a pickup

truck. Malia had an uneasy feeling, but Jaden held up his thumb. The vehicle pulled over a little beyond them. When they caught up, they saw that a young woman was driving it; Malia breathed a sigh of relief.

"Where y'all headed?" the woman asked. Malia didn't think she looked much older than her.

"Winslow," said Jaden. "We gotta get to the train station."

"I'm goin' to Winslow," she said. "Get in!"

Malia and Jaden climbed into the cab, and the woman drove away. The trip proved to be quite enjoyable. The woman liked the same kind of music that they did. They spent the time chatting about the songs that came on the radio, and she told them stories about growing up in the area. Malia felt thankful they'd found someone normal for the long drive.

It took two and a half hours to get to Winslow. The woman dropped them off in the center of town, told them where to find the train station, and wished them luck before driving away.

"Let's hope the rest of this trip goes that smoothly," Malia said as they walked up the street.

"Yeah, seriously," Jaden agreed.

They reached the train station a few minutes later. It was part of a complex that included a hotel. They crossed the parking lot and walked into the building. The main entry had led them to the hotel lobby; they followed the signs to find the train station's ticket counter.

There was someone at the counter buying tickets; Malia and Jaden waited behind them.

"Try to act older," she whispered to Jaden. "Don't slouch. We need to pass for sixteen at least."

"Yes, ma'am," he replied, standing tall.

A few minutes later, it was their turn.

"We'd like to purchase two tickets to Baltimore," Malia said to the man behind the counter. He looked younger—Malia guessed he was in his 20s.

"Minimum age to travel alone is sixteen," he said, looking at them skeptically. "Do you two have a parent or guardian nearby?"

"No, we're here on our own," Malia told him. "We're sixteen—we came here by train a few weeks ago to... uh, visit our aunt."

"I'll need to see a driver's license or ID card to verify your age."

"I'm sorry, we don't have our driver's licenses yet... and we left our school ID cards back home. But we're both sixteen—we're twins. And we're juniors in high school."

The man sighed.

"Look, I want to help you, but you two don't look sixteen to me. I could lose my job if I get caught selling tickets to you without verifying your age." He looked around to make sure nobody was around, then whispered, "Get someone older to buy the tickets for you, and you're set. They won't check for IDs once you're on the train."

"Thank you," Malia said with a smile, then walked away with Jaden.

"Well, that sucks," he said, "but at least he was cool about it."

"Yeah. Let's hope we can get someone to help us."

There was nobody else near the ticket counter. Malia led the way back to the hotel lobby. She went up to an older woman and explained their situation, and asked if she would be willing to buy the tickets for them.

"I'm sorry, I don't think so, dear," she said. "Where are your parents, anyway?"

"They're back home in Maryland, and that's where we're trying to go. We've been here visiting our aunt."

"Well, you should have her get your tickets," the woman said.

"We would, but she left town on a business trip after she dropped us off here. There was no problem doing this on the way out here, so we didn't think it would be any trouble."

"I'm sorry," the woman repeated. "I don't think I can help you."

Once Malia and Jaden had moved out of earshot, he muttered, "Stupid old lady."

"We should try someone younger," Malia suggested. "How about that guy?"

A man had just walked into the hotel. He looked like he was in his 20s. He had a mustache and goatee; he was wearing a suit jacket, but no tie. The top of his shirt was unbuttoned, revealing several gold chains.

"He looks like a pimp," Jaden whispered.

Malia giggled as they approached the man. She explained what they were trying to do and asked if he'd be willing to help.

"Well," he said, looking around the room as if he were afraid of getting caught, "what's in it for me?"

"Excuse me?" said Malia, recalling the pervert in the pickup truck.

"I mean, I'd have to charge you a service fee... say ten percent?"

"No way," said Jaden. "That's like $40. We'll find someone else."

"Jaden, we should just do it. The more people we have to hit up, the more likely someone will report us to the hotel staff."

"Fine, but we gotta talk him down—ten percent is way too much!"

"That's a lot of money," Malia said out loud.

"Yeah, we'll give you ten bucks," Jaden added.

"Twenty," said the man.

Jaden opened his mouth to speak, but Malia cut him off.

"Done!"

The man held out his hand, and Malia shook it.

"Great, give me the cash, and I'll go get your tickets."

"Not so fast," said Jaden. "We'll give it to you when we get to the ticket counter. And don't think about taking off with our money—trust me, you'd regret it."

"Lead the way," the man said, holding his hand out toward the train station.

The three of them walked over to the ticket counter. There was nobody in line, and the same agent from before was still there.

"I need two tickets to Baltimore," the man told him.

The agent gave Malia a wink. She smiled at him and gave the money to the man, who took his cut and passed the rest to the agent. He produced the tickets and said, "Have a nice trip."

"It was a pleasure doing business with you," the man said with a grin before walking back toward the hotel.

"I'm glad that worked out," said Malia, looking at the tickets. "Damn, we're stuck here till eight o'clock."

"Are you serious? That's the earliest train we can get?"

"I think it only goes through here once a day. Well, let's go make sure we can find the platform, and then we can go explore Winslow."

They headed out the back door and found the platform right behind the building.

"Easy enough," said Malia.

Turning to go back inside, she saw a man standing in front of the door. He was wearing a black suit and tie and dark sunglasses.

"Malia and Jaden Kwan, I presume?" he said with a grin.

Malia's heart leaped into her throat.

"Who the hell are you?" Jaden demanded.

"Let's just say I'm an associate of Mr. Bomani."

"Shit, Malia..." said Jaden, backing away from him.

"*Fly*!" she replied telepathically.

Malia launched herself straight into the air, high above the building. Jaden joined her a moment later.

"Now what?" he said.

"We've gotta hide," she said, turning about looking for somewhere to go. But suddenly, the man shot into the air, stopping right next to them.

"Leaving so soon?" he asked, looking at them over the rim of his sunglasses.

Malia gasped; his pupils were slits, like the being they'd seen on the video from the Martian computer.

"*Jaden—MOVE*!" she shouted in her mind.

Without wasting another moment, Malia shot to the north. Seconds later, she dropped to the ground in the busiest area she could find. It was a retail area, with stores lining both sides of the street. Jaden landed next to her.

"Malia, what the hell is he?" he asked, staring up at the sky as they hurried up the crowded sidewalk. "He can fly like us!"

"I don't know," she said. "But we can't let him catch us. We've gotta hide somewhere."

"Do you think Babcock figured out how to copy our extra genes in other people?"

"No, I don't—Jaden, did you see his eyes?"

"What? No—he had those sunglasses on."

"His eyes are like that alien we saw in the video on Mars," Malia told him. "The pupils are slits!"

"Are you serious? Do you think he's one of the missing Martians?"

"I have a funny feeling that's exactly who he is! Let's go!"

At the next intersection, Malia turned right. But just around the corner, they ran into the man—he was standing there with his arms folded across his chest, grinning at them.

"Dammit!" Jaden shouted, turning and running the other way. Malia followed him. Running across the road, they nearly got hit by a car.

"Watch out!" Malia yelled.

Jaden sprinted up the sidewalk, weaving around the people,

Malia close behind. But at the next intersection, she saw the man waiting for them across the road.

Malia stopped short, grabbing Jaden by the arm; he noticed the man, too.

"What the hell?" Jaden shouted. "We can fly like he does, but how does he keep showing up out of nowhere like that?"

"I don't know," Malia said, looking around frantically. "But this is no use! Let's get to the top of one of these buildings—maybe we can find a place to hide from up there!"

"People are going to see us!"

"It's the lesser of two evils at this point," she said. "Let's go!"

Malia launched herself into the air, landing on the top of a four-story building across the street. Jaden landed by her side a moment later.

"People saw that," he told her. "The lady next to us screamed when you went up."

"Let's hope nobody got it on video," Malia said, pulling Jaden farther from the edge, hoping to keep them out of sight from the people below. "Now, look for somewhere we can hide," she added, scanning the nearby area.

"Shit!" Jaden yelled.

The man had landed on the roof only a few feet away from them.

"I can do this all day," he said, moving toward them.

Malia reached out with her mind and threw him over the edge of the building. Rushing closer to the edge, they looked down in time to see him cross the road and start scaling the façade of the structure across from them.

"Holy shit!" said Jaden. "We can't do *that*!"

"No, but I don't think he's got telekinesis," Malia replied. "He must be using some other method to fly like that. I think that gives us an advantage!"

"If you say so," Jaden said skeptically. "We gotta move!"

The man reached the top of the building and leaped across the street. Before he could land, Malia and Jaden launched into the air.

She'd hoped going somewhere with lots of people would have discouraged their pursuer, but this hadn't proven to be the case. Somehow, he was able to avoid being seen. They needed to hide somewhere that he wouldn't be able to find them. And to do that, they'd need to get out of sight. Malia saw something on the ground that gave her an idea.

Dropping out of the sky, she landed on a street near the north end of town, next to a three-story office building. Jaden hit the ground, and she pulled him into an alley.

"This is a dead end!" he said. "Why are we doing down here?"

"Shut up and come with me," she said.

She'd noticed from the air that this building was vacant. There was a door a little farther down the alley. It was secured with a padlock; Malia reached out with her mind and ripped the bolt open. Removing it from the latch, she opened the door; once they were inside, she pulled it closed again.

"Hopefully, he didn't see us coming in here," she whispered.

"I don't like this plan," Jaden replied. "He could trap us in here."

"If he does, then we'll kick his ass," she said. "Let's go!"

She led them farther into the building. It didn't look like it had been vacant very long—it was still in good shape. They moved down a hallway lined with offices on both sides. At the end, they came to a doorway. Malia opened it and found the steps leading to the basement. Jaden closed the door behind them, and they crept down the stairs.

There were piles of boxes down here. Malia led the way but suddenly heard the door they'd used open again.

"*Shit—Malia, he found us*!" Jaden said in her mind.

"*You must not have closed the door all the way*," she replied, looking back the way they'd come. "*There's nobody there*."

She thought she heard one of the steps creak, but it must have been her imagination. They moved to the far end of the basement and hid behind a stack of wooden crates.

Malia heard footsteps. She peered around the corner but didn't see anyone.

"*What the hell*?" she said to Jaden in her mind. "*I could have sworn I heard someone*!"

"*Yeah, me too*," he replied; she could feel his fear on top of her own.

The footsteps stopped; although she still couldn't see anyone, Malia couldn't help but feel there was someone down here with them. Her heart was beating a mile a minute.

"*Jaden, I'm scared. Maybe this wasn't such a good idea*."

"*Yeah, let's get out of here*."

They emerged from behind the crates, but before they'd taken more than a few steps, the man appeared out of nowhere right in front of them.

"Whoa—shit!" Jaden yelled, stopping short.

Malia grabbed the man telekinetically and threw him across the basement. She heard him crash and saw piles of wooden crates break and scatter on the floor but couldn't see the man anymore.

"Let's go!"

Malia and Jaden ran back to the stairs and hurried up the steps. She led them out the back door and immediately shot into the air. There was a department store only a couple of blocks away. She dropped to the sidewalk, waited a second for Jaden, and then ran into the store. Malia took them to the women's clothing department and hurried over to the fitting rooms.

"I can't go in there!" said Jaden

"Yes, you can," she replied, grabbing him by the arm and pulling him inside with her.

There were several separate stalls. A woman emerged from one wearing only her underwear, spotted Jaden, squealed, and hurried back into her stall. Malia dragged Jaden into another one and closed and latched the door.

"Now what?" Jaden whispered.

"We wait here," she said. "I didn't see him anywhere when we landed—hopefully, we lost him."

"But he can make himself invisible! He could have been right next to us, and we wouldn't have seen him!"

"Well, this store is huge. He won't think to look for us in here."

There was a knock on the door.

"*Oh, he won't, huh*?" Jaden said in her mind.

Malia's heart was pounding in her chest. She unlatched the door and opened it a crack. Peering through the opening, she saw the man standing there, grinning back at her.

"Boo!" he said.

Malia shut the door again.

"*We gotta run*," she told Jaden in her mind. "*I'm gonna smash him into the wall, and then we can get out of here. Are you ready*?"

Jaden nodded.

Malia opened the door, but there was nobody there.

"Shit!" yelled Jaden.

They ran out of the fitting area, but Malia stopped short just outside of the door. A man was standing there wearing jeans and a sweatshirt, with the hood pulled tight over his head.

His pupils were slits, and the skin on his face was scaled.

Chapter Twelve: Flight Again

"Who the hell are you, now?" Jaden demanded.

"You may call me Salvatore," he said, handing Malia what looked like a cell phone. "Take this—do *not* call or text anyone, but do not lose it! I will find you—now, leave and get as far away from here as you can!"

Malia pocketed the device

"Why should we trust you?" Jaden demanded.

"Forget trust," Malia told him, grabbing him by one arm. "He's right—we gotta get out of here!"

She pulled him toward the exit, but he dragged his feet. Malia turned to yell at him but froze in her tracks. The man in black had emerged from the changing area.

"Salvatore, what a pleasant surprise," he said.

"I cannot say the same, Lucifer."

The man in black charged into Salvatore, knocking him to the floor halfway across the store. Salvatore rolled him over and straddled him; he threw a punch, but the man in black heaved him over before it connected.

They both regained their feet. The man in black threw a flurry of punches, but Salvatore managed to bob and weave out of the way. Salvatore went on the offensive, throwing blow after blow—his last one connected, tearing the man in black's shirt to shreds. Malia realized razor-sharp claws were protruding from his fingers.

The man in black shot into the air, and Salvatore followed. They exchanged punches as they hovered ten feet in the air. Shoppers below screamed, fleeing from the area. But Malia was mesmerized by this spectacle, and, she realized, so was Jaden.

Salvatore went horizontal, kicking the man in black with both feet and hurling him into the wall. The man in black crashed into the mirrors there, shattering them, and fell to the floor.

"Get out of here!" Salvatore bellowed at Malia and Jaden before dropping to the ground and charging toward the man in black.

But the man disappeared before Salvatore could reach him. Salvatore looked around frantically, trying to find him.

"We'd better go," Malia said to Jaden, afraid the man in black would come after them now.

But suddenly, something unseen slammed into Salvatore's chest, knocking him to the floor. He scrambled to his feet, but invisible claws began cutting and stabbing him.

Malia couldn't see the man in black but knew he was there. She tried to reach out with her mind and pull him away from Salvatore, but working on something she couldn't see had always been difficult for her.

Malia concentrated, imagining the man in black standing there, lashing out with his claws. She grabbed the imaginary figure with her mind and tossed him into the wall. It worked—the man in black became visible again as he bounced off the wall and hit the floor.

"Thank you—now GO!" Salvatore shouted.

Malia grabbed Jaden, and they ran out of the store. They shot into the air and landed on the roof of the nearest building.

"Now what?!" said Jaden. "Where are we gonna go?"

"Follow me!" Malia said, launching into the air again.

She took them across town to the roof of a parking garage.

"Keep an eye out for a minute," she said once they'd landed, "and let me figure something out."

She pulled the phone out of her pocket. It was some sort of Android device. She'd only ever used iPhones, but it wasn't too hard to figure out. It didn't have a security code, so she opened the web browser and found the train schedule. The train they were going to take out of Winslow made its next stop in Gallup, New Mexico, not too far beyond the border.

"I think we should still try to make our train," Malia told him. "But we can't board it here—the man in black will know to look for us there. We can cross the border into New Mexico and get on at the next stop."

"Okay, great," said Jaden. "But we should leave the phone here!"

"What? Why?"

"Malia—you saw that Salvatore dude. He's gotta be one of the missing Martians, too! He's gonna use that thing to track us—why should we trust him any more than the man in black?"

"He's *fighting* the man in black—he helped us escape!"

"Yeah, only so that he can get us later! Who knows what these people want to do with us; I don't trust any of them!"

Malia couldn't explain why, but she felt like they could trust Salvatore. At least, she didn't think his aim was to hurt them.

"No matter what, I think we have to get to Sydney and then to Uncle Brian," said Malia. "The only way we can do that is by train—and we've got the train tickets. But the man in black found us at the train station—he *knows* that was our plan. He might still find us at the station in New Mexico—he could figure out that's the next stop as easily as I did. So when he doesn't see us at the Winslow station, he could find us there. And it's going to be super hard to get away from him again.

"I don't know how Salvatore found us, but he might not know we're going by train. So if we drop the phone, there's a good chance the man in black *will* find us again, but Salvatore *won't*. I'd prefer having them *both* be able to find us again, instead of only the man in black."

"Well, I'd prefer to have *neither* of them able to find us!" Jaden insisted. "You said that the train runs once a day, right?"

"Yes."

"Okay, then let's take *tomorrow's* train, and ditch the phone. That way, if the man in black shows up to find us there tonight, and we don't show up, he'll think we went some different way. *And* the other dude won't be able to find us, either."

Malia let out a long sigh. Her desire to lose the man in black was outweighing her belief that they could trust Salvatore. She checked on the website and confirmed that they could use their tickets on a different day.

"The man in black might still look for us in Gallup again tomorrow," she pointed out.

"Maybe, but think about it. He'll look for us in Winslow tonight first. And if he doesn't find us there, there's a good chance he'll look in Gallup. But if we don't show up there either, you really think he'll look for us there again tomorrow? I mean, the guy does seem pretty persistent, so I guess it's possible. But I like our chances."

Malia had her doubts; they had no idea how he'd found them in Winslow to begin with. But she didn't argue.

"Alright. That's a plan, then. We've gotta make it to Gallup, New Mexico, and that's almost two hours away. We're gonna have to hitchhike again."

"Let's go there now," said Jaden. "We'll have to find somewhere to sleep tonight. But it's still early, so we'll have time."

Malia checked the maps app on the phone to make sure she knew where they were going, then tossed it over the edge of the building. They launched into the sky. Malia led them east, out of town. She took them down out in the desert, far enough south of the road to avoid being seen.

They made their way over to Route 66 and turned east. There weren't many cars on this road. Jaden held out his thumb every time one went by, but they all kept driving. Malia felt anxious about the police spotting them.

"I was thinking," said Jaden. "How did that man in black—Lucifer, I guess—how'd he find us in Winslow?"

"From what Bomani told us, he knew all about us," Malia replied. "He must have known about Uncle Brian, and it would be obvious that's where we'd try to go, right?"

"Yeah, probably."

"I'm sure he knew we couldn't take a plane. He was probably watching the road heading south from where we first landed with Bomani. When he didn't see us there, I bet he checked all the nearby bus and train stations. I mean, it's mostly desert out here; there aren't a lot of places we could have gone."

Jaden was silent for a moment.

"And so it was just luck that he happened to be at the Winslow train station at the same time as us?" he asked.

"I guess. I don't know."

They walked in silence for a little while. A few more cars went by, but nobody stopped. They spotted an SUV in the distance, approaching fast.

"Oh, no—Malia, I think that's a cop!"

"Damn," she replied. "Let's get off the road—quick!"

They hustled down the embankment into the desert. Moments later, they shot high into the air and watched from above. Sure enough, it was a police vehicle. It pulled over near the spot where they'd left the road, and the officer got out to look around.

"I don't think he saw us fly," said Malia. "He's not looking up."

"Good thing," Jaden replied.

A few minutes later, he got back into his vehicle and drove off. Malia and Jaden returned to the ground.

"What now?" asked Jaden.

"We keep hitchhiking," said Malia. "I don't see how else we're going to make it to Gallup. But we've got to be super careful—if we see the police again, we'll do the same thing we did just now."

They made their way back to the road and resumed their eastward trek.

"I wonder how Mom's doing," Jaden said a few minutes later.

Malia felt her heart sink.

"Me, too," she replied. "She must be devastated. I wish we could reach her somehow and let her know we're alive."

"There's gotta be some way we can contact her," Jaden said. "Once we get to Uncle Brian's, I'm sure he'll know how to do it."

"If nothing else, maybe we could use the power station in Bermuda to reach them," Malia suggested.

"Yeah, that's a great idea!" Jaden replied. "Hey, so... I was thinking. We're gonna be in New Mexico anyway; you think maybe we can visit Savannah?"

"Savannah, the girl with the confederate flag hanging in her house?"

"That wasn't *hers*; it was her grandfather's!"

"You can't be serious. Do you remember their address? I don't. And who knows if they're near the train route. We'd have to get off somewhere nearby, probably hitchhike to their place—"

"Yeah, yeah, I know. Not gonna happen," he said with a sigh. "It's too bad. She had nice... uh... a nice face."

Malia giggled.

"I know what you were gonna say!"

"Yeah, you do," he said with a grin. "It sucks, though—we're the only kids on the warship. There are literally no girls!"

"Or boys!"

"Like you care," he said. "Since when do you care about boys? You never liked anyone back home."

"That's not true—I just didn't tell *you* about it!"

"Okay, whatever. But I mean, what are we gonna do?"

"You heard Mom—they'll start having kids again once we get to that new planet."

"Yeah, but we'll be way older than them."

"We're gonna live for tens of thousands of years—in the grand scheme of things, there won't be much difference in our ages."

Jaden considered this for a minute.

"Yeah, I guess you're right. I keep forgetting about that."

A white cargo van was coming up behind them. Jaden stuck out his thumb.

"This thing looks super sketchy," said Malia. "I hope he keeps going."

The van pulled over a little farther up the road.

"Damn," Malia muttered as they ran to catch up.

An older lady was driving it. She rolled down the passenger-side window and said, "Where you kids headed?"

"Gallup, New Mexico," Malia told her.

"I'm only going as far as Holbrook, but that'll get y'all a little closer, anyway," the lady said. "Get in!"

Jaden climbed into the front seat, and Malia sat down in the back.

"You're lucky I haven't taken the backseat out yet," the woman said as they drove off. "I'll be helping my grandson move tomorrow, so I'm removing it tonight to make room."

"Great, thank you," said Malia.

They rode in silence after that. The woman was playing country music on the radio. It took nearly thirty minutes to get to Holbrook. She pulled in behind a church and parked the van.

"Well, this is the end of the road for me," she told them as they got out. "Y'all be careful—there are lots of weirdos around."

"Oh, we know," said Jaden.

"Don't' worry," Malia added. "We'll be careful."

"You'll want to keep following Route 66," she told them. "That'll take ya all the way to Gallup."

"Thank you," said Malia.

"Good luck!"

The woman went inside the church. Malia and Jaden made their way back to the main road and headed east.

"Let's get out of town before we try hitchhiking again," said Malia. "There are too many people around."

It took them twenty minutes to walk beyond the busy part of town. A few cars went by without stopping. But then, Malia spotted a police car approaching.

They left the road, heading into the desert, but it was too late. The officer pulled over and called out to them.

"Y'all come back here," he said. "I'd like a word with the two of you."

"*What do we do?*" Jaden asked in her mind. "*Fly?*"

"*I don't think so,*" said Malia. "*Right now, he thinks we're two random kids. If we fly, and word of that spreads, Babcock's bound to hear about it. Let's turn ourselves in, and we'll find a way to escape.*"

"*Okay. I hope you're right.*"

They walked back to the road and met the officer.

"Why'd you run away?" he asked.

"Uh..." said Jaden.

"We weren't running," said Malia. "We saw a rabbit down here, and we wanted to get a closer look. But he ran away."

"A rabbit, huh?" He sounded extremely skeptical. "Where are y'all headed?"

"Nowhere," said Malia. "We're just going for a walk."

"I see," the officer said, looking up and down the road. "Thing is, we've had a few reports about a couple of kids hitchhiking on this route. Now, that wouldn't be the two of you, would it?"

"Definitely not," Malia said earnestly. "Hitchhiking is dangerous—we'd never do that!"

"Uh-huh. So, you two live around here, then?"

"Yeah, in Holbrook," she said with a nod.

"Great, and what's your address?"

"It's uh... 123 Main Street."

"I see. Well, it's not very safe walking this route. People go pretty fast. So, why don't you two get in, and I'll give you a ride home."

"*He knows you're full of shit!*" Jaden said in her mind.

"*Shut up*!" Malia replied. "Sure, okay," she said out loud.

The two of them climbed into his back seat. He pulled out his phone and tapped on the display for a minute.

"This is strange," he said. "There doesn't seem to be a 123 Main Street."

"Oh, did I say 123?" Malia asked. "I'm sorry, I meant 223."

"Uh-huh. Why don't you tell me the truth? See, you two match the description we've had in the reports about the hitchhikers."

Malia let out a sigh. She didn't see any around telling him the truth—at least, part of it.

"Alright. We're trying to get to Gallup, New Mexico, so we can catch a train back home to Maryland."

"Maryland? Y'all are pretty far from home. What brought you out this way?"

"Visiting our aunt," Jaden told him. "But she left on a business trip, and she won't be back for a few weeks."

"Yeah, and we were *supposed* to get on the train back in Winslow, but, well, we were bored hanging out at the train station for the whole day. So we figured we'd get a little head start and catch our train in Gallup, instead!"

"I see. Well, thing is, hitchhiking is illegal around here. So why don't you give me your parents' phone number, and we'll give them a call and see what they'd like us to do."

"Oh, uh... our parents died, so we live with our uncle..."

"Uh-huh. And what's his phone number?"

"Uh..."

"Right," the officer said. He made a U-turn and headed back into town.

"Where are we going?" asked Malia.

"Back to the station," he said.

"You're arresting us?!" asked Jaden.

"No, nothing like that. But considering you two are minors, we'll have to contact social services and let them decide what to do with you."

"We're sixteen!" Malia told him.

"Uh-huh."

"*Told you, he knows you're full of shit!*" Jaden said in her mind.

"*Shut up.*"

It took only a few minutes to get to the Holbrook police station. The fire department shared the same building. The officer escorted them inside and told them to have a seat in the lobby. He walked through the door leading behind the counter. Malia could see him sitting down and picking up a telephone.

"What's our plan now?" Jaden whispered.

"Simple," Malia replied. "When he's not looking, we run outside and fly!"

A few minutes later, the officer joined them back in the lobby.

"There's a social worker named Susan on her way here to meet with you," he told them. "So sit tight, and she should only be a few minutes."

"Okay," Malia replied with a smile.

He went inside again, and this time, Malia couldn't see where he went. But there was still another officer sitting behind the counter, and he was keeping an eye on them.

"Can we go now?" Jaden whispered.

"Not yet," she said.

"What are we gonna tell this Susan lady?"

"I don't know—hopefully, we can leave before she gets here."

A moment later, the officer behind the counter got up and moved out of view.

"Let's go!" Malia whispered.

They got up and walked out the front door. Standing outside was Salvatore.

Malia and Jaden stopped in their tracks.

"How the hell did you find us here?" Jaden demanded.

"Police scanner," Salvatore said. "But there's no time to talk—we need to move you both away from here immediately."

"*Fly*!" Malia told Jaden telepathically.

She shot into the air, high above the police station; Jaden appeared by her side moments later. And so did Salvatore.

"Listen to me—I've incapacitated Lucifer for the moment, but he'll come looking for you very soon," he told them. "You are not safe on your own. Come with me—I will protect you."

"How do we know we can trust you?" Jaden demanded. "We don't know anything about you!"

"Come with me, and I will explain everything," he said. "If you still don't trust me, then you'll be free to go."

"*It can't hurt to hear his story,*" Malia said to Jaden telepathically.

Jaden considered this for a moment.

"Yeah, alright," he said finally. "Where are we going?"

"Follow me," Salvatore replied before shooting off to the north.

Malia and Jaden sped after him.

Chapter Thirteen: Salvatore

Salvatore returned to the ground a little north of the town; Malia and Jaden landed next to him. There was nothing but desert anywhere near them.

"What are we doing out here?" asked Jaden.

Salvatore said nothing but looked straight up to the sky. Suddenly, storm clouds gathered out of nowhere directly above them. Malia spotted a light in the clouds moving toward them. As it drew closer, she realized it was a ring of lights.

"What the hell is that?" Jaden demanded.

Malia could make out a circular object, but much of it was hidden by the clouds. Suddenly, a bright spotlight shone down on them from its center. Salvatore, Malia, and Jaden rose into the air and moved inside. The opening in the floor closed beneath them.

"Hey—what are you doing?" said Jaden. "What is this, a flying saucer or something? You didn't say anything about *this*!"

"We must move somewhere far from here to ensure that Lucifer cannot find us. Please, let me take us somewhere safe, and I promise I will explain everything."

"You're not taking us prisoner or anything?"

"You are free to leave at any time. Disembark now, if you'd

like—I will re-open the portal for you. But I urge you to hear what I have to say, first."

"Jaden, let's give him a chance," said Malia.

He thought about it for a moment longer, then said, "Yeah. Alright."

Malia took in her surroundings; it was dark here, with only enough light to make out the metal walls surrounding them.

"This will not take long," Salvatore told them.

"Where are we going?" asked Malia.

Salvatore said nothing for a few moments, then replied, "We're here."

The floor opened beneath them again, and the three of them floated down to the ground. Malia looked around her—they were standing at the base of a cliff. Stone dwellings were built into the cliff face.

"I know this place," said Malia. "We learned about this at school—these are the Pueblo cliff dwellings!"

Salvatore said nothing. He climbed a set of stone steps up to a terrace; Malia and Jaden followed him. They moved inside one of the dwellings. Salvatore took a seat in the middle of the chamber, and Malia and Jaden sat down across from him.

"We will be safe here," said Salvatore.

"How did we get here so fast?" asked Malia. "I didn't even feel your ship accelerate!"

"My people learned to master the fundamental forces of nature. The ship generates a force field that allows it to pass through the atmosphere without friction. Gravity provides the propulsion for the vessel and dampens the inertia of its passengers."

"And beams us up from the ground?" asked Jaden.

"Yes."

"So, your ship doesn't create a fireball when it enters the atmosphere from space?" asked Malia.

"Correct."

"Are you and Lucifer from Mars?" asked Jaden.

"Yes."

"But he looks different from you," said Jaden. "You've both got those weird slitted eyes, but otherwise, *he* looks human... you don't. Your skin is like a lizard's."

"He developed a holographic emitter that can render him invisible or camouflage his appearance. Using that, he makes himself look fully human."

"Then why do his eyes still look like that?" asked Malia.

"He keeps them that way by choice. You've noticed he always wears sunglasses? It adds to his mystique. When he chooses, he lowers the glasses to suggest to his victim that he might not be human."

"His victims?" asked Malia.

"For decades, he has been abducting human beings—countless thousands of them—and taking them to his underground bunker. It is located very near the location to which Bomani transported you. When he is done, he returns them to where he found them."

"Why is he abducting people?" asked Jaden.

"He has been harvesting their sperm and egg cells."

"For what purpose?" asked Malia.

"That we do not know," said Salvatore. "When we arrived here, we discovered we were no longer able to procreate. We do not know if this is a side effect of our exceptionally long cryostasis or if perhaps there is something about this planet that prevents it. I suspect that he hopes to use human cells to find a way for us to continue as a species—but how that would work, we do not know."

"How did you find out that he's harvesting cells?" asked Jaden.

"At one time, we were able to infiltrate his compound. I entered secretly but was able to penetrate only a limited area. He has a lab where he stores the human cells."

"You can't get inside anymore?" asked Jaden.

"No. Lucifer improved their security after that. We have been unable to find a way in."

"I've heard about alien abductions," said Malia. "And the men in black—like in that Will Smith movie."

"What movie?" asked Jaden.

"It's an old one—I don't think you've seen it. But the men in black show up to make people forget what they've seen after encountering aliens."

"Lucifer exists as an urban legend in your cultural consciousness," Salvatore told them. "But he is one, not many. And normally, he shows himself only to intimidate those who attempt to investigate the abductions. Most of the abductees forget their experiences without any intervention, but some recall parts of it."

"So, what does he want with us?" asked Jaden.

"I do not know for certain. Yet, to some extent, it seems obvious, no?"

"He wants us for our powers?" asked Malia.

"That is my belief," Salvatore confirmed. "He must want to use your extra genes somehow—either to give himself your powers or in conjunction with the human cells that he's been harvesting. Whatever his purpose, he will not stop until he acquires you. We must decide how to stop him."

"Our dad tried to add our extra chromosomes to regular human DNA," Malia told him, "but he couldn't do it. They don't have the technology yet."

"Lucifer possesses superior technology," Salvatore replied.

"Hang on," said Jaden. "You and Lucifer can already fly like us."

"Yes. But we do not possess telekinesis or telepathy."

"Then how do you fly?" asked Malia.

"Our species evolved on Mars where the gravity is significantly weaker than Earth's. When we relocated here, we knew our bodies would struggle endlessly against the greater mass of your planet. As I said, my people mastered gravity. We developed nanoparticles that we injected into our bloodstream that manipulate the gravitational field. They can render us weightless when we wish and provide us with the ability to move about when we leave the ground."

"Alright, then how are you able to climb buildings and shit?" asked Jaden.

"We have thousands of filaments on our hands and feet that

exert an attractive force on the molecules in whatever we touch. This gives us the ability to climb."

"Like a gecko," said Malia.

"Yes."

"*How* do you know stuff like this?" Jaden demanded.

Malia ignored him.

"We found a city beneath the face on Mars," said Malia. "And buried below the city was a vault where we found cryogenic chambers. Is that where you and Lucifer came from?"

"Yes. I will tell you the story if you wish, but it is long."

"I'd like to hear it," said Malia.

"Yeah, me too!" Jaden agreed.

"Very well. This may help you understand what you face in Lucifer." Salvatore took a deep breath. "Life evolved on Mars in much the same way as it did here on Earth. Billions of years ago, Mars had a thicker atmosphere, a strong magnetic field, and higher temperatures than it does now. Liquid water existed on the surface. As it did here on Earth, life developed from simple organic molecules.

"But a little over four billion years ago, when life on our planet was still in its early stages, the magnetic field collapsed. To this day, we have been unable to determine what caused the collapse. But in the ensuing five hundred million years or so, the solar winds stripped away most of the atmosphere.

"Mars changed, becoming the desolate world that it is now. Life continued to evolve, but these catastrophic events led to a radical change of course in that evolution. Only life forms that could adapt to life below the surface were able to survive. Over the eons, complex life evolved as it did here on Earth, but only underground.

"Our species evolved technological intelligence and became the dominant life form, as humans have done here. We developed underground cities. Due to the harsh surface conditions, our population grew to only a fraction of what humanity has attained here. The socioeconomic and geopolitical scales were smaller. Our lives were simpler; we did not acquire enormous amounts of possessions the way humans do.

"Over time, conditions on Mars continued to worsen, albeit very slowly. The atmosphere continued to thin, further depleting the oxygen supply. Tens of millions of years ago, the remaining ecosystem collapsed. Our civilization fell. Many millions of people died of starvation."

"Wait a minute," said Malia. "The Othali can synthesize food from basic proteins and fats. Why couldn't your people do that?"

"We can. Yet doing so requires chemical building blocks produced by simple organisms that were going extinct. We tried to stop it but did not possess the technology to do so. Our extinction was imminent.

"We looked into relocating to another world; we knew that complex life was already thriving on Earth. But at that time, the dinosaurs still dominated this world. We could not relocate here; it would have been far too dangerous.

"Our people had detected planets orbiting many other stars, but we had not found evidence of life on any of them. In the end, forty-five of us chose to go into cryostasis to preserve our people's existence. We hoped that one day, technologically intelligent life would develop here on Earth, though we knew it would likely take millions of years. We programmed our system to awaken us if that happened."

"How would it know?" asked Malia.

"The pyramid near the face is an antenna. It was created to monitor the Earth for artificially generated electromagnetic transmissions."

"Like radio and television?" asked Malia.

"Yes. It detected such transmissions for the first time in your year 1938. Television broadcasts. At that time, the system brought us back to life. After so many millions of years, many of the cryochambers had failed. Of those of us who remained alive, only half survived the reanimation process."

"It's incredible that *any* of you survived after so much time," said Malia. "I can't even comprehend it—nothing humans have built would last that long!"

"We designed the systems involved with keeping us alive and reawakening us to survive the ravages of time; we fortified the structures to withstand any cataclysm. Our people did not know warfare, and unlike the Othali, we never encountered a species like the Malor. Time was our only enemy, and so instead of developing technology to make weapons, we focused on building systems that could endure for ages. Yet still, time took its toll."

"But, wait—humans were using radio signals well before 1938," said Malia. "Why didn't your system wake you up then?"

"The broadcasts generated before 1938 were lower frequency—they were not able to escape the planet's ionosphere. Early television broadcasts used a higher frequency that enabled the signals to leave the atmosphere.

"We built the face on the surface to act as a beacon for any explorers who might visit our planet, in case the detection or reanimation systems failed. We hoped that such explorers would be able to find and reawaken us, but in the end, that proved unnecessary."

"Those skeletons we saw," said Jaden, "were those the people who didn't survive waking up?"

"Yes."

"And so the twelve of you who survived came to Earth?" asked Malia.

"Yes. Our goal was to revive our civilization here. We desired to peacefully co-exist with humans. But when we arrived, our plans fell apart. We found that humans were extremely warlike; we did not believe they would ever accept us."

"Why?" asked Jaden.

"World War II was raging when we arrived. We watched your societies try to destroy each other. This country unleashed nuclear weapons on its enemy. And we studied your history; we learned about the enslavement of African Americans and the genocide of the native Americans. Over and over again, societies all over the world subjugated immigrants and treated them as inferior beings. They treated other humans this way—how would they treat us?

"No, isolation was the only way we could survive. Or so most of us believed."

"Most?" asked Malia.

"Our leader, Isis, believed that we should conquer and subjugate the humans. There were only twelve of us, but so advanced was our technology compared to yours that we could have conquered the entire planet. But that is not our way. Only Lucifer supported her—which we expected him to do as her mate. The rest of us opposed her. And in the end, the only way to stop her from carrying out her plans was to kill her."

"So, Isis is dead?" asked Jaden.

"Yes."

"But Lucifer couldn't have been his name the whole time," said Malia.

"Why not?" asked Jaden.

"Because that's another name for Satan! The devil! Why would that have been his name from the beginning? Obviously, you took human names when you got here."

"We did," Salvatore said. "His name was Osiris back then."

"So, now there are eleven of you here?" asked Jaden. "Where are the others?"

"There are only eight of us left, including Lucifer," said Salvatore.

"What happened to the others?" asked Malia.

"Lucifer murdered them to avenge his mate's death. That's why we renamed him; he tried to kill us all."

"Where are the others?" Jaden asked again.

"Scattered around the world. We lived together when we arrived here, in what is now Lucifer's underground compound—although he has expanded it significantly since those days. But after he slaughtered our brethren, the rest of us fled. We are in hiding now, to ensure Lucifer cannot murder the rest of us."

"But you're here," Malia noted.

"Yes. I alone oppose him. Yet I do so mostly in secret. Rescuing the two of you was the first time I openly defied him in many years."

"So, do you live here?" asked Jaden.

"No. I live on my vessel mostly. But I come here often. This place feels like home in some ways."

"Can you use your ship to fly us to our Uncle Brian?" asked Jaden.

"I could. But I do not believe that would be wise."

"Why not?" asked Malia.

"Because he will not be able to protect you from Lucifer."

"How would he know we went there?" asked Jaden. "For that matter, how did he know we'd be at the train station in Winslow?"

"Lucifer's spies are everywhere," said Salvatore.

"I'm sorry, what does that mean, exactly?" asked Malia.

"He has eyes and ears in many places—people who work for him in some capacity. When you escaped Bomani, he probably placed his agents at every bus and train station in the area, with orders to be on the lookout for you. Once one of his people had reported your presence in Winslow, it would have taken him very little time to travel there himself."

"He has a ship like yours?" asked Malia.

"Two. He uses one for the abductions and the other for his personal transport. We had three when we came here from Mars. I've been using mine ever since we fled the compound."

"How did Lucifer know about us in the first place?" asked Malia. "Bomani told us that a man blackmailed him into bringing us to him—that must have been Lucifer."

"Yes. Lucifer knew about you for a long time. Officer Babcock told him."

"*Babcock*! But he works for the CIA!" said Jaden. "Why would he tell Lucifer about us?"

"As I said, his spies are everywhere. Lucifer heard about the project to bring you both to life through a mole he had placed within the CIA. He infiltrated Area 51 himself to learn more; Babcock caught him. In the end, Lucifer threatened to kill his son and his family unless Babcock agreed to feed him information about you.

"Lucifer decided to let things unfold. He planned to intervene once your powers manifested and take you to his compound. But then, as you well know, things spiraled out of control. When he realized the two of you were on the Othali warship, he contacted Bomani and instructed him to bring the two of you to him."

"Why didn't he come after us himself?" asked Jaden.

"I am sure he would have if Bomani had failed. But our technology is untested against the Othali. I believe their armaments to be more advanced than our own. They developed their weapons to fight the Malor; we never had to do so. Lucifer would have been reluctant to risk himself or one of his vessels against them, preferring to use that only as a last resort."

"Hang on," said Malia. "How do you know all of this?"

"I have operated in the shadows for many years, keeping tabs on Lucifer. When he confronted Babcock, I did the same. He has been giving me information ever since—he wishes to keep the two of you out of Lucifer's hands as much as I do."

"You're not going to turn us over to Babcock, are you?" Jaden demanded.

"No. And he knows that. But he is also aware that I harbor no nefarious intentions for you and considers me the lesser of two evils."

"So, Babcock told you about us," said Jaden. "How did you find out that Lucifer talked to Bomani? And how were *you* able to find us in Winslow?"

"Unbeknownst to him, I can track Lucifer. His holographic emitter uses a frequency unique to this planet. My ship's sensors detected Bomani's shuttle entering Earth orbit; I then found you by tracking Lucifer.

"He was there, his ship invisible, when you rescued your mother from the power station—he had been following the Malor to see what they would do. He saw you use your telekinesis, which is how he figured out that you were with the Othali. But he did not know that I was there as well, tracking him. And when he contacted Bomani, I was there, too."

"Can you make yourself invisible?" asked Jaden. "The way Lucifer does?"

"No, but my ship can. And its sensors enable me to watch and listen from afar."

"Why didn't you stop Bomani from going with us on the Othali ship?" asked Malia.

"I considered it, but there was no opportunity in the chaos of the Malor invasion. Very soon after he met with Lucifer, Bomani proceeded to the power station. And in any event, I did not believe he would succeed in retrieving you. In hindsight, I know I should have found a way to stop him; for that, I am sorry."

"But...how did Lucifer know about Bomani?" asked Malia.

"He had known about him for years," said Salvatore. "Bomani has developed some bad habits, and when he is under the influence, he tends to let things slip about his true identity. The locals never believe him. But Lucifer's informant knew better."

"Salvatore, can you take us to our mom?" asked Malia.

"Yes. And that may be our ultimate goal. But there are problems. If I take you there in my ship, Lucifer will detect our departure from Earth. It would not be so difficult for him to figure out that I am taking you to the Othali, and then he would pursue you. As I said, our technology is untested against theirs. It would be wise for us to consider that course of action carefully before proceeding."

"But if your ship can become invisible and doesn't generate friction in the atmosphere, how would Lucifer know if we left Earth?" asked Malia.

"The power required to achieve escape velocity would create

gravitational disturbances detectable to his sensors," Salvatore replied. "I am careful not to approach those levels when I travel."

"Oh," she said with a nod. "Well, on top of that, Bomani sabotaged the engines on the Othali ship. He told us they might not be able to fix them."

"That would hinder their ability to defend against Lucifer," said Salvatore. "All the more reason not to take you to them."

Suddenly, Malia recalled something from their trip to Earth.

"Salvatore, Bomani told us that Lucifer belongs to some organization that is planning to overthrow the world's rulers and bring peace to the planet! He said that Lucifer needs us to do it!"

"That does sound reminiscent of his mate's desire for conquest," said Salvatore. "And there is no doubt adding your powers to his would make him an even greater threat. I believe the only way we can truly guarantee your safety is to find a way to eliminate Lucifer. I think that must be our objective."

"Kill him, you mean?" said Jaden.

"Yes."

Chapter Fourteen: Showdown

"Okay, let's do it!" said Jaden. "You've got those Wolverine claws; take him out with those!"

"It won't be so easy," Salvatore replied. "Lucifer is a formidable warrior. We will need weapons and a way into his compound. I have some ideas."

"Why do we need to get inside?" asked Malia. "We could draw him out, couldn't we? He's been chasing us—why don't we lay a trap for him?"

"Yes. That would work, too."

"Where can we get weapons?" asked Jaden.

"Venus," said Salvatore.

"You have weapons on *Venus*?" said Malia. "Like, the planet?"

"No. Venus is one of my comrades. After Lucifer's treachery, she has been building and stockpiling arms."

"Great! Let's go see Venus," said Jaden, getting to his feet. "Where is she?"

"I do not know."

"What do you mean, you don't know?" Jaden asked.

"I remain purposefully ignorant of the others' locations," Salvatore explained. "If Lucifer were to capture and torture me, I would not be able to give him the locations of my comrades because I do not possess the information."

"Then, how do you communicate with each other?" asked Malia.

"We have not done so in many years."

"What the hell?" said Jaden. "Then, how are we supposed to find Venus?"

"There is a way."

"Well, what are we waiting for?" asked Jaden. "Let's do it!"

"Yes. We should begin," Salvatore agreed. He and Malia got to their feet. They left the chamber, but suddenly Salvatore stopped, cocking his head as if listening to something.

"What is it?" asked Malia.

"Lucifer is here."

"*What*?" said Jaden.

"He has found us—we must depart immediately!"

But before they could move, Malia heard a scratching noise high above them. Looking up, she spotted several people climbing down the cliff face toward their location. She pointed them out to Salvatore and Jaden.

"Who the hell are *they*?" asked Jaden.

"I do not know," said Salvatore. "Let's go!"

He leaped off the terrace, landing on the ground below; Jaden and Malia followed. But as they approached his vessel, Lucifer appeared before them.

"Leaving so soon?" he asked with a grin. "The party is just getting started."

"Oh, shit!" Jaden yelled, backpedaling toward the cliff dwelling.

Malia moved away from Lucifer, too, looking back and forth between him and the people descending the cliff face. She didn't understand who they could be—as far as she knew, only the Martians could climb a sheer rock wall like this.

Malia turned in time to see Salvatore engage Lucifer; he lunged toward him, claws extended. Lucifer ducked, grabbing Salvatore around the midsection and dropping him to the ground.

"Hey, I could use some help here!" Jaden yelled.

Malia returned her gaze to the cliff face—the people there had reached the dwellings. One by one, they jumped down to the ground, surrounding Jaden and Malia.

Malia reached out with her mind and tossed the closest one into the air. Two more rushed her; she threw them into the cliff face. The one she'd thrown into the air came to rest dozens of feet above them, then flew toward them again. Malia cast her into the cliff face with a thought.

"Let's get out of here!" Jaden yelled as he hurled two more of their pursuers away.

"No!" said Malia. "We can't leave Salvatore!"

Looking back, she saw Lucifer straddling Salvatore on the ground, landing multiple blows to his face. Malia focused and flung Lucifer off of him, into the distance. She grabbed Jaden and hurried over to Salvatore—he was directly beneath his ship, now.

"We need to get out of here!" she told Salvatore.

"Yes. Go inside my vessel; I will join you in a moment."

"Okay—how?" she asked. But looking up, she saw the portal open. A beam of light shone down on them, and she floated up into the ship with Jaden.

"What is he doing?" Jaden asked.

"I don't know!" Malia said. But a moment later, Salvatore joined them inside the metal room with a woman slung over his shoulder—one of the people from the cliff face.

The portal in the floor closed. Malia found they were moving upward, emerging in the center of a circular chamber. It was quite large, and she guessed it filled the entirety of this deck. Lining the walls were pods that resembled caskets, except that they were vertical with rounded corners.

Salvatore carried the woman over to one of the pods. She struggled and screamed the entire way. He had a hard time getting her into the pod, but she instantly calmed down once he did. Her eyes remained open, but her expression was vacant as if she were asleep.

Malia noticed that her pupils were slits; otherwise, she looked human.

"What did you do to her?" she asked.

"I sedated her. We can administer injections in the pod."

"Great," said Jaden. "What do we do now?"

"I will question her," he said to Jaden. "We need answers."

"Yeah, that's for sure," he said.

"What is your name?" Salvatore said to the woman.

"You may call me Melinda," she said, grinning slightly.

"Who are you? Where did you come from?"

"I am a child of Isis."

"I thought Isis was dead," said Malia.

"Yes," Salvatore confirmed. "Melinda, is Lucifer your father?"

"No. My father was human. I do not know his name."

"She's half-human?" asked Jaden?

"How do you know she's telling the truth?" asked Malia.

"The sedative tends to elicit truthfulness. But we will have to verify her answers.

"Melinda, how can you be the daughter of Isis? She died a long time ago."

"Osiris harvested her eggs before her death."

"Why?"

"To produce offspring. The hybrids."

"Those others who came with you—they are also the offspring of Isis?"

"Some of them. The rest are sons and daughters of Osiris."

"And they are all half-human?"

"Yes."

"That must be why he's been abducting humans!" said Malia. "He's using their DNA to create hybrids!"

"Yes," said Melinda.

"Lucifer is combining Martian DNA with human to create the hybrids?" asked Salvatore. "Using in vitro fertilization?"

"Some manipulation of the genetic code is needed, but yes."

"Who brings the fertilized eggs to term?"

"Human mothers did so in the early days. But now, hybrids do it."

"How many hybrids does Lucifer have?" asked Salvatore.

"I don't know exactly."

"Approximately."

"Over one hundred."

"Why so few?" asked Malia. "He's abducted way more humans than that over the years, hasn't he?"

"Only a tiny percentage of the humans have DNA compatible with the Martians," Melinda said. "We always need more to increase our genetic diversity."

"I don't see an emitter on her," Salvatore noted. "Melinda, is this your natural appearance?"

"Yes. But we use emitters inside the compound to prevent the humans from seeing us."

Salvatore grabbed one of her hands, examining her palm.

"You can climb walls, like Lucifer?"

"Yes. His name is Osiris."

"And you're able to defy gravity?" Salvatore asked.

"Yes. Osiris injected us with the nanoparticles."

"The hybrids live in his compound?"

"Yes. We rarely leave."

"Why has Lucifer created you?"

"It was the only way for your species to continue. One day, we will take our rightful place as the dominant life form on this planet."

Malia gasped.

"What does that mean?" she asked.

"When the time is right, we will exterminate the humans."

"How?" asked Salvatore.

"I do not know. Osiris will reveal his plan to us when the day comes."

"Let me get this straight," said Jaden. "He's created a bunch of half-human, half-Martian hybrids, who look human but can fly and climb walls like the Martians. And someday, he's going to kill every human being on the planet?"

"Yes," said Melinda.

"When will that time come?" asked Salvatore. "What is he waiting for?"

"I do not know."

"And you support this?!" asked Malia. "The hybrids are okay with murdering *billions* of people?"

"It is our great purpose," Melinda said with a gleam in her eyes. "It is the reason Osiris brought us to life. Of course, we support it."

"*All* of you do?" asked Malia. "Every last hybrid?"

"Yes."

"What is it that you and the rest of the hybrids are doing in the meantime?" asked Salvatore.

"We assist Osiris with his experiments on the humans."

"Experiments—plural?" asked Malia. "What else is he doing besides harvesting their cells?"

"I do not know," said Melinda. "We run tests. Osiris has not told us their purpose."

"Why does Lucifer want the twins, Malia and Jaden?"

"He wants their DNA so he can add their powers to those the hybrids already possess."

Salvatore regarded her for a moment longer, his expression grave. Then he turned away, moving toward the center of the chamber.

"Come with me," he said to Malia and Jaden. They joined him in the middle of the room. Suddenly, they moved upward again, emerging into another circular chamber, much smaller than the one below. There were a half dozen plush seats, and the walls were transparent. They had left the atmosphere; Malia could see the Earth far below them. They each took a seat. Malia found her backpack sitting on the floor.

"How did this get here?" she asked. "I lost it when we were on the run from Lucifer!"

"You left it in the department store," Salvatore told her. "I recovered it for you."

"Great, thank you! So... What are we doing up here?" she asked.

"Right?" said Jaden. "I didn't even know we moved!"

"How did you move the ship up here?" Malia asked. "I didn't see you use any controls."

"We control it through a neural interface."

"You mean, with your mind?" asked Jaden.

"Yes."

"Salvatore, how did Lucifer find us?" asked Malia.

"I cannot say for sure, but I believe he must have tracked us."

"How?" asked Jaden.

"You track him using his emitter, right?" asked Malia. "But you don't have one of those."

"I suspect he has found a way to track the ship—but that should not be possible. The shields block electromagnetic transmissions. I cannot imagine how he has done it. But if that is true, it means I can no longer keep you safe."

"It must be true," said Jaden. "How else could he have found us?"

"I have spent much time in the cliff dwellings in recent years," Salvatore told them. "He might have discovered that and gone looking for us there based on that knowledge. If not, then he must be tracking one of us or the ship. There are no other possibilities."

"So, what do we do now?" asked Malia.

"We *have* to stop Lucifer," said Jaden. "He's going to kill everyone if we don't!"

"Do you believe that's his plan?" asked Malia.

"I do," said Salvatore. "It has the ring of truth. Isis wanted to conquer the planet; it seems Lucifer has expanded on her plans."

"So, we gotta find that Venus chick!" said Jaden. "Get some weapons and blow up his whole compound!"

"No," said Salvatore. "I will not risk that until we determine how Lucifer is tracking us. We must not lead him to Venus. But I believe we have time. It does not seem possible that he could exterminate the entire planet with only a hundred hybrids. I do not believe the time for him to execute his plans has arrived yet."

"Okay, then what's our plan?" asked Jaden.

Salvatore seemed lost in thought for a moment.

"We must test my hypothesis," he told them, finally. "I will take us back to Earth—to a location I have never visited before.

We will see if Lucifer shows up. And if he does, then we will go our separate ways."

"*What*?" said Malia. "You can't leave us!"

"We must ascertain if he is tracking us," Salvatore replied, "and if so, how. This is the only way to accomplish that. And if I am correct that he is tracking this ship, then you will be safer on your own."

"I don't like this plan," said Jaden.

"No, neither do I!" Malia agreed.

"Take this," said Salvatore, handing Malia a cell phone—it looked identical to the one he'd given her last time. "Once we have our answer, I will find you."

Through the windows, Malia could see that they were now dropping back into the atmosphere, although she felt no acceleration. It was as if a movie were playing before her eyes, with her other senses receiving no corroboration that they were moving.

Their rapid descent ended abruptly, and she could see they had reached the ground. The land was flat, and fields stretched as far as she could see.

"Where are we?" Malia asked.

"Texas," said Salvatore. "Come with me."

He led them down through the floor to the metal chamber where they'd first entered the spacecraft. The portal in the floor opened, and they floated down to the ground.

"Now, what?" asked Jaden.

"We wait," Salvatore told him. "Lucifer is nowhere close; we will see if he shows up. Be ready to fly."

Malia took in their surroundings, turning slowly to look in every direction, but she saw no sign of Lucifer—or anyone else, for that matter. The minutes dragged by, but still, nobody approached. She felt anxious, anticipating Lucifer's arrival at any moment.

Malia heard a train whistle in the distance. Several minutes later, she spotted a freight train going by far across the field. It was the longest train she'd ever seen. There were no roads nearby.

"If he doesn't show up here, then is it safe to say that he just knew to look for you at the cliff dwellings?" asked Malia.

"We must give it more time," said Salvatore, "but yes, that would be my conclusion."

Time went by, and Malia found herself experiencing extreme boredom. Suddenly, she heard a cracking sound nearby. Wheeling around, she stared in the direction of the noise but saw nothing.

"What is it?" said Jaden.

"I thought I heard something," she replied. "It was probably nothing."

"Can you tell if Lucifer is coming?" Jaden asked Salvatore.

"No," he said. "I have not been able to detect him since we arrived here."

"Is that unusual?" asked Malia. "I thought you could track his emitter."

"It may simply mean that he isn't using it."

A few more minutes passed. Malia heard another cracking sound, closer this time. She turned to search for its source but again saw nothing.

"This time, I heard it, too," said Jaden.

"He's here," Salvatore said suddenly. "Very close now."

Malia's heart jumped into her throat. She looked around frantically but could see nobody.

Suddenly twenty people appeared out of nowhere, standing in a circle around them. She recognized several of them as the hybrids from the cliff dwellings. A moment later, Lucifer showed up, only a few feet away.

"You have something that belongs to me," he drawled. "I've come to collect."

Malia watched as Melinda floated down from the ship. She hit the ground and ran to Lucifer, standing beside him.

"You've got her back," said Salvatore. "Now, leave us be."

"Oh, I don't think so," Lucifer replied. In the next moment, he and the hybrids disappeared again.

"Fly—now!" said Salvatore.

Malia tried to take to the air but found multiple pairs of hands grasping her, holding her on the ground. Though they were invisible, she knew it must have been the hybrids. Focusing, she tried to hurl them away from her telekinetically but couldn't manage it without seeing them.

"*Malia—I can't get away*!" Jaden said in her mind; she could feel his panic.

Malia struggled to escape their grip, but it was no use; there were too many of them. Finally, she stopped. Clearing her mind, she imagined people standing next to her. Reaching out with her mind, she threw them away from her.

It worked; she was free. Next, she visualized Jaden's assailants and hurled them away, too. In the next moment, the hybrids and Lucifer became visible again. Lucifer had pinned Salvatore to the ground and had him in a chokehold. Malia moved toward them to help, but Jaden grabbed her by the arm.

"Malia, no!" he said. "We've gotta get out of here!"

But it was too late—the whole group of hybrids had converged on their position. The ones closest grabbed them again, dragging them to the ground; the rest piled on. Malia found herself lying in the dirt in a ball, her face pressed against Jaden's chest.

"*What do we do*?" he said in her mind.

"*Hold on*," she replied, squirming to cover as much of his body as she could with hers. "*I'm going to try something I've only done once.*"

"*Okay...*"

Malia concentrated. The last time she'd done this, it hadn't been intentional. She'd been under extreme stress, and it had happened on its own. But she was stronger now and believed she could repeat it by force of will.

She gathered as much energy as she could. Then, she screamed, releasing her power in every direction at once.

It worked—the hybrids flew off of them with explosive force, several slamming into the spacecraft above them. They hit the ground and moved no more.

"Now!" Malia yelled, launching herself into the air.

She soared high above the earth, searching for somewhere to go as Jaden rose to her side. Finally, she had an idea.

Malia shot across the sky. She'd spotted a freight train in the distance, moving east. It wasn't clear if it was the same one she'd seen earlier, but it didn't matter. Dropping out of the sky, she landed on the top of a boxcar. Jaden landed next to her a moment later.

"This wasn't what I had in mind when we talked about taking a train," he chided.

"Shut up," she said. "And keep your eyes open—it's still possible Lucifer was tracking the two of us somehow."

"I doubt it," he replied. "He probably found a way to track the flying saucer. Do you think Salvatore's alright?"

"He can handle himself," said Malia, hoping it to be true. "And besides, it's us Lucifer wants."

"Yeah, but you heard Salvatore—he wants to kill the rest of the Martians, too!"

Malia didn't want to think about it; she already felt terrible for fleeing like this when Salvatore appeared to be in trouble.

They sat down back to back and kept an eye out as the time dragged by. The train passed through a city eventually and then back into the countryside. Malia saw no sign of Lucifer the entire time.

It was a beautiful sunny day. People in their cars at a couple of railroad crossings spotted them and waved; Malia and Jaden waved back. Still, Lucifer did not show up.

"He must have been tracking Salvatore's ship," Jaden said, finally. "If it had been us, he would have shown up by now."

"Yeah, you're probably right," she replied. "But now I'm starting to worry why Salvatore hasn't found us yet."

"You still got that phone he gave you?"

"It's in my pocket," she told him, touching it through her jeans to make sure.

"Hey, what's that?" said Jaden.

Malia turned; he was pointing to the sky. In the distance, she saw storm clouds forming and moving toward them.

"I've got a bad feeling about this," she said, getting to her feet. "We need to move!"

"Yeah, I think you're right!"

Malia shot into the sky, flying away from the clouds as fast as she could. Jaden caught up to her as she slowed and turned to check their progress—but the clouds moved above them, and she could see a ring of lights in the middle.

"This must be Lucifer!" said Malia.

"Could be Salvatore," Jaden pointed out.

"Maybe, but then why isn't he showing himself?" Malia replied. "Let's go!"

Malia flew east, Jaden right behind her. But the spacecraft stayed above them. She turned north, and then west, but could not escape it.

Looking toward the ground, she tried to find somewhere they could hide. But it was no use—a bright light shone down from the center of the craft and lifted Malia and Jaden higher. Malia tried to resist, fighting with all her might to fly away but found she was powerless to do so. Moments later, they passed through the floor and into a metal chamber, precisely like the one in Salvatore's ship. Malia realized that Salvatore would no longer be able to track them if this ship had the same shielding as his.

And as the portal in the floor closed, someone else appeared beside Malia and Jaden: Melinda, the hybrid Salvatore had kidnapped.

"How did you find us?" Malia asked, thinking that they must have been tracking her and Jaden all along.

"Silly girl," said Melinda with a smirk. "You couldn't see me, of course, but I followed you to the train. Osiris brought me my emitter!"

Chapter Fifteen: The Bunker

Malia heard a buzzing noise and suddenly felt groggy. She couldn't remember the last time she'd slept, and now her body was trying desperately to pull her into slumber.

The next moment, Malia found herself in the center of a circular chamber, with pods lining the walls—identical to Salvatore's ship. Some unseen force moved her across the area, turned her around, and backed her into one of the pods. Across the chamber, she could see Jaden settling into one of the other pods.

Malia felt something prick the back of her neck. There was a tingling sensation there that slowly spread down her back and arms. She discovered she had lost motor control—she could no longer move her arms or legs. Her heart was hammering in her chest, and she was still breathing, but she could no longer shift her gaze.

Suddenly, Melinda appeared before her out of nowhere.

"I'm not supposed to reveal myself to abductees," she cooed, her face uncomfortably close to Malia's, "but since we've already met, I figure it's probably allowed."

Malia tried to respond but could not speak or even open her mouth.

"Oh, I'm sorry; you won't be able to move or talk for a while.

It looked like you wanted to say something, but it'll have to wait," Melinda said with a smirk. Malia felt the urge to slap her.

Melinda moved across the chamber to Jaden. Malia realized that his eyes were closed.

"I hoped you might stay awake, too," Melinda said to him with a sigh, stroking his face. "But you fell asleep like most of the humans."

Malia reached out with her mind, trying to hurl Melinda away from her brother, but nothing happened. She struggled for a few more moments, but somehow she'd lost her telekinesis.

"*Jaden*!" she called out with her mind. "*Wake up*!"

He showed no sign of having heard her. She didn't know if it was only because he was asleep, or if she'd lost her telepathy, too.

Melinda disappeared again. The minutes dragged by, and Malia was having difficulty keeping her eyes open. But suddenly, she found herself moving out of the pod. She and Jaden met in the center of the chamber, without any sign of what force might be acting on them, and descended into the metal room where they'd started. Jaden was still unconscious.

The portal in the floor opened, and they dropped to the ground. They were in the desert—there were massive rock formations nearby that looked like the ones Malia had seen when they'd first arrived in Bomani's shuttle.

Malia and Jaden floated across the desert floor toward a butte. As they drew closer, Malia realized there was an opening in its face. She and Jaden moved inside, through a short tunnel, and into what looked like a freight elevator.

They entered the elevator and turned. The door closed, and she felt them going down very fast. They stopped abruptly, and the door opened again.

Malia found herself gazing down a long tunnel with walls of stone and metal doors lining either side. They moved halfway down the corridor and passed through a doorway into a dark chamber. As her eyes adjusted, she saw that there were exam tables here. The unseen force took her to one and lay her down on her back. In the corner of her eye, she could see Jaden lying on a nearby table.

Malia struggled to stay awake but could no longer resist. Her eyes closed, and slumber stole her away.

Malia opened her eyes. It took her a few seconds to remember where she was and what had happened. She tried to look around the room but found she still had no motor control. Jaden was still lying on a nearby table. She could barely see him at the edge of her vision and couldn't be sure, but it looked like he was naked now.

Malia abruptly realized that she was naked, too. She struggled mightily to roll off the table but could not move a muscle. Summoning her telekinesis, she tried moving herself to the floor, but nothing happened.

Suddenly, she saw an egg-shaped object appear above her. It hovered over her face and touched her forehead for a moment. Malia felt her heart rate increasing with her anxiety. What was this thing? It moved over her heart and came to rest again. What was it doing to her? It moved to her lower abdomen. It touched her briefly, and she felt a pinprick—it was only mildly painful. But her leg involuntarily flinched when it happened. Malia tried to repeat the movement consciously but could not.

With a spasm of fear, she realized that the device had pricked her directly above her ovary. Salvatore had told them Lucifer was harvesting sex cells—was that what had just happened? Did this mean they now possessed her DNA?

A man appeared out of nowhere, standing beside her. He held the egg-shaped device in one hand. He wore a white lab coat, and she realized that the pupils of his eyes were slits. For a moment, he grinned down at her, then disappeared again, along with his device.

Malia felt herself growing sleepy again. They must have been using some sort of drug to paralyze her, rob her of her powers, and render her unconscious. She thought back to the time she'd healed the cut on her finger back on the Othali warship. Then, she'd imagined the coagulant streaming to the wound. Now, she tried to visualize the drug they'd used coursing through her veins and her immune cells attacking it.

For a few moments, it seemed to be working. Malia could feel her head clearing a bit. She tried to flex her fingers—nothing happened at first. But then, her index finger flinched. It wasn't much, but she felt sure it was voluntary.

She struggled to move again but found drowsiness overcoming her. Moments later, she fell asleep.

When Malia awakened again, she found herself lying on the floor inside an enormous room that resembled an aircraft hangar.

She was clothed now, much to her relief. And she could move. Getting to her feet, she took in her surroundings.

The Othali shuttle Bomani had used to take them to Earth was nearby. A flying saucer was hovering in the middle of the chamber. There were bay doors at the far end of the room. There were windows at the closer end, and beyond them stood Lucifer, staring back at her.

Malia moved toward him. Reaching out with her mind, she tried to slam him into the window. Nothing happened.

"Welcome," Lucifer's voice said over loudspeakers somewhere high on the walls. "As I assume you just discovered, these walls shield me from your powers."

"Yeah, I noticed," she said, glaring at him. "Just like Babcock's torture chamber in Area 51."

"Ah, Ms. Kwan," he replied, "who do you think provided them with the technology for this kind of shielding?"

"You?" she guessed.

"I would like you to use your telekinesis to lift the shuttle off the ground," he said.

"Why should I?"

Malia felt intense pain jolt her body—it seemed to emanate from the back of her neck. It was excruciating but lasted only a moment. When it subsided, she realized she'd dropped to her knees.

"You did that?" she said, getting back to her feet.

"And I will do it again if you fail to comply," he drawled. "Now, lift the shuttle."

"How high?" she asked, glaring at him again.

"Ten feet."

Malia turned to face the shuttle. Reaching out with her thoughts, she lifted the vessel into the air, to her best approximation of ten feet.

"You may set it down," he said.

Malia let it drop. It crashed to the floor, and she again felt excruciating pain course through her body. She fell down screaming.

"Gently, next time," Lucifer said when the pain stopped.

Malia stood up again, tears streaming down her cheeks.

"Lift it again," he commanded.

She reached out with her mind but found the shuttle was much heavier this time. Again she moved it roughly ten feet off the ground, but this time, it was much more difficult. After a few seconds, she set it down gently.

"How did you do that?" she asked. "You made it heavier."

"Again," Lucifer said a moment later, ignoring her question.

This time it took every ounce of strength she could muster. She managed to move the ship off the ground but could barely get it as high as he wanted. It took enormous effort to place it down again without letting it crash.

"Again."

Malia tried, but this time, the shuttle was too heavy for her to move. She struggled for several seconds but couldn't lift it an inch.

Extreme pain wracked her body. Malia fell to the floor, writhing and screaming. When it stopped, she found herself panting and sobbing.

"How can you punish me for that?" she screamed as she regained her feet, stumbling toward Lucifer. "You made it too heavy! I can't lift that!"

"Again," he said with a grin.

How did he expect her to accomplish this?

Malia returned to the shuttle. Taking a deep breath, she did her best to clear her mind. Reaching out, she focused on the shuttle. With all her might, she tried to lift it. Nothing happened, and she concentrated ever harder. Her whole body began shaking, and she started sweating.

Suddenly, something snapped, and she felt power coursing through her limbs. The shuttle shot into the air and slammed into the ceiling. In her shock, Malia lost control of it. But as it fell, she reached out again and hurled it into the windows toward Lucifer.

The entire room rang like a gong as the shuttle smashed into the wall. It fell apart, the pieces crashing to the floor. Malia knew her power must have interacted with the planet's magnetic field to make her so strong. She only wished she could tap into it at will—as before, this had happened subconsciously.

"Impressive," Lucifer said, stepping back from the wall, "but most unwise."

Unimaginable pain ripped through Malia's body; she hit the floor, writhing and screaming. She couldn't think; there was only agony, and she wanted to die.

Finally, the pain stopped. Malia was sobbing and felt too weak to stand.

"You broke Bomani's shuttle," Lucifer said with a tone of amusement. "No matter, we'll find something else for your brother."

"You're a monster!" she screamed. "I know what you're planning—you're going to kill every human on the planet!"

"Humanity has had its chance, and look what they've done with the place," he drawled. "And we won't be killing *all* of the humans—only 99.9% of them."

"So you and your hybrids can rule the world," she said with disgust.

"The hybrids, as you call them, are a superior race, and they know it. They are the future of this world. Sleep, now."

"*Jaden...*" Malia called out with her mind as darkness engulfed her.

Malia's eyes fluttered open. She was back in the room with the exam tables. But it was different—it was brighter here, and she could see the walls. She didn't think this was the same room from before.

"Good morning, sunshine," a voice cooed from somewhere behind her.

Malia couldn't move to see who was there. But Melinda moved into her field of view. She was wearing a white lab coat.

"I heard you had a rough time," she said with a smile, standing right next to her now. Malia realized that her eyes looked normal this time—her pupils were round. "It will do you no good to resist Osiris."

Malia tried to reply or reach out and grab Melinda by the throat, but her muscles refused to work. She tried to reach out with her mind to throw her across the room, but her powers were disabled.

"Leave her alone, you bitch," a voice said.

Malia noticed there was someone else in the room with them. It was a girl, probably a few years older than Malia, lying in one of the other exam beds. She was fully clothed.

"Wendy, this is Malia. The two of you will be spending some time together today."

"Go screw yourself!"

"Goodnight, Wendy," Melinda said with a sigh. The girl didn't say anything else. "She can get a little feisty sometimes," Melinda said to Malia. "I figured you two should meet before Osiris begins his experiments. He's going to see if he can use your DNA to give Wendy your powers! We're more than a little excited about this—if it works, we'll be next!"

Malia felt her heart racing. She was right—Lucifer had their DNA. Salvatore had told them that his technology was superior to what the humans possessed—she was willing to bet his experiment would be successful.

She tried to imagine the hybrids adding her powers to their own; the thought was terrifying. It was like Lucifer was trying to raise an army.

"Well, I must be going," said Melinda, walking out of the room. "Back to sleep now."

Malia felt the drowsiness creeping over her again. She tried to sense their drug in her veins and direct her body to resist. Closing her eyes, she visualized her immune system battling the chemical.

Slowly, she felt the lethargy receding. She tried flexing her fingers—at first, nothing happened. But she kept trying and finally managed to make a fist.

She tried to sit up or swing her legs off the table, but this proved too much. Beyond her fingers and toes, she was still unable to move.

"*Jaden*!" she called out with her mind. "*Can you hear me*?"

There was no response. But suddenly, she heard a different voice in her mind.

"*Malia? Is that you*?"

"*Bomani*?!"

"*Hey, yeah, it's me—listen, I'm so sorry for what I did. I let myself give in to fear; that was wrong.*"

"*Lucifer reneged on his promise, didn't he*?" she asked. "*He's not letting you go.*"

"*How'd you know*?"

"*It's pretty obvious. You wouldn't be apologizing otherwise.*"

"*No, seriously, I've realized the error in my ways. I'm a new man, I swear*!"

"*Right. What do you want?*"

"*Well, I was wondering... Can you get us out of here? Using your powers*?"

Malia ignored him. She tried again to get up from the exam table but felt herself growing groggy.

"*Malia, can you hear me*?"

She focused with all her might, trying to imagine the alien drug leaving her system. But it was no use. She succumbed to sleep moments later.

When she woke up, she was lying on the floor in the hangar again. Sitting up, she saw Wendy lying nearby on the floor, unconscious. Lucifer was watching them through the windows.

Malia stood up.

"You gave her our powers?" she asked.

"That remains to be seen," he drawled.

"But you gave her our extra chromosomes?"

Lucifer ignored her. A few minutes later, Wendy stirred and woke up.

"Where am I?" she asked, sitting up and taking in her surroundings.

"It's a hangar, I think," said Malia.

"How long was I out?" she asked, slowly getting to her feet.

"I have no idea."

"Enough chit-chat, ladies," Lucifer said over the loudspeakers. "Ms. Bell, we have completed the procedure. I would like you to try to move Ms. Kwan with your mind."

"Are you really telekinetic?" Wendy asked Malia. "He told me you and your brother both are and that he was giving me some of your DNA somehow. But it sounds like a bunch of bullshit to me."

"Perhaps a little demonstration is in order, Ms. Kwan?" said Lucifer.

Malia focused on Wendy and lifted her a few feet into the air.

"Whoa! Holy shit!"

Malia set her down on the floor.

"Your turn, Ms. Bell."

"You've gotta be kidding me—I can't do that!"

Wendy screamed and collapsed on the floor, writhing in pain. Malia knew Lucifer was responsible; it stopped a moment later.

"What the hell was that?" Wendy asked, regaining her feet, tears streaming down her cheeks.

"He'll do it again if you don't do what he wants," Malia warned her.

"But I don't know how to move you with my mind!"

"Take a deep breath," said Malia. "Imagine me rising off the floor. You've got to concentrate as hard as you can."

"Alright..."

Wendy breathed deeply. She stared at Malia for a few moments, but nothing happened.

"I can't—"

She screamed, falling to the floor again, this time curling up in a ball.

"Stop it!" Malia shouted. "It takes time—you can't expect her to do it so fast!"

Wendy relaxed, flopping onto her back; she was sobbing.

"Again," Lucifer said over the loudspeakers.

Malia helped Wendy to her feet.

"You can do it," she told her. "Take a few deep breaths, and then you have to focus. Visualize what you want to happen and then make it so."

Malia backed away several feet, and Wendy tried again. She took several deep breaths and then concentrated on Malia.

Moments later, Malia found herself lifting off the floor—only a few inches, but Wendy had done it.

"Yeah! That's it!" said Malia before dropping back to the floor.

Wendy gasped.

"That was incredible!"

"Ms. Kwan," said Lucifer. "I want you to communicate telepathically with Ms. Bell. You will tell her the name of the person who brought you back here to Earth."

"*Wendy, can you hear me*?" Malia called out with her mind. "*Wendy*?"

"I can hear you!" she said out loud.

"*His name is Bomani.*"

"Bomani? What kind of name is that?"

"Ms. Bell, you will now tell Ms. Kwan the name of the town where you grew up. Telepathically."

Wendy opened her mouth to protest but thought better of it. Malia nodded to her encouragingly. Wendy focused on her, but nothing happened.

"*Say it in your mind*," Malia told her. "*Concentrate on me, and say it in your mind.*"

Still, she couldn't do it.

"Ms. Kwan?" said Lucifer.

Knowing what was coming if he knew she'd failed, Malia decided to take a guess.

"Boise."

Wendy screamed in pain, falling to the floor again.

"Leave her alone!" Malia shouted. "Stop it!"

"Perhaps you're right," he said. Wendy stopped screaming. "It's already clear the experiment is a success."

Malia suddenly felt extremely drowsy. She thought of fighting it again but didn't want Lucifer to know she could do that. Instead, she allowed the drug to put her to sleep.

When Malia woke up again, she was back on her exam table. She couldn't move. Focusing on the drug flowing through her veins, she willed her immune system to expel it from her system. Slowly, she gained the ability to wiggle her fingers and toes, but she kept going. Summoning her full power, she concentrated on expelling the chemical from every muscle in her body.

Finally, she moved her arms and her legs. Sitting up, she looked around the room. Jaden was lying on another exam table across the room. Wendy was here too, halfway between them.

Malia slipped off the table and tiptoed over to Wendy. She was awake but strapped to the table.

"Hey," Malia whispered. "I'm sorry about what happened back there."

"What are you talking about?"

Malia shushed her, turning to see if anyone would walk in on them. She was afraid if they found her on her feet, they'd give her a more potent drug.

"In the hangar with Lucifer," she whispered. "I would have stopped him if I could, but the walls in there are shielded. They block our powers."

"I'm sorry, I don't have the first clue what you're referring to," Wendy said.

"Don't you remember him taking us to the hangar? Making you try your powers?"

"Powers? What powers?"

Malia didn't understand what was going on. They must have given her something to interfere with her memory.

"Never mind," she said. "Forget it."

She crept over to Jaden. His eyes were closed; Malia shook him by one arm.

"Jaden!" she whispered. "Wake up!"

He didn't move.

"*Jaden! You have to wake up*!"

It was no use. He remained unconscious.

Malia reached out with her thoughts, trying to probe into his mind. She could sense his feelings—he must have been dreaming. There was anxiety and anger. Focusing harder, she caught images of Lucifer and the hybrids chasing them through a forest.

"*Jaden*!" she called out again. "*Can you hear me*?"

"*Malia? Where are you*?"

"*I'm right beside you—you're dreaming. You have to wake up*!"

"*Lucifer—he killed Salvatore—we have to get away! We have to get back to the ship*!"

"*Jaden, no—it's only a dream. We're in Lucifer's compound. I need you to wake up—we have to get out of here*!"

It wasn't working—he wouldn't come out of it. The drugs were still working on his system.

Malia probed deeper still, trying to penetrate his subconscious. She focused on *his* immune system, willing it to eliminate the chemical from his body the same way she'd done for herself. Slowly, it started to work. She could sense his conscious mind beginning to wake up.

"*Jaden*," she called out. "*You have to help me. We have to expel the drugs from your body*!"

She felt his mind relax. He wasn't dreaming about Lucifer anymore. New images formed in her mind—the girl they'd met in New Mexico. Jaden was swimming with her; she was removing her bikini top.

"*Jaden! I don't need to see this! Wake up!*"

Malia focused with all her might. She could feel his immune system working to eliminate the toxin. With every bit of energy she could muster, she willed his body to fight.

Suddenly, Jaden's eyes fluttered open.

"*Malia? What's happening? I can't move*!"

"*They drugged you—I've been helping you eliminate it from your body.*"

"*I can feel you in my head with me—how are you doing that*?!"

"*Don't worry about that now—concentrate on your immune system expelling the chemicals from your bloodstream*!"

She could feel him focusing. Slowly, he grew stronger; the toxin was leaving his muscles. Finally, he sat up.

"Holy shit!" he said out loud.

"Shut up!" Malia hissed. "They'll hear us!"

"You were inside my head! I could feel you with me in my dreams—did you see Savannah?"

Malia giggled.

"That's not cool—those are my private thoughts!"

"I won't do it again, I promise! We've got to get out of here!"

Chapter Sixteen: Light at the End of the Tunnel

They took a few steps toward the door, but Malia heard footsteps approaching.

"Quick—back on the exam table!" she whispered to Jaden. "Pretend you're asleep!"

She hurried back to her own table, lay down on it, and closed her eyes. The footsteps moved into their room.

"Wendy Bell," a voice said, "we need you." It sounded like Melinda, but her voice lacked its usual cooing quality.

Malia opened her eyes a crack. Melinda was standing by Wendy's table. As she watched, Melinda released her straps and helped her off the table.

"I don't understand what you people want with me," said Wendy. Malia closed her eyes again as they walked past her. "Why don't you let me go?"

Malia opened her eyes again in time to see them walk out of the room. She waited a few moments, then dropped to the floor.

"Jaden, let's go!" she whispered.

He hurried over, and they moved to the exit. Although there was no door in the opening, Malia could not see through it. She stuck her head through and saw the long corridor they'd used when they first arrived; their room was at the opposite end from the elevator. She didn't see anyone.

Pulling her head back into the room, she grabbed Jaden by the arm and said, "Come on."

They moved into the hallway. She heard someone wailing somewhere farther down the corridor.

"Now what?" Jaden whispered. "How do we get out of here?"

Malia shushed him, listening intently. That voice seemed familiar.

"That sounds like Lucifer," she said.

"What's wrong with him?"

"I don't know. Let's see if we can find out."

They crept down the hall toward the elevator. A few doors down, they came to the source of the noise. The door to the room looked like metal, but her finger went right through it when Malia touched it. She poked her head inside. The room was only dimly lit, and she couldn't see the walls. There were exam tables, most of them empty. But there were several people in lab coats gathered around one of the tables, and that was the source of the wailing.

The people were blocking her view, so Malia couldn't see who was on the table, but it sounded like Lucifer. Something was wrong with him. She spotted Bomani in the group. Wendy was lying on one of the other exam tables, Melinda hovering over her.

Pulling her head back out of the room, she told Jaden what she saw.

"What's wrong with Lucifer?" he asked.

"I don't know, but I have an idea—I'm going to reach out to Bomani."

"What's to stop him from ratting us out? If he tells them we're out here, then we're screwed."

"He talked to me earlier—telepathically. Lucifer's turned on him. He wants to escape too—and he might know a way out of here!"

"Are you kidding? How can you possibly trust him after what he's done?"

"I *don't* trust him—but we might be able to use him. Once we escape, we can decide what to do with him."

"Alright," said Jaden. "Do it."

She focused her thoughts on Bomani.

"*What's going on in there? Is that Lucifer?*"

"*Malia? Where are you?*"

"*We're getting out of here. You can come with us if you want, but if you tell them what we're doing, we'll let you rot down here.*"

"*Agreed! This isn't going to be easy, though—you have a plan?*"

"*Not yet. We're in the hallway—come out here, and we can figure something out.*"

Bomani emerged from the doorway moments later.

"They'll see us out here—come with me."

He led them a little farther down the hall and into one of the other rooms.

"Okay, tell us what's wrong with Lucifer," Malia said.

"I'm not sure exactly, but he's messed up. I helped him use your

DNA to create a virus he could inject into that girl's cerebellum—what's her name..?"

"Wendy?" asked Malia.

"Yeah, her. And it worked—he tested her with you, right? In the hangar?"

"Yes," Malia confirmed. "She has telekinesis and telepathy—but they made her forget all about it after. Why the cerebellum?"

"*What* is a cerebellum?" asked Jaden.

"It's a structure in the brain, in the back of your head," Bomani told them. "It's responsible for motor control and communication and plays a role in thinking. That's basically where your powers reside. By introducing the virus into Wendy's cerebellum, we were able to alter her DNA. The virus spreads the DNA to the entire structure. Once Lucifer confirmed that it had worked on Wendy, he made me inject him."

"*What*?!" said Malia.

"So, he has our powers, now?" asked Jaden.

"No, man—I mean, I don't know. He collapsed and went into convulsions. I told him the DNA might not be compatible with his system, but he wouldn't listen. He wants to give it to these hybrids but insisted on testing it on himself, first."

"Do Martians *have* a cerebellum?" asked Malia.

"They've got something comparable," he said.

"Is he dying?" asked Jaden.

"No idea. The seizure stopped eventually, but now he can't walk or talk or anything, and he keeps screaming. They're trying to figure out what they can do for him. Melinda wants to give him an infusion of human growth hormone—that's why she took Wendy in there. And this might give us a chance to get out of here—they're all distracted!"

"Can we go up the elevator they used to bring us down here?" asked Malia.

"Not a chance," said Bomani. "I tried it, and they knew what I was doing right away. They caught me."

"Wait, they've allowed you to move about freely?" asked Malia.

"Limited movement," he said. "Mostly, they've had me in the lab working on the virus. I had to sneak out to try the elevator."

"Okay, so what do we do?" asked Jaden.

"If we can get to the hangar, we could leave in the shuttle. He's got the place locked down, but I'm pretty sure we could blast our way through those bay doors."

"Uh... actually, I kind of... well, destroyed the shuttle," Malia told him.

"What the hell did you do that for?" he asked.

"I was upset. It's a long story. But we'll have to find another way."

"I found a map of the complex on the terminal they had me working on," he told them. "If we can get up to the lab, we can use that to find another way out. Hopefully."

"Where's the lab?" asked Malia.

"Two levels up."

"How'd you get up there if you couldn't use the elevator?" asked Jaden.

"Oh, I used the elevator, but one of the hybrids escorted me back and forth."

"There must be another way to move between levels, right?" said Malia. "What if they lost power or something—if the elevator failed, they'd be trapped down here? That doesn't seem right."

"I don't know, but I haven't seen any stairs or anything if that's what you're thinking," said Bomani. "Come to think of it, we never did find any stairs back in that Martian city, either."

"Yeah, but that was built around an open pit," Malia replied. "There's nothing like that here... Wait a minute. I noticed these tracks running up and down the walls in that city—they reminded me of sidewalks, except that they were vertical."

"Well, that would make sense, right?" said Jaden. "They're basically lizards, and they can scale walls and shit. They probably used the sidewalks to go up and down between levels. They wouldn't need stairs."

"Yeah!" Malia agreed. "So there must be something like that here!"

"We need to find it," said Bomani. "Then you two could use your powers to get us up there."

Malia stuck her head through the doorway to make sure the coast was clear. Then the three of them moved into the hallway. They crept down the corridor, looking inside each door they passed to find something that looked like a pathway or tunnel between levels. But they found only exam rooms.

They'd checked all but the last three doorways when Malia heard a noise—voices followed by footsteps. She caught a glimpse of three people emerging from the last door on the left before grabbing Jaden and Bomani and pulling them through the nearest doorway.

"Someone's coming," she whispered by way of explanation.

They waited a minute but didn't hear anyone go by.

Malia poked her head back into the hallway but didn't see anyone. They crept back into the corridor.

"Where'd they go?" Jaden whispered.

They checked the last couple of rooms. The last one on the right was where they'd started; Wendy had not returned yet. Across from that was the doorway through which the people had emerged.

"Careful," said Bomani.

Malia poked her head through quickly, affording her only a brief glimpse inside.

"Looks like a control room or something," she told them. "I saw displays on the far wall. But there's no one in there."

"Where the hell did those people go?" said Jaden.

Malia had an idea. She touched the wall at the end of the hallway, and her hand moved right through it. Sticking her head through, she found a tunnel extending vertically in both directions. She saw nobody below her, but looking up, spotted someone scaling the tunnel wall.

"This is it," she told them, pulling her head out of the wall.

"Great, so, what are we waiting for?" asked Bomani.

"There's someone in there," she told him. "A few levels above us. We have to go two levels up?"

Bomani nodded.

Malia waited a few more moments, then rechecked the tunnel. It was clear. She and Jaden used their telekinesis to take the three of them up two levels. They emerged into the corridor there. But as they hurried toward the lab, one of the hybrids stepped out of another doorway right next to them.

Malia wasted no time—they couldn't risk getting caught. She reached out with her mind and threw the man into the wall, slamming his head into the stone. He slumped to the floor unconscious.

"What do we do with him?" asked Jaden. "Someone's gonna see him if we leave him here."

"Does anyone else use your lab?" Malia asked Bomani.

"I've been the only one in there since I got here."

"Perfect," she said. Using her mind to lift the hybrid off the floor, they continued to the lab. Once inside, she set him down on the floor in the far corner.

Bomani ran over to a display on the wall. He tapped it a couple of times and then said, "Here it is!"

There was a diagram of the entire compound.

"We're here," said Bomani, pointing to a chamber. "That's the elevator, and this is the tunnel we just used."

Malia examined the diagram. There were two more levels below the one where they'd been keeping her and Jaden. The bottom floor had only a few rooms—one of them significantly larger than the hangar.

"I wonder what's in there?" said Jaden, pointing to the massive area.

"I don't know, but this looks like it must be the power generator," said Malia, tapping a smaller chamber at the far end. She spotted two lines extending at an angle deep into the Earth. "If they're running on geothermal energy like the Martian city, then these must be the conduits for the heat pumps."

"That won't do us any good," said Bomani. "Those systems pump fluid into the ground to transfer the heat. It's a dead end unless you want to be boiled like a lobster."

"Yeah, but what's this third line between them?" asked Malia. "There's another at the end that goes from that one straight up to the surface."

"Could be service tunnels," Bomani suggested.

"Is there any reason we can't just go to the top of that tunnel we just used?" asked Jaden.

"It looks like it comes out above ground," said Malia. "The top of it appears to be inside of a mesa, like the elevator shaft."

"That's probably monitored, too," said Bomani.

"Salvatore did say that Lucifer beefed up his security after he broke in," said Malia.

"We've got four choices, kids," Bomani told them. "It's the elevator, the tunnel we just used, the hangar, or the service tunnel for the geothermal system. And I'm betting the service tunnel is the only one that has any chance of getting us out of here undetected."

"I agree," said Malia. "Let's go."

They moved back into the corridor. As they crept toward the tunnel, Jaden spoke to Malia telepathically.

"Are you sure about this—I still don't trust him!"

"Neither do I! But don't worry—once we get out of here, we'll take care of him."

At the end of the corridor, Malia poked her head through the wall. Two people were climbing down the wall from above. She pulled her head out immediately. A minute later, she checked again—this time, the tunnel was empty.

Malia and Jaden used their powers to lower them to the bottom. They moved through the wall and found themselves in a long corridor, broader than those above.

"The generator's down at the far end," said Malia. "Let's go!"

"Hold on," said Jaden. "I want to check out that huge room and see what's in there!"

Malia had to admit that she was curious, too. They ran down the hall. There was a door on the left, halfway down; Malia peered inside.

"Whoa," she said, moving into the room.

Jaden and Bomani followed her in.

The chamber was vastly larger than the hangar—more so than was apparent in the diagram. It was twice as high as the rooms on the upper levels. And lining one entire wall were rows of rectangular hatches.

"Guys, this looks like a gigantic morgue," Bomani said. "I think we should get out of here."

"Wait," said Malia.

She opened one of the nearest hatches. There was a sound of pressure releasing, and clouds of vapor poured out of the opening. A table slid out, seemingly suspended in midair. And sure enough, there was a corpse lying on it. Malia stifled a scream.

"What the hell?" said Jaden. "He's dead, right?"

"And frozen," Bomani replied.

It was a white man; he looked fully human, probably in his mid-60s at the time of death.

"Is this one of his hybrids, or... what?" asked Jaden.

"I don't think so," said Malia.

She reached out to lift one of his eyelids but pulled her hand away at the last second. She couldn't bring herself to touch a dead body. Instead, she reached out with her mind and opened one eye. The man's pupil was circular.

"Human," she said.

Malia pushed the table; it withdrew into the wall, the hatch closing behind it. She checked two more—an older Asian woman and a young Black man—they were human, too.

"I don't get it," said Jaden. "I thought Salvatore told us that Lucifer lets the people go after he abducts them. This makes it look like they all die in here."

"I don't know," Malia replied. "But I don't like it here. Let's go."

They returned to the corridor. Before they'd taken two steps, three hybrids emerged from the tunnel wall.

"What are you three doing down here?" one of them said.

An alarm sounded, its siren echoing off the walls.

"Shit!" said Jaden.

Malia reached out with her mind, smashing all three of them repeatedly into the wall. They fell to the floor and didn't move.

"Hurry!" she yelled, taking off down the hall, Jaden and Bomani right behind her.

At the far end, they found another chamber housing the power generator.

"Let's find that service tunnel!" said Bomani.

The generator looked similar to the one on Mars but smaller. Beyond it, Malia found what looked like a manhole cover in the floor.

"This must be it!"

Jaden and Bomani joined her.

Malia focused and used her mind to lift the cover out of the floor. It was a metal cylinder. Casting it aside, she looked down the tunnel. It was barely wide enough for one person and descended at a steep angle. Although it was dark inside, there was a faint glow—she couldn't determine its source.

"Ladies first," Bomani suggested.

"Not a chance," said Malia. "You go first—I'll replace the cover once we're all in."

Bomani lowered himself inside and began sliding down. Jaden went next. Malia brought up the rear, pulling the cover in behind her. The siren continued blaring. She hoped they could make it to the bottom and get to the surface before they realized where they'd gone.

For the first couple of minutes, the tunnel was so steep that they had no problem sliding along its length. But it leveled out after a while.

"This sucks," Bomani said. "I can squirm along, but I barely fit in here. There's not much room to move my arms or legs—this is going to take forever!"

"Jaden—" said Malia.

"I'm on it," he replied before she could finish her sentence.

Jaden and Bomani took off down the tunnel. Malia used her powers to speed along behind them. The temperature rose as they continued; she wished they still had their spacesuits. But they were in her backpack on Salvatore's ship.

Finally, they reached a small, cubical chamber, quite small for the three of them. Malia barely had room to stand up straight.

There was a tunnel directly above them, equally as narrow as the first. Far above, Malia could see daylight.

"This is it," she said. "Straight up to freedom."

"Uh, guys, there's no ladder or anything," said Bomani.

"I got you," Jaden replied.

"I'll go first this time," said Malia.

Using her telekinesis, she propelled herself up the shaft, slowing down as she reached the top. There was a metal grate covering the opening; before she could move it, someone on the outside pulled it off. The next moment, there was a face staring down at her—with eyes like a cat's.

Chapter Seventeen: Intrusion

Malia felt her heart sink—for a moment, she thought it was Lucifer. But then, a voice said, "Malia, Jaden—is that you?"

It was Salvatore. He reached out and helped her out of the shaft; Jaden and Bomani followed close behind.

"I was about to go down there looking for you," Salvatore told them. "How did you escape?" he added, eyeing Bomani.

"It's a long story. But we'd better get out of here, first," said Malia.

"Yes, of course," Salvatore agreed. "Come with me."

He led them across the desert only a short distance. Out of nowhere, his spacecraft appeared directly above them. The beam shone down from the center, and they rose into the vessel.

"Whoa!" said Bomani.

"Relax," Jaden told him. "This is normal."

Once the portal had closed below them, they moved up to the central chamber.

"I need to talk to you—alone," Malia whispered to Salvatore.

He nodded.

"*Keep an eye on Bomani,*" Malia said to Jaden in her head. "*Let me know if he tries anything. I'll be right back.*"

Malia and Salvatore moved up to the top level. They each took a seat, turning to face each other.

"What happened to you out there?" Malia asked.

"Soon after your departure, I managed to get back on board and flee the scene as well," he told her. "I moved the ship to a remote location. Minutes later, Lucifer arrived. You were still in Texas, moving slowly eastward, so I had my answer: he'd found a way to track this ship.

"I fled again, and Lucifer gave chase. After a careful search, I discovered he'd somehow found a way to place a tracking beacon on the ship. Once I'd destroyed it, he was no longer able to follow."

"How did he get the beacon on board?" asked Malia.

"I suspect it has been here since before the rest of us left the compound. And it was a passive beacon—I believe that's why I never detected it before. Instead of emitting a constant signal, it only responded to a ping from Lucifer's ship. He sent the command signal as I was listening for unauthorized emissions. On top of that, it used an extremely high frequency that allowed it to pass through the shields."

"How did you know to look for us in Lucifer's compound?" she asked. "Once he took us inside his ship, you couldn't track us anymore, right?"

"Correct. But when your signal abruptly disappeared, I knew he must have captured you. Do you know how he found you?"

"Yes—Melinda followed us. He must have given her an emitter because she was invisible until she went up inside his ship with us.

"Salvatore, Lucifer did it—he took our DNA. Bomani helped him create a virus with it and injected Lucifer with the virus. But something went wrong!"

Malia told him the whole story.

"This is disturbing," Salvatore said when she was done, "yet encouraging. Lucifer's medical distress may mean that your DNA is not compatible with ours. And if Lucifer couldn't give himself your powers, he may not be able to give them to the hybrids, either."

"On the way out, we found an enormous room," she said. "It looked like a morgue—there were dead bodies in there—hundreds, maybe thousands of them. The ones we saw were human. I thought you said that Lucifer lets them go after he abducts them?"

"To the best of my knowledge, that is true. I do not know where the corpses are coming from."

"We have another problem," Malia told him. "Bomani. He helped us escape, but I still don't trust him. I think he must be up to something. Can we give him the drug you gave Melinda and see if we can get the truth out of him?"

"Yes. Come with me."

They returned to the central chamber. Bomani was examining one of the pods, Jaden watching him like a hawk.

"Oh, hey," said Bomani, backing away from the pod when he noticed them. "This is some pretty neat tech you've got here. What does it do, exactly?"

"They are medical pods," Salvatore told him. "Get in, and I will give you a demonstration."

"No, no—that's okay. You don't have to do that."

"I insist," Salvatore said, moving toward him.

"Whoa, hey—what's going on here?" Bomani asked, sidestepping him.

Malia reached out with her mind and threw him into the pod. Salvatore must have injected him because moments later, he relaxed, and his eyes glazed over.

"Why are you here?" Salvatore asked.

"I came here with the twins; I helped them escape."

"What do you plan to do next?"

"I… I don't know. You're in charge."

"Are you working for Lucifer?"

"Who?"

"Osiris," said Malia. "The man in black."

"I was—not anymore. He blackmailed me into bringing the twins back to Earth; he made me give him their DNA. But he reneged on our deal—he refused to let me leave."

"You are no longer working on his behalf?" asked Salvatore.

"I… uh… no."

"He's lying," said Malia. "I'm sure of it."

"Some people can resist the drug," Salvatore told her. "Or at least omit certain elements of the truth. His hesitancy suggests to me that he is withholding something. I'm sorry."

"It's okay," Malia replied. "Leave it to me."

"Oh—you're gonna go inside his head, aren't you?" said Jaden. "Like you did to me?"

Malia said nothing. She stared deep into Bomani's eyes, reaching out to him with her mind.

"*I know you're lying,*" she told him. "*Tell me why you're here.*"

"I came with you! You wouldn't have escaped if it weren't for me!" he said out loud.

Malia forced herself into his thoughts. She could feel his emotions—he was afraid.

"What are you doing? Get out of my head!" he yelled.

Malia could feel his fear escalating, verging on panic. Closing her eyes, she probed deeper. Images flashed in her mind—Lucifer finding Bomani after he arrived on Earth with her and Jaden. He took him and the shuttle into his compound.

The scene changed: Lucifer and Bomani were in his lab.

"You made me a promise," Bomani was saying to him. "I brought you what you wanted—it's time to let me go!"

"Yet, you lost them," Lucifer replied. "In the end, I had to acquire them myself. I'm afraid you failed to live up to your side of the agreement."

"Oh, come on, man! I risked my life to get them to Earth—I took care of the hard part!"

"I will give you a chance to redeem yourself. The twins are here; we have their DNA. You will help me introduce their extra chromosomes to my body."

"That's insane—we have no idea if their DNA is compatible with yours."

"Your expertise is in genetics, is it not?"

"Well, sure, but what if—"

"We will test it on one of our human subjects, first," Lucifer told him. "If that works, then we will proceed with me."

The scene changed once more. Bomani and Lucifer were together again, but this time in one of the exam rooms. A couple of the hybrids stood nearby. Lucifer must not have been using his emitter because he no longer looked human. He was lying naked on one of the tables; his skin was scaled.

"Before you proceed," Lucifer drawled, "I have one more assignment for you."

"What? Are you kidding me?" said Bomani. "I've done everything you've asked—this is it. This injection should give you their powers. I'm done after this!"

"You will help the twins escape this facility," Lucifer told him. "And make sure they regroup with Salvatore."

"What? Are you crazy? I told you—if this doesn't work, we're going to need them. This will add their extra chromosomes to the cells in your cerebellum, and it *should* give you their powers. But we may need to augment your neural pathways, too, and if we do, we're going to have to use their brains as a guide!"

"Get them to Salvatore," Lucifer insisted. "I will take care of recapturing them."

"No. I won't do it. Giving you this marks the end of the road!"

One of the hybrids moved toward him, his expression menacing.

"I will sweeten the pot," Lucifer drawled. "Take the twins to Salvatore, and we will make you governor of your little island once we've taken over. You will be free to conduct your business as you see fit, and we will leave you alone. Fail, and face the consequences."

Bomani glanced at the hybrid.

"This deal keeps getting worse," he muttered. Malia could sense that he still harbored serious doubts about the "new order" Lucifer claimed his organization would be establishing—and about Lucifer's sanity. But he didn't feel that he had a choice. "Yeah, alright. But how am I supposed to get them out of here?"

"There is a service tunnel that provides access to the geothermal conduits. That is not monitored. Let Melinda know when you are ready—she will stop the drug keeping the twins unconscious. You have to convince them that you're helping them escape—they must not know that we are letting them go!"

"Alright, but where do I find that tunnel?" Bomani asked.

"You'll figure it out," Lucifer said with a grin.

Bomani agreed. He gave Lucifer the injection, inserting the needle in the side of his neck, below the base of his skull. For a few moments, nothing happened. But then Lucifer went into convulsions, wailing in pain.

Malia withdrew from Bomani's memories, stunned yet hardly surprised. This only confirmed that they couldn't trust him. And now that he was with them, he would continue to be a problem.

"*You only helped us escape because Lucifer ordered it*!"

"I wanted to get out of there anyway—and you two were already in the process of escaping before I did anything! I'm not working for him anymore, I swear!"

Malia told Salvatore and Jaden everything she'd learned.

"This is troubling," said Salvatore. "Lucifer believed he would be able to track us again with you here."

He turned to face Bomani; his pod began humming.

"What are you doing?" asked Jaden.

"A full scan," Salvatore replied. Seconds later, he added, "Lucifer implanted a chip in the back of his neck. I will remove it."

A moment later, he held out his hand. Malia could see a tiny black square in his palm.

"What is it?" asked Jaden.

"A tracking beacon, among other things," said Salvatore.

"That must be how he did it!" said Malia.

"Did what?" asked Jaden.

"When I was in the hangar, and Lucifer was running his tests, he was able to inflict terrible pain when I didn't cooperate."

"Yes. You may have chips, too," said Salvatore. "We must remove them. Please, get into a pod—both of you."

Malia got to her feet and backed into one of the pods; Jaden took the one next to her. She felt a pinprick on the back of her neck.

"That's it," said Salvatore, holding out his hand. "Come see."

Malia and Jaden stepped out of the pods and joined Salvatore near the center of the chamber. In his hand were now three small wafers.

"Stand back, and I will destroy them," he told them.

He placed the squares on the floor, and the three of them backed away. An energy beam shot down from the ceiling and vaporized the trackers.

"So, that's it, right?" said Jaden. "He won't be able to find us anymore?"

"That is correct."

"And if he's got our extra chromosomes now, he won't need us anymore, right?" he added. "So we can go find Mom, now?"

"He will still wish to destroy me," said Salvatore. "And he will be able to detect us if we generate enough power to escape the planet's gravity."

"Not only that," said Malia, "but we don't know for sure if he's got our powers now. Bomani said he might still need us to alter his neural pathways."

"We must assume he will still be seeking you," said Salvatore.

"What do we do with him?" Malia asked, indicating Bomani. "He'll cause us more trouble the first chance he gets."

"I agree," said Salvatore, considering the situation for a moment. "I will put him into a state of hibernation."

Bomani's eyes closed, a peaceful expression coming over his face.

"We won't have to worry about him anymore," Salvatore told them.

"So, what do we do now?" asked Jaden.

"We find Venus," said Salvatore. "I believe destroying Lucifer and his hybrids should still be our goal."

"I agree," said Malia. "Especially if he has our powers. He'll give them to the hybrids next, and that will get him closer than ever to being able to wipe out humanity."

"Very well," Salvatore replied. "I will begin the search."

He ascended to the upper chamber. Jaden and Malia sat down on the floor, as far from Bomani as they could get.

"Hey, you wanna teach me how to do the stuff you did to Bomani and me?" asked Jaden.

"Not particularly," she said. "I'd have to be your guinea pig, and I don't want you inside my head!"

"It's only fair," he retorted. "You've been inside mine!"

"Yeah, and there's a *lot* of empty space in there!"

"Shut up, Malia. I'm serious right now."

"Look, I'm sorry for invading your privacy, but it was *necessary* to get us out of there! There's no *need* for you to be inside my mind."

"Well, no, there's not right now. But what if I need to do it at some point? I'm not gonna be able to figure that out on my own!"

Malia felt extremely reluctant to allow this. There was a lot she'd kept from Jaden over the years—personal thoughts and feelings. They'd always been close, but there was a line she didn't want to cross.

But she couldn't escape his logic. It *could* prove useful for him to learn this skill. After everything they'd seen and experienced, she knew the stronger they *both* were, the better.

"Alright, fine," she said. "But you have to *swear* to me that anything you see will stay secret."

"You have my word."

"And you're not allowed to make fun of me for anything you find out!"

"That's gonna be tough..."

"Jaden!"

"Okay, already. I promise."

"Alright," she said with her mind. *"Listen to my voice in your head, and reach out with your mind. Find the source of the voice—find* me."

"But you're sitting right in front of me."

"Close your eyes," she suggested. *"This will be easier that way."*

"Okay..."

"Now, imagine you're going inside my head. Try to feel what I'm feeling."

"I can hear you, but I can't feel you..."

"Follow my voice. You have to reach out the way you do when you move something with your mind. But instead of touching an object, you have to touch my mind."

"Whoa—yeah, I can feel it. This is you!"

Malia could sense his mind touching hers.

"Yes—that's it! I can feel you. Now, keep going. Come all the way inside."

She could sense that he'd done it—he was inside her mind, now.

"Wow! This is crazy! I can feel how tired you are from doing this to Bomani!"

"Yes, you've got it. Now try to find some memories."

Malia tried to let her mind go blank. She could sense Jaden's presence inside of her. It made her feel profoundly vulnerable. The thought of Lucifer and his hybrids acquiring this power was terrifying.

Images surfaced in her mind of the night their father died. Malia could see the police entering their house. The gunfire. And the explosion she'd caused.

"*Whoa*," Jaden said in her mind. "*This is incredible*!"

The scene changed. Malia was back in Lucifer's compound, in the hangar. The shuttle was too heavy to lift, but she tapped into the Earth's magnetic field. It slammed into the ceiling, and then she hurled it at Lucifer.

"*I hate to admit this, but I think you're right—you* are *more powerful than I am*," Jaden told her. "*I can't do some of the stuff that you do*."

The image dissolved. Malia was back at their house in Marlton, Maryland, wearing a fancy black dress. The doorbell rang; her mom opened the door. One of the varsity football players was there, wearing a tuxedo and holding a corsage: he was taking her to the prom. A fantasy she'd had about him began to surface.

"*NO*!"

Malia opened her eyes. Jaden was staring at her, eyes wide; she was mortified.

"You kicked me out of your mind!" he said. "How did you do that!"

"Easy," she replied, averting her eyes. "You said it yourself—I'm stronger than you."

"Yeah… So, uh… you have a crush on Vinnie Barbieri?"

"Ugh! This is exactly what I was worried about. That is *none* of your business!"

"Hey, you saw me with Savannah. But I told you I'd keep it a secret. Not like we're ever going to see either of them again, anyway."

"Yeah, that's true," she said with a sigh.

"Alright, you do me now. I wanna see if I can kick you out of my head like you did."

"*Not a chance*," she said in his head.

Focusing on him with her mind, she penetrated his thoughts. This was becoming easier every time.

"*Damn—that was fast*!"

Malia immediately brought out his fantasy of Savannah. Images of Jaden kissing her flashed in her mind.

"*Hey! This is private! Get outta here*!"

"*Make me*!" she chided.

The scene became increasingly steamy—Malia hoped he would kick her out quickly. She didn't want to see where this was going. But she had nothing to worry about—choosing these thoughts had provided him with ample motivation. Jaden expelled her from his mind moments later.

"Figures you'd go for that!" he said, opening his eyes and glaring at her.

"Had to get even for Vinnie!"

"It worked, though! I got you out of my head!"

"You did," she confirmed. "And not a moment too soon!"

"Yeah, that's for sure..."

This time, Jaden was the one averting his eyes.

"I wonder if we'll ever be able to do that on humans," said Malia. "Full humans, I mean. I sometimes forget that we're half-Othali."

"Me, too," Jaden agreed. "I don't know—it kinda started

working with the Malor. We might get it with humans eventually. Or Martians."

"Yeah, we should try it on Salvatore!" said Malia. "Hang on."

Malia closed her eyes and focused on Salvatore.

"*Salvatore, can you hear me*?" she called out in her mind. "*Salvatore?!*"

There was no reply.

"Not working," she said to Jaden. "I guess Martians aren't compatible."

"If Lucifer does get our powers—or the hybrids, then we'd be able to do it on them, for sure," he said.

"Probably," she agreed. "Having our DNA would make them compatible. But let's hope it didn't work. I don't want to imagine what they'd do if it did."

Salvatore descended into the chamber.

"Is everything alright?" he asked. "I thought I heard one of you calling out to me?"

Jaden looked at Malia, his eyes wide.

"That was me," Malia said to Salvatore. "But it was telepathic—I didn't say your name out loud!"

"Intriguing," he said. "Do it again."

"*Salvatore—can you hear me*?"

"Yes!"

"*Say something back to me in your mind,*" she suggested.

"Did you hear that?" he asked out loud a moment later.

"No," she said. "Hang on."

Malia reached out with her mind, trying to probe Salvatore's thoughts the way she'd done with Jaden. But despite her intense focus, she was not able to communicate with him this way.

"It seems like it only goes one way," she said with a sigh.

"That's still pretty cool, though," said Jaden.

"We can work on this more some other time," Salvatore told her. "But now, I need to show you both something. Come with me."

Chapter Eighteen: Entanglement

Malia and Jaden followed him up to the top level of the spacecraft. They each took a seat. Malia noticed that they were hovering high in the sky somewhere—a blanket of cumulus clouds spread out beneath them. In the center of the chamber, a holographic image of the Earth appeared.

"This is our present location," Salvatore told them, pointing out a red dot that had appeared above the center of North America. "And here is my oracle—it is the key to finding Venus," he added, showing them another dot in the middle of Asia, down on the ground.

"Like the Oracle of Delphi?" asked Malia.

"No. It is a device, not a person," said Salvatore.

"Well, what are we waiting for?" asked Jaden. "Let's go!"

"We will not arrive in time," Salvatore told him.

"In time for what?" asked Malia.

"It is going to move elsewhere in a few minutes."

"What? I don't get it," said Jaden. "Who's going to move it?"

"The oracle is a quantum computer. We constructed one for each of us after fleeing Lucifer. The others carry theirs with them whenever they relocate. However, due to my constant proximity to Lucifer, I felt it would be safer not to keep mine with me. I built a drone that houses it and moves it at regular intervals to a new location—always somewhere remote. There are synchronized atomic clocks on this ship and the drone, so I can always calculate *when* it is going to move."

"I don't understand," said Malia. "What is a quantum computer, exactly? And how is that going to help us find Venus?"

"The oracles are entangled with each other," said Salvatore. "When one of them moves, its new location is shared instantaneously with the others. Once we retrieve mine, it will tell us the location of the others—including Venus."

"Entangled? What does that mean?" asked Jaden.

"In quantum mechanics, particles can become entangled when they interact with each other. They will then share the same state even if they become separated by great distances. Thus changes to one particle's state will instantaneously alter the entangled particle's state, no matter how far away it is. Our oracles take advantage of this effect to make our locations known to each other in a way that Lucifer cannot trace."

"But that's impossible," said Malia. "Nothing can travel faster than light—information can't be transmitted across the world instantaneously—nothing can."

"In the case of quantum entanglement, nothing is traveling—and thus nothing can be intercepted, by Lucifer or by anyone else," Salvatore replied. "The particles can no longer be described separately—once entangled, they are part of the same system.

"Wherever Venus is now, her oracle will have recorded her

location. That information exists on each oracle. We must retrieve mine to acquire it."

"But that means that you can find them, but they can't find you," Jaden observed.

"Correct. But they know I monitor Lucifer."

"Where is your oracle going to go next?" asked Malia.

"I do not know yet," said Salvatore. "The drone uses a formula to decide its next location based on solar activity levels measured in real-time. We will measure solar activity over the same period as the drone to determine its next location."

"This seems incredibly complicated," Malia observed.

"It is. But it ensures that Lucifer cannot find my oracle. Were he to capture me, he could not torture the information out of me because I do not have the formula memorized."

"What if he captures your ship and finds the formula?" asked Jaden.

"This vessel responds only to my commands," Salvatore told him. "It scans my DNA and brain waves to verify my identity; the drone does the same. The others keep their oracles in vaults that implement similar measures. The entire system is extremely secure."

"You and our Uncle Brian would get along great," Malia said with a grin.

"How much longer before it moves again?" asked Jaden.

"Moments," said Salvatore. "We are measuring solar activity now... That's it."

Malia watched the hologram as the dot in Asia disappeared.

A new one appeared in the middle of the Pacific ocean. Looking out the windows, she saw that they were now racing through the atmosphere; the clouds below went by in a blur. Minutes later, they descended toward the ocean.

"There it is," said Salvatore, "on that island."

Malia looked where he was pointing. It wasn't so much an island as it was a mountain sticking out of the sea. Plumes of smoke poured from its peak.

"This looks like a volcano," Jaden noted.

"Yes," Salvatore confirmed. "We must hurry."

Malia and Jaden followed him down to the bottom level of the spacecraft. The portal in the floor opened beneath them. Looking down, Malia saw ocean waves roiling below. The three of them descended through the portal. Salvatore led the way, and they flew to the island. They landed at the top, on the rim of the caldera. Far below, Malia could see magma glowing through cracks in the surface.

"Where's the drone?" asked Jaden.

"There," said Salvatore, pointing.

Hovering near the center of the caldera, maybe fifty feet above the surface, was a metal sphere. Malia could only catch glimpses of it through the smoke rising from the cracks below.

"How are we supposed to get to it?" asked Jaden.

"We're not," said Salvatore. "I'm hoping one of you might be able to bring it to us."

Malia waited until there was an opening in the smoke. Once she could see the sphere again, she reached out with her mind and tried to bring it toward them. It resisted. Malia focused, pulling ever harder. Slowly, the sphere began moving toward them.

It had nearly reached them when suddenly, it disappeared. Malia had lost control of it and could not find it again.

"What the hell?" asked Jaden.

"It's moved to its next location," said Salvatore. "Quickly, back to the ship!"

They followed him through the air, back through the portal, and into his vessel. Moving up to the top level, they sat down and examined the hologram.

"There it is!" said Malia, pointing to the new red dot that had appeared over northern Africa.

"We will have to wait," said Salvatore. "There is not enough time to get there before it moves again."

"You couldn't have made this easier?" Jaden asked with a sigh.

"Only eight of my kind remain. Protecting them is of the utmost importance."

Minutes passed, and finally, the red dot over Africa disappeared. A new one formed over northern Canada.

The ship raced away from the volcanic island. Below, the sea moved by in a blur. Before long, they were over land. They came to rest abruptly high above a snowy landscape. Malia spotted the sphere out ahead of them. Salvatore moved the ship directly above it.

The three of them moved down to the main deck as the sphere rose through the floor. Salvatore placed his hands on its surface, and the top half disappeared, exposing a golden pyramid within.

"That's the oracle?" asked Malia.

"Yes."

"Great!" said Jaden. "So, how do you figure out where Venus is?"

"I just did," said Salvatore.

The top of the sphere reappeared.

"So, where is she?" asked Jaden.

"You'll see." He picked up the sphere. "I think I'll hold onto this now. Once we eliminate Lucifer, there will be no need to keep it hidden anymore."

They followed him back up to the top level. The ship raced above the snowy terrain below. Minutes later, they flew over the mountains and then the sea. More time passed, and nothing was visible around them but the ocean. Finally, they moved over land again; it was another landscape of white snow.

"Um... where are we?" asked Jaden as they abruptly stopped moving.

They were surrounded by snow, as far as Malia could see. Here and there, rocky hills poked through the desolation.

"I'm going to guess Antarctica?" she said.

"Correct," said Salvatore.

"How the hell did you know that?" asked Jaden. "And I thought Antarctica was all ice and snow—how can there be rocks and dirt and stuff?"

"You're thinking of the *arctic*," said Malia. "That's only ice. Antarctica is a continent—there's land underneath the snow. But I always thought it was *entirely* covered in ice."

"Most of it is," Salvatore confirmed. "The ice sheet averages about a mile in thickness. But it is thinnest in this area, and I suspect Venus dug out a lot of what you're seeing."

"And why is Venus in Antarctica?"

"We will soon find out," said Salvatore. "Venus, this is Salvatore. Are you there?"

"How is she going to hear you from here?" asked Jaden.

"Radio transmission," he said. "Venus, can you hear me?"

There was no reply.

"You're sure this is where she is?" asked Malia. "I don't see any buildings or anything."

"She is here," said Salvatore. "I am detecting a large underground cavern. But she is either not receiving our signal or choosing to ignore it. We will need to go down there. You should both change into your spacesuits—you will not survive the temperatures out there without them."

Jaden and Salvatore moved down to the main level to give Malia a chance to change into her suit. She joined them and had Jaden seal her in. He went to change next. Malia closed the back of his suit when he returned, and they put their helmets on.

"What about you?" Malia asked Salvatore.

"I can endure temperature extremes far better than humans," he said.

The three of them moved down to the surface.

"Where are we going?" asked Jaden. "There's nothing here!"

"This way," said Salvatore.

They followed him across the frozen landscape. Not too far away, they arrived at a valley in the snowy terrain. Making their way down to the bottom, they came to a vast cavern in the ice. Malia and Jaden followed Salvatore inside.

At first, the ground was ice and snow. But as they moved farther inside, it gave way to rock and dirt. Near the far end of the cavern, they found a metal hatch. It had no handles—there was no obvious way to get inside.

"Can you open this?" Salvatore asked them.

"We can try," said Malia.

She reached out with her mind and tried to open the hatch. Jaden added his power to her own, but it was no use.

"It's locked from the inside," said Malia. "Without being able to see how the mechanism works, we can't control it."

"Now what?" asked Jaden.

"We knock," said Salvatore, stomping on the hatch with his boot. The noise echoed ominously off the cavern walls.

He waited a few moments and then stomped a few more times. Still, there was no response.

"Maybe she's not home," Jaden suggested.

Salvatore led them back toward the cavern opening. But at that moment, several people moved into view, each carrying a cylindrical object on their shoulders that Malia thought might be bazookas.

"Who are you?" Salvatore demanded.

"Venus commands you to go back to your ship and leave this place," their leader shouted.

"We have urgent matters to discuss with her," Salvatore replied. "You must take us to see her."

"Negative," the man said. "Our orders are to execute you if you refuse to leave."

"You want us to take care of them?" Jaden whispered.

"No," said Salvatore. "This situation calls for patience."

They moved out of the cavern. The men with the bazookas followed them back to the ship and watched as they boarded.

Salvatore led them up to the top level.

"Venus, we must speak with you," he said. "Lucifer is planning to exterminate humanity. We must stop him, but we need your help."

There was no reply.

"We are not leaving until you hear what we have to say."

Minutes passed in silence.

"I don't think she cares," said Jaden. "She's holed herself up down here in Penguin Land with her personal army and can't be bothered with the rest of the world. And I gotta tell you, it does *not* look like she needs your protection. I don't think Lucifer could touch her down here."

But before Salvatore could reply, they spotted movement on a nearby hill. At first, it looked like a small avalanche of rock and snow slipping down its face. But then, Malia spotted a sliver of bright light extending across the hillside. It grew in thickness, finally revealing a hangar within.

"It would seem Venus is ready to listen," said Salvatore.

He moved the ship inside the hangar; the enormous bay door

closed behind them. Malia spotted another flying saucer farther inside the cavernous chamber.

"I thought only you and Lucifer had ships like this?" she asked.

"So did I," Salvatore said.

A dozen men ran into view, each carrying a bazooka over his shoulder and pointing it at the ship.

"Exit your vessel," a male voice said through a speaker somewhere in the floor. "Venus will see you now."

"Let's go," said Salvatore.

Malia and Jaden followed him down to the lower level; they each removed their helmet. The portal opened, and they descended to the cavern floor.

The men with the bazookas rushed over, forming a semi-circle around them. They moved closer, prodding them forward with their weapons.

Salvatore moved ahead, Malia and Jaden close behind. At the far end of the hangar, they came to a tunnel. One of the men took the lead, while the rest remained behind. He led them through the shaft to a set of metal doors. They opened, sliding into the walls; Malia thought they must have been at least three feet thick. The soldier directed them inside, following them into a foyer.

There were marble steps before them, leading to an upper level. Persian rugs covered the floor, and giant oil paintings hung from the walls. Malia thought they had entered a palace.

The soldier led them around the staircase to a set of wooden doors. He opened them and directed them inside but remained in the foyer as the doors closed behind them.

An enormous wooden table occupied the middle of the space. A woman sat at the head of the table, wearing a thick robe. Her dark hair fell about her shoulders, and her skin was scaled.

"Salvatore, what the hell do you want?" she said, without getting up from her chair. "And who are they?"

"*Not exactly the emotional reunion I would have expected for two old friends who haven't seen each other in decades,*" Malia commented to Jaden telepathically.

"*Meh. These Martians don't seem like the emotional types.*"

"Venus," he said, bowing slightly. "It has been too long."

"Yes, yes," she replied impatiently. "Come in and sit down and tell me what is going on."

Chapter Nineteen: Venus

They joined her at the table, Salvatore sitting adjacent to her, and Malia and Jaden across from him. Salvatore told her everything that had happened with Lucifer and the twins.

"I see," said Venus, eyeing Malia and Jaden when he was done. "So you two are the ones who defeated those Malor invaders?"

"That's us," Jaden said; Malia nodded.

Venus considered them for a few moments.

"Salvatore, I have to be honest with you; I'm not sure I have any interest in helping you," she said finally.

"Why not?"

"Lucifer's going to destroy humanity, you say? Why not let him? To stop him now is only prolonging the inevitable. These humans seem determined to annihilate themselves anyway."

"Not all of them," said Salvatore. "It is our duty to stop Lucifer. Violence is not our way."

"Well, it never was before—when we were home. But now we're here. And after everything we've seen, it has become *my* way. When we went our separate ways, it fell to me to build and stockpile weapons to protect ourselves from Lucifer should he come calling.

That is what I have done; I have built us an impregnable fortress. If he attempts to harm the rest of us, we can survive here indefinitely.

"But I have built this for *us*—not for the humans. And I built it for *defensive* purposes. I do not wish to initiate an attack."

Salvatore sat back in his chair, considering her words.

"You have done well here," he said. "This fortress appears to be a palace as well."

"And why not? We lived in caves of austerity our entire lives. This is one area where I believe humans have the right idea. I live like a queen here. Join me, Salvatore—you can be my king. I have missed you these long years."

"Might I ask how you paid for all of this?" he asked.

"I have become an arms dealer, my dear," she said with a smile. "Oh, don't worry—I will never sell the weapons I have developed for *our* security. But I have also developed conventional arms that I sell on the black market for a substantial profit."

"And the men we encountered when we arrived?"

"A small mercenary unit I keep on the payroll, darling. They have sworn fealty to me, and I pay them well. And they cannot take our weapons with them, you see, as they have no way to leave here without my help."

They were silent for a moment.

"Venus, you must understand that the dynamic has changed. Lucifer has harvested the twins' DNA. He has tried to give himself their powers. We do not yet know if he succeeded, but even if he has not, it is only a matter of time before he does. You know him. He will never back down. And once he gives his hybrids these powers, we are doomed. Perhaps not today, but I tell you he is building an army. And the day will come when we can no longer withstand the force with which he will attack us—even with the arsenal you have collected here."

"You've always had a flair for the dramatic," said Venus, gazing at Malia and Jaden again. "Would you be willing to provide me with a demonstration of their powers?"

Salvatore looked to the twins; they nodded in agreement. They followed Venus back out to the hangar. Her mercenary unit was waiting for them there.

"You, girl," she said to Malia. "Captain Flint will face off with you. Show us what you can do."

Malia felt a stab of anxiety. The mercenary grabbed her by the arm and escorted her to the middle of the hangar. Throwing her to the floor, he mounted the bazooka on his shoulder and pointed it at her.

Malia regained her feet. Reaching out with her mind, she tossed the soldier's weapon through the air. She lifted him off his feet and flung him into the back wall of the hangar. He smashed into the rock, fell to the floor, and did not move.

Venus gestured to the rest of the soldiers. They ran out and surrounded Malia. Before they could hoist their weapons on their shoulders, she grabbed them all, hurling them across the hangar. She lifted the soldiers into the air, ten feet off the ground.

"I don't want to hurt them," she called out to Venus.

"No need," Venus replied. "This has been an extremely effective presentation. You may put them down."

Malia returned the soldiers to the floor. She moved past them to rejoin Salvatore, Venus, and Jaden; the mercenaries gave her a wide berth.

"Salvatore, you don't need me," said Venus. "These two should be able to take out Lucifer."

"Perhaps," he conceded. "But don't forget, he may have their abilities now. And he has at least one hundred hybrids who may also share those powers. Such a force will be overwhelming. And we must destroy his compound as well. We need your help."

Venus regarded him for a moment in silence.

"Let me consider this," she said finally. "Why don't the three of you avail yourself of my dining room, and I will join you shortly."

"We do not require food at this time," Salvatore told her.

"Speak for yourself," said Jaden. "I'm starving—I can't even remember the last time we ate!"

Venus showed them back to the dining room and left their company. As the three of them sat down, a waiter came to take their order.

"What kind of food do you have here?" asked Jaden. "Please tell me it's not that artificial crap we had to eat on the Othali ship!"

"We have a full kitchen, with provisions restocked weekly from the mainland," the waiter told him.

"Can I get a steak?" asked Jaden. The waiter nodded. "And maybe some lobster?"

"Jaden!" said Malia. "Don't take advantage!"

"And for the lady?" the waiter asked.

Malia looked from Jaden to the waiter, finding that her stomach was growling.

"Do you actually have lobster?"

The waiter nodded with a grin.

"Sir?" he said to Salvatore.

"Nothing, thank you," he said.

The waiter scurried off through a door on the side of the room.

"So, what do you think?" Malia asked Salvatore. "Will she help us?"

"It's hard to tell. She must realize the threat that Lucifer represents."

"Well, at least she hasn't said 'no' yet!" said Jaden.

Their food arrived soon after, and they ate in silence.

Malia thought about what they were setting out to do. She had an uneasy feeling about the whole thing.

"Salvatore, do you think there's a way to save some of the hybrids?" she asked. "I mean, I get that Lucifer is hellbent on destroying humanity, and Melinda seemed to believe that the hybrids are unanimous in supporting his agenda. But being hybrids doesn't make them inherently bad. Jaden and I are hybrids if you think about it—but we're half-Othali instead of half-Martian."

"Oh jeez, here we go again," said Jaden. "It's the Malor all over again. Malia, they want to kill *everybody*. And they'll do it if we don't get rid of them!"

"By the sounds of it, Lucifer has raised those people for this single-minded purpose," said Salvatore. "Of course, they are not inherently evil. But he has indoctrinated them their entire lives—he has built a cult-like devotion in them. If any of them survive, I believe they would do everything in their power to carry out his agenda."

"Couldn't we give them some kind of warning?" asked Malia. "Give them a chance to surrender and renounce Lucifer before we kill them all?"

"Our success will depend on secrecy and surprise," said Salvatore. "If we were to warn them somehow, they would report our plans to Lucifer. I think your sentiments are admirable, but I do not see any way we can accomplish this."

Malia let out a long sigh. She couldn't think of a way, either.

"They're planning on killing *billions* of people," said Jaden. "This is the only way to stop them."

"Okay," she said finally. "I don't have to like it, though."

By the time they'd finished eating, Venus had returned.

"I've made my decision," she said, sitting at the head of the table. "It does seem that these new developments will lead inexorably to Lucifer hunting us down. And as the humans like to say, the best defense is a good offense..."

"So, you'll help us?" asked Jaden.

"Yes. Truth be told, if Lucifer were to exterminate the humans, it would put me out of business, and I've grown to quite enjoy this lifestyle.

"I will provide you with weapons, nothing more. I will not risk myself or my men for this. And… I will help with logistics. You have schematics of his compound, I assume?"

"Yes. I will transmit them to you now," Salvatore replied.

"Very well. Come with me."

They followed her out a door in the back of the room and into a conference room beyond. Venus sat at the head of a long table, Salvatore to her right, and the twins to her left. A three-dimensional hologram of Lucifer's compound appeared above the table.

"I have developed this from detailed scans taken from my ship," said Salvatore. "Perhaps the two of you can guide us through what you saw in there?"

Malia pointed out the elevator, the level with the exam rooms, the hangar, the vertical walkway, the lower level with the morgue and power generator, and the service tunnel they'd used to escape.

"This shaft where we came out goes down to this small chamber," she told them. "Then the service tunnel goes from there to the generator room. Lucifer told Bomani that the service tunnel is the only entry that's not monitored."

"He fortified his security after finding out that I'd breached the compound," Salvatore told her. "The hangar bay doors are blast-resistant—I cannot penetrate them with the weapons on my ship."

"I could with the plasma cannons on *my* ship, but I'm not letting you have that," said Venus. "Your only way in is that service tunnel, but that much is obvious. Will Lucifer expect you to attack?"

"I do not believe so," Salvatore replied. "But we have no way of knowing."

"You will have to enter stealthily. If you can get inside undetected, this fool's errand may just succeed."

"We should go soon," said Salvatore. "Lucifer may still be incapacitated—that would improve our chances."

"I will provide you with fusion fireballs. A few of those should be enough to obliterate his entire compound," Venus told him. "And I will let you take one of the shoulder-mounted plasma cannons. It doesn't pack the same wallop as the ones on my ship, of course, but it should do the job. And I daresay you two hardly need additional weapons," she added to the twins.

"Oh, man," Jaden complained. "I was hoping I could get one of those, too."

Venus raised an eyebrow at him.

"And you?" she asked Malia.

"I mean, it would be useful..."

"Okay, I will provide three," Venus said with a grin. "But we'll need to train you on them before you leave."

"What exactly are fusion fireballs?" asked Malia.

"They're essentially grenades, but a fusion reaction provides their explosive yield," Venus told her. "They're only a couple of kilotons each, but that should do the job."

"You're saying it's a nuclear weapon?" asked Malia, shocked that she would suggest using such a thing. "What about the fallout?"

"There is no fallout," said Venus. "And there's no gamma-ray burst or electromagnetic pulse, either. Unlike the hydrogen bombs the humans have created, our weapons have no fission component.

They use a pure hydrogen fusion reaction. They produce a flash of neutron radiation, but otherwise, helium and lots of blast energy are the only byproducts. I recommend placing one at each end of the lower level and a third inside the hangar bay. Set the detonator to give yourselves enough time to get out of there, and that should do it."

They went back to the hangar. One of the soldiers led Malia, Jaden, and Salvatore to a massive storage area, where he retrieved three plasma cannons, handing one to each of them.

Jaden hoisted his over his shoulder, saying, "I'm the Terminator!"

"You're an idiot," Malia told him.

"We'll be going outside to train you on these," the soldier said. "Follow me."

He led them down a long tunnel. At the end, there was a ladder leading up through a narrow shaft in the ceiling. Jaden and Malia attached their helmets. Climbing to the top, they emerged through the hatch into the ice cave they'd found earlier. They moved out of the cavern and climbed out of the valley.

"We'll do some target practice on that rocky hillside over there," he told them. "This weapon is powerful but alarmingly simple to use." He hoisted it onto his shoulder. "This lever here is the safety—you'll want to keep that engaged until you need the weapon." He slid the lever back. "Now, get the target in the sight and pull the trigger."

The soldier aimed the weapon and fired. A fireball shot out of the end of it, streaking toward the hillside. It hit a large boulder at the top, shattering it into a million pieces.

"And that's it," he said. "She designed these things with

inertial dampeners, so there's zero recoil. Much easier to use than a conventional firearm."

Salvatore raised his weapon onto his shoulder. He aimed and fired, creating a crater in the hillside. Debris sprayed into the air, and a small landslide ensued.

"Nice shot," said the soldier. "Your turn," he added to Jaden.

"Hell, yeah," he said, lifting the cannon onto his shoulder. He fired the weapon, and the fireball blew a hole in the top of the hill.

"That's it," said the soldier. "You're next."

Malia had never fired any kind of gun before. Jaden at least had played paintball and lots of video games—experiences she hadn't shared. She hoisted the weapon onto her shoulder. Using the sight, she targeted a boulder near the base of the hill. She pulled the trigger, but nothing happened.

"Don't forget the safety," the soldier told her. Jaden sniggered.

"Shut up, Jaden," she said, flipping the lever.

Malia aimed again and fired. The fireball obliterated the boulder.

"That was easy," she said.

"Yes, that's the thing about these weapons—they require little to no training," the soldier replied. "It's a good thing Venus doesn't sell this stuff. I shudder to think about what would happen if garden variety criminals could get their hands on this kind of tech."

They returned to the hangar; Jaden and Malia removed their helmets. The soldier retrieved a wooden box from the storage area. He opened it, showing them the contents. There were three black metal objects inside, each the size and shape of a hockey puck.

"These are the fireballs," he said, pulling one out of the box. There was a small display, two buttons, and a switch on one face. "Set the timer with these buttons, flip the switch to arm it, and then haul ass. The base is magnetic, so you can attach it to a bulkhead or something if you want."

He closed the box and handed it to Salvatore. They dropped off the weapons inside his ship and then returned to the dining room to say farewell to Venus.

"Once you've taken care of Lucifer, maybe you can return and spend some time here with me," she said to Salvatore, embracing him. "Your work will finally be done."

"Yes, perhaps," he said.

"At the very least, come back and let me know that you've succeeded?"

"I will," he replied.

The two of them kissed passionately.

"*Did we know they were they were romantically involved*?" Malia asked Jaden telepathically.

"*Uh... no, I don't think I remember him mentioning that.*"

They both looked the other way.

"Farewell, and good luck," Venus said to them a moment later. "You'll have to come back and visit again once this is done."

Jaden and Malia followed Salvatore back to the ship. They moved up to the top level, and each took a seat.

"So... is Venus your wife?" Malia asked.

"We were mates," he told her.

"Aw," said Malia with a grin. "You should come live here with her once we're done!"

"We'll see," Salvatore replied. "Let us focus first on the task at hand."

"Hey, can we go get the Othali now and get them to help?" asked Jaden.

"The dynamic there has not changed," said Salvatore. "We do not know if they have restored their engines. And if we leave the atmosphere, Lucifer could follow. I do not advise that course of action."

"Yeah, you're right," Jaden replied with a sigh.

"We have a good plan. I will take us in low and keep the shields up—they should not detect our arrival. We will enter the compound through the service tunnel. Once inside, we will use the walkway to move up to the hangar. We will plant one of the grenades there and then move back down to the lower level. Once we've placed the other two grenades, we'll move back out through the service tunnel.

"I will take care of the grenades. You two will need to cover me—use your cannons if Lucifer or any of the hybrids approach."

"Shoot on sight?" asked Jaden.

"Yes."

Malia and Jaden both nodded.

"Are we ready?" asked Salvatore.

"Let's do it!" said Jaden.

Chapter Twenty: Execute

The hangar bay door opened, and Salvatore guided the ship outside. Once beyond the opening, they shot into the sky. Minutes later, they passed over the water.

Though she felt confident, Malia had some butterflies in her stomach.

"I'm a little nervous," she said.

"Don't worry, we've got this," Jaden replied with a grin, patting his cannon.

They moved over land, and then Salvatore took them in low over the desert floor. The landscape went by in a blur.

"We're invisible now?" asked Malia.

"Yes."

The ship stopped abruptly. Looking around, Malia recognized the nearby buttes and mesas from the last time they were here. The sun was setting in the west; she realized she and Jaden had arrived here with Bomani that same morning.

"Lucifer is here," Salvatore told them. "I am detecting his emitter."

"So, he must be using it?" asked Malia. "That must mean he's better. Let's hope he doesn't have our powers..."

"Yeah, that would suck," said Jaden.

"We still have the element of surprise," Salvatore told them.

"And plasma cannons," Jaden added.

They moved down to the lower level, using the straps to sling the cannons over their shoulders. Salvatore carried the box of grenades in one hand. The portal opened below them, and they dropped to the ground.

"This way," Salvatore said, leading them off into the desert.

Jaden took off behind him, Malia bringing up the rear. The cannon bounced against her back as they ran. Minutes later, they found the service tunnel.

"I'll go first," Salvatore told them. "They shouldn't have detected us yet, but I suspect Lucifer might have lied to Bomani about the service tunnel not being monitored."

"So, they'll know we're here by the time we get to the generator room?" Malia asked.

"Possibly. Be ready for anything."

"Now, you tell us," Jaden muttered.

Salvatore pinned his cannon against his side, lowered himself into the shaft, and dropped out of view. Jaden went next, and then Malia. They regrouped in the small, cubical chamber far below.

Salvatore moved into the service tunnel and took off into the distance. Jaden and Malia followed. Minutes later, they reached the cover at the far end.

"This is too heavy," Salvatore whispered. "One of you will have to move it—quietly, please!"

"I've got it," Jaden whispered.

As he pushed the cover out of the opening, light from the generator room spilled into the shaft. They moved out of the tunnel.

Malia felt her pulse quickening. She hoisted the cannon onto her shoulder and released the safety; Jaden did the same.

Salvatore led the way out into the corridor; there was nobody here. They hurried to the opposite end. He stuck his head through the wall to check the shaft for the vertical passage.

"Two hybrids a couple of levels above us," he reported.

They waited a few moments, and then he checked again.

"Let's go," he said.

They moved into the shaft and flew up to the hangar level. As they emerged into the corridor, Malia spotted two hybrids moving toward them. She aimed the cannon at one of them and fired. A fireball ripped a hole the size of a basketball in his torso; he gazed at his wound in surprise for a moment before collapsing on the floor. Jaden hit the second one a moment later.

"Nice shooting," Salvatore whispered.

They hurried down the hall and ducked inside the only door on this level. Malia recognized the room with the windows from which Lucifer had watched her during her tests. She didn't see anyone inside the hangar. Both flying saucers were here, hovering on the far end by the bay doors.

"We'll put this one in the hangar," Salvatore told them, pulling one of the grenades out of the box. "On the bulkhead in that back corner, I think."

They followed him inside, running over to the opposite corner. But suddenly, Malia heard footsteps behind her. Turning, she pointed her cannon, ready to fire.

"Malia?! It's me—don't shoot!"

Standing there was her uncle, Brian Kwan.

"Uncle Brian!" she said, lowering the weapon. "What are you doing here?"

"I could ask you the same thing!" he said, pulling her into a hug.

Jaden and Salvatore had stopped short, regrouping with Malia.

"Uncle Brian?" said Jaden, his face registering shock.

"Jaden!" he said, hugging him, too. "I thought you two would be somewhere in interstellar space by now—what's going on?"

"It's a long story," said Malia. "But there's no time for that—we're here to blow this place up!"

"Nuclear grenades," Jaden added with a grin, pointing to the one in Salvatore's hands.

"No—you can't!" said Brian. "Not yet—they've got Sydney! I'm here to rescue her!"

"*What*?!" Malia and Jaden said together.

"This man in black—he's abducting people and bringing them here."

"Yeah, we know!" said Malia. "How did you get in?"

"Elevator—I managed to hack the control system and disable the security. Who is this?"

"Salvatore—he's a good guy," Malia told him. "We'll explain later."

"Let's get Sydney," Brian replied, eyeing him skeptically, "and then you can carry through with your plans. Any idea where they might be holding her?"

"Medical level," she said, turning to Salvatore.

He nodded, replacing the grenade in its box.

"We have to hurry," he said.

They moved back out to the corridor; there was nobody here. Malia led the way to the end of the hall and poked her head through the wall; the walkway shaft was empty.

"Coast is clear," she told the others. "There's no ladder or anything, so I'll carry you down," she added to Brian.

She reached out with her mind and brought him into the shaft with her. They moved down to the medical level and emerged into the corridor. Salvatore and Jaden joined them moments later.

"Now we have to figure out which room she's in!" said Jaden.

But just then, one of the hybrids walked out of a nearby doorway. Malia hoisted her cannon onto her shoulder, aimed, and fired as the woman turned and spotted them. The fireball blasted through her chest, and she fell to the floor.

"Is that a plasma cannon?" Brian asked, his eyes wide. "Where did you get that?"

"Another long story," she said. "Come on."

Malia poked her head through the first door. Wendy was inside, lying on her table. Malia hadn't expected Sydney to be in this room but wanted to make sure.

"In here," Jaden said from the next door.

They followed him inside. The room was dark; Malia could not see the walls. But lying on one of the exam tables was Sydney. She was naked and unconscious.

"See if you can wake her," said Salvatore. "But do it quickly. Otherwise, we will have to carry her—but either way, we need to hurry!"

Malia hurried over to Sydney, slinging the cannon over her shoulder by its strap. Shaking Sydney by her shoulder, she tried to wake her up. But something was wrong—she didn't seem to be breathing. Malia started to panic—was she dead?

But suddenly, Sydney vanished. Someone else appeared in her place: Melinda. She opened her eyes. Looking up at Malia, she cooed, "Welcome back!"

"I don't understand," said Malia, backing away and staring at the others.

"Silly, stupid girl," Brian drawled, smirking at her. But the next moment, he transformed, and Malia found herself facing Lucifer in his black suit and sunglasses.

"What the hell!" Jaden shouted, lifting his cannon onto his shoulder; Malia did the same.

But an instant later, a dozen hybrids appeared out of thin air. Malia aimed her weapon and fired at Lucifer, but the nearest hybrid grabbed the barrel, and the fireball hit the ceiling, spraying them with sparks.

Malia reached out with her mind and threw the hybrid across the room. Jaden tried to shoot Lucifer, too, but another hybrid grabbed his cannon. His shot blasted a hole in the wall.

"It's a trap!" Salvatore yelled.

Several things happened at once: Lucifer snatched the box of grenades out of Salvatore's hands; three hybrids converged on Jaden, two of them grabbing him by the arms while the third took his cannon; three more hybrids lunged at Malia. She focused, blasting them away from her. She pointed her cannon at Lucifer as one of the hybrids pointed Jaden's cannon at her.

"Seems we have something of a standoff," Lucifer drawled.

"You tricked us with your emitter!" said Malia, feeling angry with herself for falling for the deception. "I should've seen that coming."

"Yes, you should have," Lucifer told her with a smirk.

Malia reached out with her mind, attempting to take the box of grenades from him. But nothing happened. She tried to fling him into the wall instead, but that didn't work either.

"What have you done?" she demanded, her heart hammering in her chest.

"Oh, I'm sorry—were you trying to use your powers on me?" he asked, his tone falsely sympathetic. "I'm afraid that it will no longer be possible. Injecting myself with your DNA failed to give me your abilities, so I had to find some other way to level the playing field. I've been able to adapt my emitter to shield me from your telekinesis. Quite a clever little piece of engineering, if I do say so myself."

"But... I moved you through the tunnel!" said Malia, struggling to comprehend what was happening.

"No, that was all me—you forget that we can manipulate

gravity. But I allowed you to believe that you were doing the work," he told her. "But speaking of clever, would you care to reveal how you managed to shake off the drugs we gave you? Your dosage was strong enough for a man twice your size."

Malia glared at him.

"Nothing to say? Well, it would seem you have more powers than we realized."

Malia tried once more to take the grenades with her telekinesis, but it didn't work. It sounded like Lucifer's emitter would protect only him. She focused on the hybrid's cannon, trying to point it up in the air; that worked, but he pulled the trigger, hitting the ceiling with a fireball. Malia reached out with her mind and snapped the hybrid's cannon in half. It exploded, knocking down several hybrids. Malia pointed her cannon at Lucifer and fired—but he'd vanished. The fireball hit the hybrid behind him, killing her instantly.

"Let's get out of here!" Jaden yelled.

Malia reached out with her mind and flung every hybrid in the room up into the ceiling. She ran to the door, Salvatore and Jaden right behind her, as the siren started blaring. They bolted to the end of the corridor, dropping down the shaft without bothering to check if there was anyone inside.

Reaching the bottom, they hurried into the corridor. Three hybrids were running toward them. Malia lifted the cannon onto her shoulder and fired at one of them. Salvatore shot another, and Jaden slammed the third one into the wall repeatedly.

They raced down the corridor and into the generator room. Two hybrids were guarding the entrance to the service tunnel. Malia fired her cannon at one of them, and Salvatore took care of the other. One of them had fallen on the cover to the shaft, so Malia reached out with her mind and moved the corpse out of the way.

Jaden lifted the cover out of the opening and tossed it aside. He dropped into the shaft, sliding out of view. Salvatore jumped in after him, holding his cannon tight to his side. Malia went last. They emerged in the small chamber and then shot up through the second shaft.

Malia emerged from the hole right behind the other two and took in her surroundings. Dusk had fallen on the desert, and there was nobody in sight.

Salvatore led the way, and they hurried back to his ship.

"I can't believe you destroyed my cannon!" said Jaden. "You could've taken it away and given it back to me!"

"I'm sorry; it was the first thing that came to mind!"

As they approached the ship, Malia heard a metallic clink. Looking up, she spotted something attached to the hull. It was shaped like a hockey puck.

"Oh, no!"

Reaching out with her mind, she grabbed it and hurled it across the desert, using her powers to accelerate it as much as she could.

"Jaden—put on your helmet!" she yelled, attaching hers.

He threw it over his head and closed the seal. Moments later, there was a blinding explosion that sent a mushroom cloud high into the air. The shockwave hit them, knocking the three of them to the ground and sending the ship a hundred feet away from them.

"What just happened?" Jaden yelled, regaining his feet.

"Fusion grenade!" Malia told them. "Someone's here—they threw it onto the ship!"

At that moment, a dozen hybrids appeared out of thin air, converging on their position. Malia and Salvatore both fired their cannons, taking out one at a time. Jaden used his powers to throw two more into the underside of the ship. But a dozen more hybrids showed up to take their place.

"*Jaden, fly—get out of here, fast*!" Malia told him telepathically.

She found Salvatore, tackled him, and pinned him to the ground. Then she gathered her strength and released it with explosive force. The hybrids flew through the air, hitting the desert floor and not moving anymore.

"Quickly," said Salvatore as they got to their feet. "We must board the ship!"

"*Come back*," Malia called out to Jaden. "*It's time to leave*!"

Jaden met them beneath the flying saucer. But before they could board, Malia saw Lucifer appear out of nowhere. He threw something at them before disappearing again.

"Oh, shit!" said Jaden, catching the object: it was another grenade.

Malia snatched it from him, flew high into the air, and threw the grenade as far as she could, accelerating it with her telekinesis. It exploded moments later in a blinding flash. The shockwave hit her, and she tumbled from the sky.

Malia screamed, hurtling out of control and unable to get

her bearings. She stopped abruptly, moments before hitting the ground—Jaden had broken her fall at the last moment.

"Malia!" he yelled, running over to her with Salvatore close behind. "Are you alright?!"

"I'm fine, thanks to you! Let's get out of here!"

They ran to the ship, which had drifted even farther away in the shockwave. Once on board, they moved to the upper level. Malia and Salvatore set their cannons down on the floor. Through the windows, she could see the second mushroom cloud rising into the sky.

"Oh, shit—look!" Jaden yelled, pointing to a nearby cliff face.

Malia spotted two flying saucers emerging from the shadows.

"Lucifer," she said.

Chapter Twenty-one: Hide and Seek

Their ship accelerated, rising straight into the sky. Lucifer's saucers pursued them, firing lasers at them. It looked like they hit Salvatore's vessel, but Malia didn't feel anything. Lucifer's saucers vanished. She saw their own weapons return fire; the other two ships became visible again momentarily when the lasers hit them.

"They hit us?" asked Jaden.

"Yes," Salvatore confirmed. "Our shields absorbed the energy—we did not take any damage."

Barely a minute later, Malia saw the atmosphere around them give way to the blackness of space. Turning, she couldn't see the other two saucers.

"We're leaving Earth!" said Jaden. "Where are we going?"

"Low Earth orbit," Salvatore told them.

"How are they able to follow us?" asked Malia. "I thought they could only track us if you achieved escape velocity?"

"That is true from a distance," said Salvatore. "At close range, they can detect our power output at lower levels. Cutting engines now."

Lucifer's vessels became partially visible as they fired their weapons again. Malia could see their lasers impact Salvatore's ship.

"How can they still hit us?" she asked. "If you cut engines, and our shields are up, they shouldn't be able to find us now, right?"

"They can calculate our position based on our velocity and last known position when we cut engines," said Salvatore. "I was hoping to have put more distance between us by the time we cut engines—that would have reduced their accuracy."

"But their weapons aren't hurting us," said Jaden. "What's the worst they can do?"

"Shields are down to seventy percent," Salvatore replied. "They will fail eventually. Without them, they will be able to disable our engines."

"Oh," said Jaden. "Well, that sucks."

"We can see part of the ships when they fire," said Malia. "Let's use our powers to push them away from us!"

"Great idea!" said Jaden.

Malia reached out with her mind, trying to move Lucifer's vessels back toward Earth. She could feel Jaden's power adding to her own, but they had no effect.

"Damn!" said Jaden.

"Lucifer must have augmented his shields to block our telekinesis!" said Malia.

"Can the two of you move us from inside the ship?" asked Salvatore. "They cannot detect your powers, and that would make it harder for them to find us."

"We can try," said Jaden, "but we've never been able to do that before."

"It *should* be possible," Malia added. "We can move ourselves, so moving a vehicle from the inside must be doable, too."

"Let's try it!" said Jaden.

"See if you can take us farther from Earth," Salvatore suggested. "That should slow us down relative to our pursuers, and they will fly past us."

Malia reached out with her mind, focusing on the entire ship. She imagined it moving away from the planet below. Lucifer's lasers hit them again.

"No change," Salvatore reported. "Shields at fifty percent."

She focused harder. This was nothing but a mental block—she was sure of it. She closed her eyes, imagining that she wasn't on board the ship, but floating out in space, watching the scene from afar. Again, she concentrated on moving the saucer away from the Earth.

"It's working!" Salvatore told them. "Keep doing what you're doing!"

Moments later, she saw Lucifer's ships fire on them again, but the lasers shot out into space. Malia focused harder, using all her strength to keep them moving. Soon, she could feel Jaden's power adding to her own.

The enemy saucers began firing in random directions. Malia could see them only briefly each time they engaged their weapons.

"He's fishing for us now," Salvatore reported.

One of the shots hit them. Lucifer must have detected the impact because both ships began concentrating their fire on their position.

"Damn!" said Jaden. "They found us!"

"Yes," Salvatore replied. "You may stop now. Our proximity limited our chances."

Malia relaxed. She was thrilled that she'd finally been able to overcome this particular mental block but disheartened that it had been for nothing.

"We can try again—it should work better if I can increase our lead," said Salvatore.

Malia realized they were moving again. Lucifer's saucers continued shooting lasers at them; Salvatore returned fire.

"Engines are at full power," said Salvatore. "We're moving away from them very slowly."

"But how is that possible?" asked Malia. "Aren't his ships identical to yours? They should be able to keep up."

"Yes, but it seems they are carrying more mass at the moment."

"More mass?" asked Jaden. "What would that be?"

"Hybrids!" said Malia. "Lucifer's not alone!"

"That is likely the case," Salvatore agreed. "The amount of extra mass he is carrying on each vessel would suggest that most, if not all, of his hybrids have joined him. Should it come to a ground battle, we will have our hands full."

"It's astonishing that he'd risk them all this way," said Malia.

"It should give you some idea how desperately he wishes to acquire the two of you," Salvatore replied.

As the minutes passed, Malia realized where he was taking them.

"We're going to the Moon?"

"Correct," said Salvatore. "I have an idea."

Minutes dragged by, the Moon growing ever larger before them. Malia noticed that Lucifer's ships had stopped firing on them, which meant they could no longer see them.

"Why aren't they shooting anymore?" she asked.

"Our lead has continued to increase, and we've moved beyond their range," said Salvatore.

"But lasers keep going forever, don't they?" asked Jaden. "They're just light beams."

"The light waves do diverge gradually over distance," Salvatore told him. "Move far enough away, and the energy is no longer sufficiently concentrated to do any damage."

They reached the Moon and entered orbit. After circling the far side, Salvatore stopped them abruptly and dropped them into a crater only slightly wider than the ship.

"What are we doing down here?" asked Malia.

"Losing them, I hope," said Salvatore. "I have calculated their trajectory based on their last known position. As long as they fail to see us on their way by, we will accelerate back toward Earth once they have passed."

"How will we know if they've seen us?" asked Jaden.

"If they fire on us, then we'll know."

"Oh, great," Jaden muttered.

Malia found herself holding her breath in anticipation.

"They should be passing over us now," said Salvatore.

Nothing happened. Malia let out a long sigh.

"It's time," said Salvatore. "Could the two of you take care of liftoff? If we can begin our journey back without engines, we may be able to evade detection completely."

"Sure thing," Jaden replied.

Malia closed her eyes, again pretending she was observing the spacecraft from afar. She focused on moving them away from the Moon. Opening her eyes, she could see that it was working. The ship had moved out of the crater, and they were accelerating toward Earth. They kept it up for a few more minutes until finally, Salvatore told them they could stop.

"We can fire engines now," he told them. "We'll keep the power output low to avoid their notice."

Suddenly, there was a banging sound somewhere from within the ship.

"What was that?" asked Jaden.

"We have a problem," said Salvatore. A hologram appeared in the middle of the chamber. Malia didn't know what it was showing—something mechanical—and there was a flashing red circle on one side of it.

"What's happening?" she asked.

"Partial engine failure," he told them.

"Can you fix it?" asked Jaden.

"Yes. But the failure generated a flash of energy that Lucifer's sure to have detected."

"Uh-oh," said Malia.

"Wait here," said Salvatore. "I will make the repairs."

He dropped down to the main deck. Malia stared back toward

the Moon, waiting with bated breath. Suddenly, she saw lasers firing all around them. Most streaked by harmlessly, but finally, one of them hit their ship.

"Oh, damn!" yelled Jaden.

They'd found them. Both ships concentrated fire on them, now.

"Salvatore, we're in trouble!" Malia said, dropping to the main deck, Jaden right behind her.

She found Salvatore dropping a panel back into place in the floor.

"More than you know," he said, fear in his eyes. "They've affixed something to our hull—I believe it is the last fusion grenade!"

"What?!" said Malia.

"We cannot remove it from inside the ship!" Salvatore added.

"Oh, shit!" yelled Jaden.

Malia knew what she had to do.

"I'm going out there," she said, checking to make sure her helmet was still sealed. "Open the portal for me!"

She dropped to the lower level. The portal opened below her, and she moved out of the spacecraft. She spotted the grenade immediately, only a few meters away.

Using her powers, she propelled herself to the device, snatched it off the hull, and flew toward one of Lucifer's saucers. But at that moment, they stopped firing their lasers, and she lost sight of them. She knew they must be moving away to get out of the blast radius.

Malia hurled the grenade in the direction she'd last seen the saucer. Then, she turned, finding that Salvatore's ship was visible only by its open portal. Focusing, she reached out with her mind, hurling herself and their saucer away from the imminent explosion.

Seconds later, though she neither felt nor heard anything, she saw intensely bright light reflecting off her spacesuit. She knew the grenade had exploded and that they'd cleared the blast radius. Turning, she saw a spherical cloud of light quickly dissipating. She could not find either of Lucifer's saucers.

Looking back, she could no longer see Salvatore's ship, either. She'd saved them, but she was now floating in the blackness of space, somewhere between the Moon and the Earth.

Malia panicked; she felt her heartbeat pounding in her chest, and her breathing was rapid and shallow.

"*Jaden! Where are you? Help me*!"

There was no reply. The ship must have survived the explosion—she had without the benefit of its shields. What was happening? Where were they?

"*Jaden?!*"

Malia forced herself to calm down. She inhaled deeply, letting her breath out slowly. The Earth was out there in front of her, a magnificent sight from the depths of space. She took in the wonder of the scene before her and refused to despair. Salvatore would find her. And if he didn't soon, she could use her powers to return to Earth.

Of course, that would present its own problems. How long would it take her to get back to the planet? Malia couldn't move as fast as Salvatore's ship—would her oxygen supply last long enough?

And what about re-entry—she'd have to slow down enough to avoid burning up in the atmosphere.

Malia started to panic again.

"*Jaden, where are you?*"

"*Malia! Don't move—we're coming for you!*"

A moment later, she saw the portal open directly above her. Malia propelled herself inside, and the opening closed below her feet. She moved up to the main deck, and Jaden grabbed her in a big hug.

"Holy shit!" he said. "That was the craziest thing I've ever seen!"

Salvatore was standing nearby, grinning at her.

"What happened?" she asked. "One minute, I could see the portal, but then it was gone! I lost you!"

"I do apologize," he said. "We had to close it to protect against the radiation from the blast."

"I threw the grenade at one of Lucifer's ships—did it work? Is it gone?"

"I believe so," said Salvatore. "The mass of the debris field is consistent with one of the saucers. He is down to one ship."

"Yes!" said Malia, removing her helmet.

"Do we know if we got the ship Lucifer was on?" asked Jaden.

"No," he said. "There is no way to tell."

"Were you able to fix the engines?" asked Malia.

"Yes, they are back to one hundred percent," Salvatore told them. "But shields are down to thirty percent. We are heading back to Earth, but I am keeping power output low enough to avoid detection."

They moved back to the upper level. Taking her seat and gazing out the windows, Malia could see nothing behind them but the Moon.

"Where is the other saucer now?" she asked.

"Unknown," said Salvatore. "It moved away to escape the blast. We have had no contact since then. I believe we may be out of range now, but that is not certain."

The Earth grew larger in the window. Suddenly, Malia spotted laser blasts flying past them.

"They've caught up to us," said Salvatore.

Malia turned toward the source of the lasers. She caught a glimpse of the saucer each time it fired. One of the blasts hit them. Salvatore returned fire.

"I'm cutting power," he said as they reached the Earth. "We're going to enter the atmosphere in a freefall."

"What? Why?" asked Malia.

"With no power output, they won't be able to detect us. And unlike in space, we will experience chaotic motion as we pass through the atmosphere—the various air currents and pressure gradients will bounce us around in an entirely unpredictable manner. This will make it virtually impossible for them to find us."

"But what about the fireball?" asked Jaden. "All that air friction is gonna give us away, right?"

"No, remember—he told us they have force fields that eliminate the friction," said Malia.

"Correct," Salvatore confirmed.

Sure enough, as they passed into the atmosphere, the lasers stopped hitting them, flying wide instead. Eventually, they ceased altogether.

As they plummeted toward the ground, Malia realized they were headed toward the United Kingdom, somewhere far north. It was nighttime here, but she could recognize the area from the lights—London in the south, and Ireland to the west. They continued falling, and soon, she worried they would crash. Malia let out a little scream, but a moment later, they stopped quite abruptly, only meters above a long, narrow lake.

"That was close," she said, breathing a sigh of relief.

"Where are we?" asked Jaden.

"Somewhere in England," said Malia.

"Scotland, actually," Salvatore told them. "Loch Ness, to be precise."

As he spoke, the ship lowered slowly into the lake.

"Wait, are you serious?" asked Jaden. "We can't go in here—what if the monster finds us?"

"Jaden, that's a myth," Malia said with a chuckle. "There is no Loch Ness Monster."

"Oh, yeah? Only a week ago, we thought aliens were a myth too, and now what?" he said, looking pointedly at Salvatore.

"Relax," said Malia, shaking her head. "But, what *are* we doing down here?"

"Hiding," said Salvatore.

Slowly, the ship dropped to the bottom of the lake. The water outside was dark and murky, and Malia could not see very far. A school of fish swam by the window.

"Now, what?" asked Jaden. "We're just gonna hang out in the lake?"

"We must determine our next course of action," said Salvatore, sitting back in his chair. "Somehow, we should determine if Lucifer still lives. And then, we need a new plan."

"Yeah, that first plan didn't work out so well," said Jaden.

"Can you detect his emitter?" asked Malia.

"No, but if he were aboard the remaining saucer, its shields would prevent us from doing so," Salvatore replied. "Taking out the remaining hybrids and their compound will be easier if Lucifer is gone. But if he survived, we are starting from what you humans call 'square one.'"

"We're going to need more help," said Malia. "Either Venus or the Othali—we can't do this on our own."

Just then, laser fire lit up the water around them.

Chapter Twenty-two: Chernobyl

"They found us!" said Malia.

Salvatore moved them out of the water, and they shot into the sky. He flew erratically—moving evasively to dodge enemy fire and try to lose the other saucer. Across the Scottish countryside and over the North Sea, they fled, but their pursuer followed their every move, firing weapons the entire way.

"Our shields are down to ten percent," Salvatore told them.

"What about theirs?" asked Malia. "We've been hitting them this whole time, too!"

"Yes, but we were dividing our attack between two ships at first. They're still at forty percent."

"What about the plasma cannons?" she asked. "Can we use these?"

"You'd have to hang out of the portal," he told her.

"Open it—I'll do it," she said.

"No way," said Jaden. "You got to do the spacewalk—it's my turn to do something cool! Hand it over!"

"This isn't a game!" she told him. "We're fighting for our lives here!"

"Yeah, no shit—so give me the cannon and stop wasting time!"

"Ugh, fine!" She handed him the weapon.

"The portal is open," Salvatore told him. "Lower yourself through, and the ship will keep you suspended just beyond the hull."

Jaden slung the strap over his shoulder and moved down to the lower level. Moments later, a hologram appeared, showing him dropping through the portal. He raised the cannon onto his shoulder, aimed, and fired. Watching through the window, Malia saw the fireball hit the other saucer.

"Direct hit," said Salvatore. "Their shields are down to twenty percent! One more shot like that, and we might be able to disable their engines."

The saucer stopped shooting its lasers, making it impossible to see them. By the time they fired again, Malia could see that they'd fallen behind. Jaden fired again, but this time, the fireball failed to find its target.

"Damn!" Malia yelled.

They flew at a breakneck pace, streaking eastward over northern Europe; Malia wasn't sure exactly where they were anymore. The other saucer became visible again, firing its lasers. Jaden fired again. The enemy ship became visible briefly when the fireball hit them.

"Our shields have failed; theirs are still at five percent," said Salvatore. "Get Jaden back up here—he's got no protection down there!"

"Jaden, our shields are down! You're not safe out there—get back inside, now!"

Malia watched him on the hologram moving back up through

the portal. He joined them on the upper deck moments later. As he sat down, the enemy fire hit them again.

"We're going to lose engines if this keeps up," Salvatore told them. "I'm taking us lower."

Malia spotted the silhouette of a city up ahead, but there were no lights—it looked like a ghost town. Salvatore steered them directly toward it.

"Where are we?" Malia asked.

"Pripyat, Ukraine," he said.

"Never heard of it," said Jaden.

"The city was built to support Chernobyl," Salvatore replied.

"The power plant that had the nuclear disaster back in the 1980s?" asked Malia.

"Yes. They evacuated the city, and nobody has lived here since."

"Why are we doing there?" she asked.

"Lots of places to hide," said Salvatore, "and no people to get in the way."

Salvatore weaved around the buildings. The other saucer was close behind, firing weapons. They were able to dodge the lasers, which blew chunks out of the nearby buildings instead. But as they looped around a building at the western end of the city, they took a direct hit.

"Engines are down," Salvatore told them. "We're going to make an emergency landing."

Malia didn't understand how this was going to work. They were still moving very fast. Salvatore steered them closer to the ground.

They touched down on a city street; Malia could hear the bottom of the saucer grinding against the pavement as they hopped and skidded along. The ship was slowing down, but not quickly enough—there was a four-story building at the end of this road, and they were headed directly for it.

"Brace yourselves," Salvatore told them. "This is going to get rough if the inertial dampers fail!"

They held, but the ship bounced off the pavement near the end of the street, lodging itself in the building's second floor.

"We need to get off the ship quickly," Salvatore told them. "Our impact has compromised the structural integrity of this building."

"You mean it's about to fall on top of us?" asked Jaden.

"Yes. Put your helmets on—the radiation levels here are still very high."

Malia and Jaden threw their helmets over their heads, sealing them in place. Salvatore handed them each one of the plasma cannons. The three of them moved down to the main deck—and Malia saw Bomani in his pod.

"Wait—what do we do with him?" she asked.

"There's no time—leave him!" said Salvatore.

They dropped to the lower level and climbed out of the portal.

There was a narrow gap between the bottom of the saucer and the building's concrete deck; Malia found she had to crawl to make it through. She led the way, Jaden behind her and Salvatore bringing up the rear. As they moved, she heard the building groaning and cracking.

"Hurry," said Salvatore. "Collapse is imminent."

But at that moment, there was a loud crashing noise. Malia was about to fly out of the structure, but Jaden yelled, "Malia—wait!"

Looking back, she saw that a crater had opened in the concrete below the saucer—and Salvatore was nowhere to be seen.

"He fell in!" Jaden told her.

"Salvatore!" she yelled, moving to the edge of the breach.

Looking down, she could see his head and shoulders far below—he was pinned beneath a slab of concrete.

"We'll get you out!" she yelled, reaching out with her mind to move the debris.

"There's no time!" he told her. "You two get out—now!"

Malia heard a rumbling sound above them. She gathered her energy to clear the rubble off of Salvatore, but at that moment, Jaden reached out with his mind, grabbed hold of her, and flew them out of the building. They landed on the street a couple of blocks away, turning in time to see the structure hit the ground in a heap of rubble.

"Salvatore!" Malia screamed, tears slipping down her cheeks.

"I'm sorry," said Jaden, "we'd be in there, too, if we didn't move."

"*Salvatore*!" she called out in her mind. "*Can you hear me*?"

There was no reply.

"Jaden, we can rescue him—we have to move the rubble! I need your help!" she said out loud.

"Malia, no—we need to move!" said Jaden, grabbing her by one arm. "Look!"

Turning, she saw that the other saucer was hovering over the street directly behind them, completely visible now.

"Fly!" Malia yelled.

She took to the air, Jaden right behind her. But before they'd risen above the nearby buildings, dozens of hybrids appeared, forming a dome above and around them. Malia reached out with her powers and threw the nearest few away. But as she moved to fly through the gap she'd created, others took their places, grabbing her and flinging her back to the ground. Jaden landed by her side.

"What the hell are we gonna do?" he demanded.

Malia raised the cannon onto her shoulder and blasted several hybrids out of the air in rapid succession. Shouldering the weapon by its strap, she shot into the air again, trying to fly through the opening she'd created. But once again, more hybrids filled the hole, grabbing her and throwing her to the earth as she tried to pass.

"Damn!" she yelled, rejoining Jaden.

A hybrid flew toward them; Malia used her powers to slam him into the ground. Another came in behind them; Jaden used his cannon to take her down.

"It's no use," said Malia. "There are too many of them!"

"Right! So what's the plan?"

"Follow me!"

Malia ran toward the nearest building. A nearby hybrid dropped to the ground and charged toward her. Leaping over him, she flew through a missing window and into the abandoned structure, Jaden right behind her.

Looking to her right, she saw hybrids streaming into the building in pursuit. Malia ran to the left, reached the end of the corridor, and turned right. There was a stairway at the end of the hall. When Jaden caught up to her, she flew up the middle of the stairwell.

Sticking her head out the window there, she saw that the hybrids had reformed their dome directly above them.

"They're making sure we can't fly away!" she told Jaden.

"Shit! What do we do?"

"I've got an idea—come with me!"

Malia jumped out of the window, flying across the street and through a window in the opposite building. She landed in another stairwell, Jaden right behind her. They leaped over the railing and dropped to the basement.

Jaden started running down the corridor, but Malia grabbed him by one arm and said, "Wait."

Seconds later, they heard the footsteps of dozens of people hurrying down the stairs.

"Let's go!" said Jaden.

"Hang on!" Malia insisted.

When the first couple of hybrids reached the basement, she used her mind to throw them into the wall, then said, "Okay, move!"

Malia flew down the corridor. Looking back from the stairwell at its end, she saw dozens of hybrids pursuing them. She flew up to ground level and hurried out of the building, stopping short when they hit the street.

Turning to Jaden, she said, "Bring it down."

"Huh? Oh—the building!"

Malia reached out with her powers, focusing on all three stories of this concrete edifice. Gathering all of her strength, she focused on reducing it to rubble. She felt Jaden's power joining her own. As the first couple of hybrids emerged from the exit, she felt the building starting to shake. Moments later, there was a deep rumbling sound, and the building collapsed on itself.

Malia and Jaden had to fly away to escape the cloud of dirt and debris. But there were still many more hybrids keeping formation above them.

"Shit," said Jaden. "We hardly made a dent!"

"I know," Malia replied with a sigh. "There should have been only fifty or sixty hybrids left—but it seems like there are way more!"

Several hybrids shot toward them from the sky.

"Let's go!" Malia yelled.

They flew through the adjacent building and out the other side. They dove through a window across the street, dropped down a stairwell, and flew across the basement. Moving up the next set of stairs, they emerged at street level.

Jaden turned and fired his cannon at the hybrids who had followed them out the exit. Malia shot three more who were coming at them from the air.

They flew into the next building, several hybrids hurrying after them. Malia turned and took them out with her cannon.

At the far end of the structure, they emerged into a giant plaza.

No more hybrids were chasing them, and looking up, Malia didn't see any more above them, either.

"Where'd they go?" Jaden asked, scanning the sky.

"I don't know," said Malia. "But I don't like this—they're up to something."

They looked around for another minute, slowly crossing the plaza, but there was nobody around. The night was silent.

"They couldn't have given up," said Jaden. "I mean, I know we're pretty badass, but we're not *that* badass..."

"Well, let's get out of here," said Malia.

She took off into the sky. But a hybrid appeared out of nowhere, slamming her into the façade of a nearby building and pinning her there.

Malia reached out with her powers and flung the woman off of her. But another appeared out of thin air to take her place. She tossed him away and flew off before the next one could move in. But as she flew above the buildings, she heard her brother in her mind.

"*Malia—help*!"

Looking down, she spotted Jaden in the middle of the plaza. Three hybrids had managed to gain control of him.

Malia dropped to the ground. One by one, she flung the hybrids away from him. But in the next moment, the flying saucer appeared directly above the plaza. A beam of light shone down from its center, and Jaden floated up into the spacecraft.

"NO!" Malia screamed, backpedaling away from the ship.

But as she moved, it disappeared. Hoisting the plasma cannon onto her shoulder, she fired straight up into the air. The saucer became visible again. But before she could fire another shot, a voice called out to her.

"That's enough, Ms. Kwan," it said.

Lucifer was standing directly in front of her. Malia fired her cannon at him before he could move. The fireball tore a hole through his chest.

His expression showed surprise as he looked down at the wound. But then he collapsed to the pavement, returning to his natural lizard-like appearance, and moved no more.

Malia gasped, unable to believe her own eyes. But suddenly, she heard dozens of screams as the hybrids became visible. They hit the ground, several of them grabbing her at once, the rest converging on her position.

Malia used her powers to throw the nearest ones off of her, but others took their place. She tried to fire the cannon, but they stripped it away from her. Dropping to a knee, she gathered all her energy and released it explosively. The hybrids within a twenty-foot radius flew away from her, but before she could escape, more moved in, grabbing onto her as she tried to take off.

And then the saucer moved directly above her. The beam of light shone down from the middle, and she found herself floating up into the spacecraft, unable to resist its pull.

As she floated upward, she spotted Lucifer's form lying on the ground. And as she watched, he sat up, his torso reconstituting itself: he'd acquired their power of healing. He looked up at her and grinned; Malia's heart sank.

Inside the metal chamber, Malia heard a buzzing noise. She instantly felt groggy, finding it difficult to keep her eyes open. Moving up into the central area, she spotted Jaden in one of the pods, his eyes closed. The unseen force backed her into the unit next to his.

Something pricked the back of her neck, and she knew they were drugging her. She could feel the chemical coursing through her veins, spreading from her neck down her arms and back.

Malia focused on eliminating the drug from her system, but it was too much. Lucifer knew she'd fought it off last time, and he'd increased the dosage tenfold. The force of it overwhelmed her, and she sank slowly into darkness.

Epilogue

Venus sat in her dining hall, thrumming her fingers impatiently on the arm of her chair, the oracle on the table in front of her. Taking another sip of brandy, she accessed the oracle with her neural implants for probably the hundredth time that day. A holographic representation of the Earth appeared over the table, visible only to her.

Salvatore—or his oracle, at least—had come to rest in an abandoned ghost city in Ukraine and not moved in hours. Near that nuclear disaster site that the idiot humans had created. She'd watched his progress with excitement initially—to Lucifer's compound, out to the Moon and back, and then racing across northern Europe. But now, hours of nothing.

She rechecked the oracle the moment she woke up the next morning. Still in the ghost city. Something was wrong. Maybe he'd simply lost his oracle somehow, but given that he was engaging Lucifer, some sort of disaster seemed much more likely.

Venus had to laugh at herself. She was becoming more like the humans every day she spent here. It was unlike her people to experience such deep and volatile emotions. All at once, she felt love, worry, anger, rage, despair, and more than anything else, impatience—that in particular a byproduct of spending so much time with humanity. But she *had* to know what was happening.

She changed into the leather jumpsuit she always wore on the rare occasion that she left her compound. It was formfitting, allowing for total freedom of movement if she needed to fight. She decided to leave her oracle behind; she was worried she might be walking into a trap and didn't want to take the risk that the oracle might be alerting anyone to her arrival.

Venus met Lieutenant Perry in the hangar. She let him know where she was going and that he'd be in charge until her return. Flint was in traction in the medical bay after his altercation with that girl, and Perry was next in line. She grabbed a plasma cannon and boarded her saucer. Moments later, she sped out of the hangar bay.

Her anxiety rose as she grew closer to the ghost city. She had a bad feeling that Lucifer might be there waiting for her.

Arriving at the coordinates the oracle had provided, she found a pile of debris. Salvatore's oracle was somewhere underneath it. Using her ship's gravity beam, she moved the rubble out of the way, finally revealing Salvatore's saucer. She detected Martian life signs somewhere beneath the saucer—they were faint. There was another set of life signs on board the ship. These were unfamiliar—neither Martian nor human. Very curious.

She moved Salvatore's saucer out to the street. There was more debris to remove, and then she finally found the source of the life signs. Using the gravity beam, she raised the body into her ship.

Hurrying down to the main deck, she found Salvatore lying

on the floor. She took a knee by his side. He was unconscious and barely breathing.

"Oh, my love, what happened to you," she said, stroking his face. A tear slipped down her cheek. Damn these emotions. She engaged the internal gravity beam to move him into a medical pod.

Salvatore had sustained grave injuries, including a broken skull and a punctured lung. She worried there might be brain damage, but it would be impossible to know for sure until he recovered. And he *would* recover—she would make sure of it. They hadn't survived eons of cryostasis for him to die here. It would take weeks, maybe more, but she would see it through.

Venus shouldered the plasma cannon and moved down to the street. Salvatore's ship was a mess, but she believed this, too, could be salvaged. The portal had been left open. Moving inside, she found a man in one of the medical pods. Despite engine failure, the ship still had main power, and the pod was active. The man was in some sort of deep hibernation. He looked human, but his life signs were different. She guessed this was the Othali Salvatore had told her about—the one who had betrayed his own people.

The ship's gravitational generators were disabled, so this traitor was going to have to stay where he was for the ride home. She wasn't about to carry him.

Venus returned to her ship. She moved directly above the other saucer and lifted it off the ground with the gravitational beam. Her shields wouldn't mask the second vessel—any humans who happened to be looking in the right direction would see it streaking across the sky. *Oh, well*, she thought—wouldn't be the first time.

She plotted a course back to her compound and sped into the sky.

To be continued...

Made in the USA
Coppell, TX
08 August 2021